# Funeral Rites

WORKS BY JEAN GENET

Published by Grove Press

The Balcony
The Blacks
Funeral Rites
The Maids & Deathwatch
Miracle of the Rose
Our Lady of the Flowers
Querelle
The Screens
The Thief's Journal

# Funeral Rites
# by Jean Genet

Translated by Bernard Frechtman

GROVE PRESS
NEW YORK

Published by Grove Press
a division of Wheatland Corporation
920 Broadway
New York, N.Y. 10010

Originally published in Paris, France, as *Pompes Funèbres*
in: Jean Genet, *Oeuvres Complètes*, copyright © 1953 by
Editions Gallimard

First Grove Press Edition 1969
New Evergreen Edition 1988
ISBN: 0-8021-3087-9 (pbk.)
Library of Congress Catalog Card Number: 68-58157

Manufactured in the United States of America
10   9   8   7   6   5   4   3   2   1

*to Jean Decarnin*

*Publisher's Note*

Bernard Frechtman had completed the first draft and first revisions of this translation at the time of his death. The final editing and verification of the text was completed by Helen R. Lane.

# Funeral Rites

The newspapers that appeared at the time of the Liberation of Paris, in August 1944, give a fair idea of what those days of childish heroism, when the body was steaming with bravura and boldness, were really like.

"PARIS ALIVE!" "PARISIANS ALL IN THE STREETS!" "THE AMERICAN ARMY IS ON THE MARCH IN PARIS." "STREET FIGHTING CONTINUES." "THE BOCHES HAVE SURRENDERED." "TO THE BARRICADES!" "DEATH TO THE TRAITORS!" . . .

As we turn the pages of the old sheets, we see once again the stern and smiling faces, gray with the dust of the streets, with fatigue, with four or five days' growth of beard. Shortly thereafter, these papers bring before us the Hitlerian massacres and the games, which others call sadistic, of a police that recruited its torturers from among the French. Photographs still show dismembered, mutilated corpses and villages in ruins, Oradour and Montsauche, burned by German soldiers. It is within the framework of this tragedy that the event is set: the death of Jean D., which is the ostensible reason for this book.

When I returned from the morgue, where his fiancée had taken me (she was an eighteen-year-old housemaid, an orphan from the age of twelve. She used to stand next

to her mother and beg in the Bois de Boulogne, offering
to the passers-by, with a dull face of which only the eyes
were beautiful, a few songs in a beggar-girl's voice. Her
humbleness was already such that at times she would accept only the small coins of the money that the ladies
offered her as they strolled by. She was woebegone, and
so dejected that in all seasons one saw around her the stiff
rushes and pure puddles of a swamp. I don't know where
Jean picked her up, but he loved her), when I returned
alone from the morgue, darkness had set in. As I walked
up the Rue de la Chaussée-d'Antin, swimming on waves
of sadness and grief and thinking about death, I raised
my head and saw a huge stone angel, dark as night, loom-
ing up at the end of the street. Three seconds later, I
realized it was the bulk of the Church of the Trinity, but
for three seconds I had felt the horror of my condition,
of my poor helplessness in the presence of what seemed
in the darkness (and less in the August darkness of Paris
than in the thicker darkness of my dismal thoughts) to be
the angel of death and death itself, both of them as unyielding as a rock. And a moment ago, when writing the
word "Hitlerian," in which Hitler is contained, it was the
Church of the Trinity, dark and formless enough to look
like the eagle of the Reich, that I saw moving toward me.
For a very brief instant, I relived the three seconds in
which it was as if I were petrified, appallingly attracted
by those stones, the horror of which I felt but from which
my trapped gaze could not flee. I felt it *was evil* to gaze
in that way, with that insistence and that abandon, yet
I kept gazing. It is not yet the moment for me to know
whether the Führer of the Germans is, in general, to
personify death, but I shall speak of him, inspired by my
love for Jean, for his soldiers, and perhaps shall learn
what secret role they play in my heart.

I shall never keep close enough to the conditions under which I am writing this book. Though its avowed aim is to tell of the glory of Jean D., it perhaps has more unforeseeable secondary aims. To write is to choose among ten materials that are offered you. I wonder why I was willing to set down in words one fact rather than another of equal importance. Why is my choice limited and why do I see myself depicting before long the third funeral in each of my three books? Even before I knew Jean, I had chosen the funeral of the bastard child of the unwed mother which, disguised by the words, prettified, decorated by them, disfigured, you will read about later. It is disturbing that a gruesome theme was offered me long ago so that I would deal with it today and incorporate it, despite myself, into a work meant to decompose the gleam of light (composed mainly of love and pain) that is projected by my grieving heart. I am writing this book near a monastery that stands deep in the woods, among rocks and thorns. As I walk by the torrent, I enjoy reliving the anguish of Erik, the handsome Boche tank-driver, of Paulo, of Riton. I shall write freely. But I wish to emphasize the strangeness of the fate that made me describe at the beginning of *Our Lady of the Flowers* a funeral I was to conduct two years later in accordance with the secret rites of the heart and mind. The first was not exactly the prefiguration of the second. Life brings its modifications, and yet the same disturbance (though one that, paradoxically, would spring from the end of a conflict—for example, when the concentric waves in a pond move away from the point at which the stone fell, when they move farther and farther away and diminish into calm, the water must feel, when this calm is attained, a kind of shudder which is no longer propagated in its matter but in its soul. It knows the plenitude of being water). The

funeral of Jean D. brings back to my mouth the cry that
left it, and its return causes me an uneasiness that is due
to having found peace once again. That burial, that death,
the ceremonies lock me up in a monument of murmurs,
of whisperings in my ear, and of funereal exhalations. They
were to make me aware of my love and friendship for
Jean when the object of all that love and friendship disappeared. Yet now that the great eddying is over, I am
calm. One of my destinies seems to have just been fulfilled. Jean's mother appeared to understand this when
she said to me:

"That set you off."

"Set me off?"

She was arranging books on the sideboard. She hesitated a bit, nervously pushed a volume that struck the
photograph of her husband, and, without looking at me,
she uttered a sentence of which I understood only the
last words:

". . . the candles."

I made no reply, perhaps out of laziness, and, it seems
to me, so as to be less alive. Indeed, every act that was too
precise, too explicit, put me back into the life from which
my grief tried to uproot me. I felt ashamed, at the time,
of still living when Jean was dead, and it caused me great
suffering to rise to my own surface. Nevertheless, in my
pitiful, illogical mind, which was drifting more and more
into vagueness, those two words, which probably referred
to the candles on the sideboard, arranged themselves in
the following sentence:

"You're setting yourself off amidst the candles."

No longer remembering what preceded these few
words, I am surprised to recall the following statement
by Jean's mother, who was staring at me:

"People can say what they like but breeding will tell."

I looked at her and said nothing. Her chin was cupped in the hollow of her right hand.

"Jean took after his grandmother a bit in that respect."

"Yes, he might have been distinguished. He was quite refined."

Her gaze turned away from me and rested on the polished surface of a service plate, lying on the sideboard, in which, with her head bent forward, she was admiring herself as she tucked her hair back into place:

"My mother was very distinguished. She was a society woman. It was I who inherited the aristocracy in the family."

A gesture with which she arranged the candles had released that confidence. The mother wanted to prove to me that she was worthy of such a son and her son worthy of me.

She raised her head and, without looking at me, left silently. She was going to inform Erik of my arrival. She had never loved Jean, but his sudden death nevertheless glorified her maternal conscience. Four days after the funeral I received a letter from her thanking me—did she mean to thank me for my grief?—and asking me to come to see her. It was the little housemaid who opened the door to me. Jean's mother had taken her in despite her disgust at the fact that the girl was a maid and the daughter of a beggar. Juliette ushered me into the living room and left. I waited. Jean's mother was no longer in mourning. She was wearing a white, very low-necked, sleeveless dress. She wore mourning, that is, in the manner of queens. I knew that she had been hiding a German soldier in her small three-room apartment since the insurrection of Paris, but an emotion very much akin to fear gripped my throat and heart when Erik appeared at her side.

"Monsieur Genet," she said, simpering and putting out her white, flabby, plump hand, "this is my friend."

Erik was smiling. He was pale despite the memory of a sun tan. When he tried to be attentive, his nostrils grew tense and white. Without consciously formulating the thought that he must have been quick-tempered, I felt the kind of discomfort one feels in the presence of a man who is ready to bite. Undoubtedly he had been the lover of the Berlin executioner. His face, however, was veiled with a kind of shame in my presence, and that shame later led me to imagine him in a posture which I shall speak of. He was wearing civilian clothes. I first saw his frightening neck, which emerged from a blue shirt, and his muscular arms in his rolled-up sleeves. His hand was heavy and steady, though the fingernails were bitten. He said:

"I know about your friendship with Jean. . . ."

I was very surprised to hear a very soft, almost humble, voice speak to me. Its timbre had the roughness of Prussian voices, but it was softened by a kind of gentleness when I discerned in it what might be called shrill notes, the vibrations of which he tried—deliberately or not—to muffle. The smiles of both the woman and the soldier were so hard, perhaps because of the stiffness and immobility of the curl of the lips, that I suddenly felt as if I were caught in a trap and being watched by the smiles, which were as alarming as the inevitable jaw of a wolf-trap. We sat down.

"Jean was so gentle. . . ."

"That's true, Monsieur. I don't know anyone. . . ."

"But you're not going to call each other Monsieur," said the mother laughingly. "After all, you're a friend. And besides, it's too long. It makes for endless formality."

Erik and I looked at each other hesitantly. For a

moment, we were ill at ease. Then, moved by some force or other, I immediately put out my hand first and smiled. Confronted with mine, the two other smiles lost their cruelty. I crossed my legs and a really friendly atmosphere was created.

Erik coughed. Two dry little gasps that were in perfect harmony with his pallor.

"He's very shy, you know."

"He'll get used to me. I'm not a monster."

The word "monster" must have been awakened by the echo of the words "get used to." Was it possible that in my personal life I was accepting without anguish one of those against whom Jean had fought to the death? For the quiet death of that twenty-year-old Communist who, on August 19, 1944, was picked off at the barricades by the bullet of a charming young collaborator, a boy whose grace and age were his adornment, puts my life to shame.

I ruminated for perhaps six seconds on the words "get used to" and felt a kind of very slight melancholy that can be expressed only by the image of a pile of sand or rubbish. Jean's delicacy was somewhat akin (since it suggests it) to the grave sadness that issues—along with a very particular odor—from mortar and broken bricks which, whether hollow or solid, are made of apparently very soft clay. The youngster's face was always ready to crumble, and the words "get used to" have just crumbled it. Amidst the debris of buildings being demolished, I sometimes step on ruins whose redness is toned down by the dust, and they are so delicate, discreet, and fragrant with humility that I have the impression I am placing the sole of my shoe on Jean's face. I had met him four years before, in August 1940. He was sixteen at the time.

At present, I am horrified with myself for containing—having devoured him—the dearest and only lover who

ever loved me. I am his tomb. The earth is nothing. Dead.
Staves and orchards* issue from my mouth. His. Perfume
my chest, which is wide, wide open. A greengage plum
swells his silence. The bees escape from his eyes, from his
sockets where the liquid pupils have flowed from under
the flaccid eyelids. To eat a youngster shot on the barricades, to devour a young hero, is no easy thing. We all
love the sun. My mouth is bloody. So are my fingers. I
tore the flesh to shreds with my teeth. Corpses do not
usually bleed. His did.

He died on the barricades of August 19, 1944, but his
staff had already stained my mouth with blood in May,
in the orchards. When he was alive, his beauty frightened
me, as did the chastity and beauty of his language. At
the time, I wanted him to live in a grave, in a dark, deep
tomb, the only dwelling worthy of his monstrous presence.
It would be lit by candle, and he would live in it on his
knees or crouching. He would be questioned through a
slit in the slab. Is that the way he lives inside me, exhaling
through my mouth, anus, and nose the odors that the
chemistry of his decaying accumulates within me?

I still love him. Love for a woman or girl is not to be
compared to a man's love for an adolescent boy. The
delicacy of his face and the elegance of his body have
crept over me like leprosy. Here is a description of him:
his hair was blond and curly, and he wore it very long.
His eyes were gray, blue, or green, but extraordinarily
clear. The concave curve of his nose was gentle, childish.
He held his head high on a rather long, supple neck. His
small mouth, the lower lip of which had a distinct curl,
was almost always closed. His body was thin and flexible,
his gait rapid and lazy.

---

* "Staves and orchards" renders an untranslatable play on words:
*les verges et les vergers. Verge* is the zoological word for penis.
—*Translator's note.*

My heart is heavy and succumbs to nausea. I puke on my white feet, at the foot of the tomb which is my unclothed body.

Erik had sat down in a chair with his back to the window draped with long, white lace curtains. The air was dense, painful. It was obvious that the windows were always kept closed. The soldier's legs were spread, so that the wooden front of the chair on which he put his hand was visible. The blue workman's trousers he was wearing were too tight for his thighs and behind. Perhaps they had been Jean's. Erik was handsome. I don't know what suddenly made me conceive the notion that his sitting on a straw-bottomed chair cramped his *"oeil de Gabès."** I remembered an evening on the Rue des Martyrs, and in a few seconds I relived it. Between the dizzying cliffs of the houses the street climbed uphill toward a stormy sky that paid heed to the melody of the gait and gestures of the group of three kids and a *bataillonnaire*, who were all delighted with a story the soldier was telling. As they went by, the shopping bags of the bareheaded women hit against their calves.

". . . that was all I wanted, so I stuck my finger in his eye."

The *Joyeux* pronounced *oeil* (eye) like *ail* (garlic). The three youngsters, who were walking at the same pace, with their heads down and shoulders slightly bent and their hands in their pockets pressing against the muscles of their taut thighs, were a bit winded by the climb. The *Joyeux's* story had a fleshy presence. They said nothing.

---

* A few French terms have been retained in this and the following paragraphs. *L'oeil de Gabès* ("the eye of Gabès") was African Batallion slang for the anus. A member of the Batallion, which was referred to familiarly as the Bat-d'Af (Bataillon d'Afrique) was a *bataillonnaire* or, familiarly, a *Joyeux* (a Merry Boy).

*—Translator's note.*

Within them hatched an egg from which emerged an excitement charged with cautious love-making under a mosquito net. Their muteness allowed the excitement to make its way quiveringly to their very marrow. It would have taken very little for the kind of love that was developing within them for the first time to escape from their mouths in the guise of a song, poem, or oath. Embarrassment made them curt. The youngest walked with his head high, eye pure, lips slightly parted. He was nibbling his nails. Because of his weakness he was not always able to be calm or self-controlled, but he felt deeply grateful to those who brought him peace by dominating him.

He turned his head a little. His open mouth was already a fissure through which all his tenderness passed and through which the world entered to possess him. He gazed docilely at the *Joyeux*. The sensitive *Joyeux* understood and was pained by the excitement he had aroused. He drew his head back proudly. His little foot, which was surer, mastered a conqueror. He snickered a bit:

". . . In the oye, I'm tellin' ya, in the oyye!"

He came down hard on the *o* so as to let the *yye* stream out. Then, a slight silence. And he ended the sentence so bombastically that the story became the relation of a deed witnessed in the land of the gods, at Gabès,* or at Gabès in the broiling, sumptuous country of a lofty disease, of a sacred fever. Pierrot stumbled over a stone. He said nothing. Without moving the fists in his pockets, the soldier again threw back his round little burned head, which was as brown as a pebble of the wadis, and added with his hoarse laugh, in which the blue tattooed dot at the outer angle of his left eyelid seemed to be painted:

---

* Gabès is in southern Tunisia.—*Translator's note.*

". . . of Gabès! In the eye of Habès! And bango!"

It is not a matter of indifference that my book, which is peopled with the truest of soldiers, should start with the rarest expression that brands the punished soldier, that most prudent being confusing the warrior with the thief, war with theft. The *Joyeux* likewise gave the name "bronze eye" to what is also called the "jujube," the "plug," the "onion," the "meanie," the "tokas," the "moon," the "crap basket." Later, when they return to their hometowns, they secretly preserve the sacrament of the Bat-d'Af, just as the princes of the Pope, Emperor, or King glorified in having been, a thousand years ago, simple brigands in a heroic band. The *bataillonnaire* thinks fondly of his youth, of the sun, of the blows of the guards, of the prison queers, of the prickly-pear trees, the leaves of which are also called the *Joyeux's* wife; he thinks of the sand, of the marches in the desert, of the flexible palm tree whose elegance and vigor are exactly those of his prick and his boy friend; he thinks of the grave, of the gallows, of the eye.

The veneration I feel for that part of the body and the great tenderness that I have bestowed on the children who have allowed me to enter it, the grace and sweetness of their gift, oblige me to speak of all this with respect. It is not profaning the most beloved of the dead to speak, in the guise of a poem whose tone is still unknowable, of the happiness he offered me when my face was buried in a fleece that was damp with my sweat and saliva and that stuck together in little locks of hair which dried after love-making and remained stiff. My teeth went at it desperately at times, and my pupils were full of images that are organizing themselves today where, at the back of a funeral parlor, the angel of the resurrection of the death of Jean, proud, aloft in the clouds, dominated in his fierce-

ness the handsomest soldier of the Reich. For at times it is
the opposite of what he was that is evoked by the wonderful child who was mowed down by the August bullets, the
purity and iciness of which frighten me, for they make
him greater than I. Yet I place my story, if that is what
I must call the prismatic decomposition of my love and
grief, under the aegis of that dead boy. The words "low"
and "sordid" will be meaningless if anyone dares apply
them to the tone of this book which I am writing in homage. I loved the violence of his prick, its quivering, its size,
the curls of his hairs, the child's eyes, and the back of his
neck, and the dark, ultimate treasure, the "bronze eye,"
which he did not grant me until very late, about a month
before his death.

On the day of the funeral, the church door opened at
four in the afternoon on a black hole into which I made
my way solemnly or, rather, was borne by the power of
the grand funeral to the nocturnal sanctuary and prepared
for a service which is the sublime image of the one performed at each grieving of the fallen prick. A funereal
flavor has often filled my mouth after love.

Upon entering the church:

"It's as dark here as up a nigger's asshole."

It was that dark there, and I entered the place with
the same slow solemnity. At the far end twinkled the
tobacco-colored iris of the *"oeil de Gabès,"* and, in the
middle of it, haloed, savage, silent, awfully pale, was that
buggered tank-driver, god of my night, Erik Seiler.

Despite the trembling of the tapers, from the black-
draped church door there could be discerned on Erik's
chest, as he stood on top of an altar supporting all the
flowers of a stripped garden, the location of the mortal
hole that will be made by a Frenchman's bullet.

My staring eyes followed Jean's coffin. My hand played

for a few seconds with a small matchbox in the pocket of my jacket, the same box that my fingers were kneading when Jean's mother said to me:

"Erik's from Berlin. Yes, I know. Can I hold it against him? One's not responsible. One doesn't choose one's birthplace."

Not knowing how to answer, I raised my eyebrows as if to say, "Obviously."

Erik's hand, which was between his thighs, was pressed against the wood of the chair. He shrugged and looked at me with somewhat anxious eyes. Actually I was seeing him for the second time, and I had long known that he was Jean's mother's lover. Since his force and vigor compensated for what (despite great austerity) was too frail in Jean's grace, I have ever since made great efforts to live his life as a Berlin youngster, but particularly when he stood up and went to the window to look into the street. With a gesture of needless caution he held one of the double, red velvet curtains in front of his body. He stood that way for a few seconds, then turned around without letting go of the curtain, so that he was almost completely wrapped in its folds, and I saw an image of one of the young Nazis who paraded in Berlin with unfurled flags on their shoulders, wrapped in folds of red cloth buffeted by the wind. For a second, Erik was one of those kids. He looked at me, again turned his head with a brief movement toward the closed window from which the street could be seen through the lace, then let go of the curtain so that he could raise his wrist and see the time. He realized that he no longer had a watch. Jean's mother was standing quietly by the sideboard and smiling. She saw his gaze—I did too—and the three of us immediately looked in the direction of a small table near a couch where two wristwatches were lying side by side.

I blushed:

"Look, your watch is over there."

The mother went to get the smaller one and brought it to the soldier. He took it without a word and put it into his pocket.

The woman did not see the look he gave her, and I myself did not understand the meaning of it. He said:

"It's all over."

I thought that everything was over for him, me, and Jean's mother. Nevertheless, I said:

"Not at all, nothing's over."

This was an obvious answer, but I hardly thought about what I was saying, since, inspired by the image of Erik in the folds of the curtain, I was in the process of going back to his childhood, of living it in his stead. He sat down on the chair again, fidgeted, stood up, and sat down a third time. I knew that he had hated Jean, whose severity did not allow for indulging his mother. Not that he condemned her, but the child who went all over Paris with valises full of guns and anti-German pamphlets had no time to smile. He also realized that the slightest truckling, the slightest witticism, might relax his attitude, which he wanted to keep rigid. I even wonder whether he felt any tenderness toward me.

On the sideboard in a frame adorned with flowers and shellwork foliage was a portrait-photograph of him. When I went to see him at the morgue, I was hoping that his perfectly scrubbed, clean, naked, white skeleton, which was composed of very dry scraped bones, of a skull admirable in shape and matter, and particularly of thin finger joints that were rigid and severe, had been laid out on a bed of roses and gladiolas. I had bought armfuls of flowers, but they were at the foot of the trestle that supported the coffin. They were stuck in a roll of straw and formed, with the oak or ivy leaves that had been added, ridiculous wreaths. I had got my money's worth, but the fervor with which I myself would have strewn the roses was lacking. It was indeed roses that I had wanted, for their petals are sensitive enough to register every sorrow and then convey them to the corpse, which is aware of everything. A huge straw cushion, lastly, decorated with laurel leaves, was leaning against the coffin. Jean had been taken from the refrigerator. The reception room of the morgue, which had been transformed into a mortuary chapel, was thronged with people walking through it. Jean's mother, who was sitting next to me veiled in crape, murmured to me:

"Before, it was Juliette. Now it's my turn."

Four months earlier, Juliette had lost a new-born baby, and the fact that Jean was its father had infuriated his mother. She had cursed them, foolishly, and now she herself was a child weeping over her son's death.

"It's hardly . . . ," she added.

The phrase was completed by a tremendous sigh, and though my thoughts were far away I gathered that she meant: "Hardly worth my being in charge of the funeral."

My grief did not prevent me from seeing beside me the young man I had met beside the tree near which Jean had died. He was wearing the same fur-lined leather coat. I was sure he was Paulo, Jean's very slightly older brother. He said nothing. He was not crying. His arms hung at his side. Even if Jean had never spoken about it, I would have recognized his nastiness. It gave great sobriety to all his gestures. He had a tendency to put his hands into his pockets. He stood there without moving. He was shutting himself up in his indifference to evil and unhappiness.

Despite the crowd, I bent forward to contemplate the

child who, by the miracle of machine-gun fire, had become that very delicate thing, a dead youth. The precious corpse of an adolescent shrouded in cloth. And when the crowd bent over him at the edge of the coffin, it saw a thin, pale, slightly green face, doubtless the very face of death, but so commonplace in its fixity that I wonder why Death, movie stars, touring virtuosi, queens in exile, and banished kings have a body, face, and hands. Their fascination is owing to something other than a human charm, and, without betraying the enthusiasm of the peasant women trying to catch a glimpse of her at the door of her train, Sarah Bernhardt could have appeared in the form of a small box of safety matches. We had not come to see a face but the dead Jean D., and our expectation was so fervent that he had a right to manifest himself, without surprising us, in any way whatever.

"They don't go in for style these days," she said.

Heavy and gleaming, like the most gorgeous of dahlias, Jean's mother, who was still very beautiful, had raised her mourning veil. Her eyes were dry, but the tears had left a subtle and luminous snail track on her pink, plump face from the eyes to the chin. She looked at the pine wood of the coffin.

"Oh, you can't expect quality nowadays," replied another woman in deep mourning who was next to her.

I was looking at the narrow coffin and at Jean's leaden face, which was overlaid with flesh that was sunken and cold, not with the coldness of death, but the iciness of the refrigerator. At twilight, accompanied by the muted fanfares of fear, almost naked and knowing I was naked in my corduroy trousers and under my coarse, blue, V-necked shirt, the sleeves of which were rolled up above my bare arms, I walked down silent hills in sandals, in the simple posture of the stroller, that is, with one hand closed in my pocket and the other leaning on a flexible stick. In the middle of a glade, I had just offered funereal worship to the moon that was rising in my sky.

An assistant brought in the lid of the coffin and I was torn apart. It was screwed on. After the rigidity of the body, the ice of which was invisible, breakable, even deniable, this was the first brutal separation. It was hateful because of the imbecility of a pine board, which was fragile and yet absolutely reliable, a hypocritical, light, porous board that a more depraved soul than Jean's could dissolve, a board cut from one of the trees that cover my slopes, trees that are black and haughty but frightened by my cold eyes, by the sureness of my footing beneath the branches, for they are the witnesses to my visits on the heights where love receives me without display. Jean was taken away from me.

"It has no style."

It was an agony for me to see the boy go off in the dissolution of a ceremony whose funereal pompousness was as much a mocking as familiarity would have been. The people walked around the coffin and left. The undertaker's assistants took the coffin, and I followed the black-clad family. Someone loaded the hearse with wreaths the way one garners bundles of hay. Each action wounded me. Jean needed a compensation. My heart was preparing to offer him the pomp that men refused him. No doubt the source of this feeling was deeper than defiance of the shallow sensitivity indicated by men's acts, but it was while I was following the coffin that friendship rose within me as the star of the dead rises at night in the sky. I stepped into the hearse. I gave the chauffeur twenty francs. Nothing was preventing the inner revelation of my friendship for Jean. The moon was more solemn that evening and rose slowly. It spread peace, but grief too, over my depopulated earth. At a crossing, the hearse had to stop so that an American convoy could pass, and it took another street, when suddenly the silence, contained amidst the houses, welcomed me with such nobility that I thought for a moment death would be at the end of the street to receive me and its valets would lower the running board. I put my right hand to my chest, under my jacket. The beating of my heart revealed the presence within me of a tribe that dances to the sound of the tomtom. I was hungry for Jean. The car turned. Undoubtedly I was made aware of my friendship by the grief that Jean's death was causing me, and little by little I became terribly afraid that since the friendship would have no external object on which to expand itself it might consume me by its fervor and cause my death. Its fire (the rims of my eyelids were already burning) would, I thought, turn against me, who contain and detain Jean's image and allow it to merge with myself within me.

"Monsieur! Monsieur! Hey! Monsieur, please stay with the men!"

Of course. I must stay with the men. The director of the funeral was wearing knee breeches, black stockings, a black dress coat, and black pumps and was carrying an ivory-headed cane entwined with a black silk cord at the end of which was a silver tassel. Someone was playing the harmonium.

Paulo was walking stiffly in front of me. He was a monolithic block, the angles of which must have scraped space, the air, and the azure. His nastiness made one think he was noble. I was sure that he felt no grief at his brother's death, and I myself felt no hatred for that indifference against which my tenderness was about to crash.

The procession stopped for a second, and I saw the

profile of Paulo's mouth. I mused upon his soul, which cannot be defined better than by the following comparison: one speaks of the bore of a gun,* which is the inner wall—less than the wall itself—of the gun. It is the thing that no longer exists, it is the gleaming, steely, icy vacuum that limits the air column and the steel tube, the vacuum and the metal; worse: the vacuum and the coldness of the metal. Paulo's soul was perceptible in his parted lips and vacuous eyes.

The procession stirred, then got under way again. Paulo's body hesitated. He was his brother's chief mourner, as a king is a king's, and led the cortège like a caparisoned horse charged with a nobility of fire, silver, and velvet. His pace was slow and heavy. He was a lady of Versailles, dignified and unfeeling.

When Jean had diarrhea, he said to me, "I've got the trots." Why did that word have to come back to me just as I was watching Paulo's solemn and almost motionless backside, why did I have to call that barely indicated dance the trots?

Roses have the irritability, curtness, and magnetic edginess of certain mediums. It was they who were performing the actual service.

The coffin was slid onto the catafalque through an opening at one end. This sudden theatrical stunt, the conjuring away of the coffin, greatly amused me. Acts without overtones, without extension, empty acts, were reflecting the same desolation as the death being reflected on the black-draped chairs, on the little trick of a catafalque, on the *Dies Irae.* Jean's death was duplicating itself in another death, was making itself visible, was projecting itself upon

---

* The French word *âme* means both "soul" and "bore" of a gun.
—*Translator's note.*

trappings as dark and ugly as the details with which inter-
ments are surrounded. It seemed to me an inane, doubly
useless act, like the condemnation of an innocent man. I
deeply regretted that processions of handsome boys,
naked or in underpants, sober or laughing—for it was important that his death be an occasion for play and laughter—had not accompanied Jean from a bed of state to his
grave. I would have loved to gaze at their thighs and arms
and the backs of their necks, to have imagined their woolly
sex under their blue woolen underpants.

I had sat down. I saw people kneeling. Out of respect
for Jean, I suppose, and in order not to attract attention,
I wanted to kneel too. I mechanically put my hand into
my jacket pocket and encountered my little matchbox. It
was empty. Instead of throwing it away, I had inadvertently put it back into my pocket.

"There's a little matchbox in my pocket."

It was quite natural for me to recall at that moment
the comparison a fellow prisoner once made while telling
me about the packages which the inmates were allowed
to receive:

"You're allowed one package a week. Whether it's a
coffin or a box of matches, it's the same thing, it's a
package."

No doubt. A matchbox or a coffin, it's the same thing,
I said to myself. I have a little coffin in my pocket.

As I stood up in order to kneel, a cloud must have
passed in front of the sun, and the church was darkened
by it. Was the priest censing the catafalque? The harmonium played more softly, or so it seemed, as soon as
I was on my knees, with my head between my hands. This
posture immediately brought me into contact with God.

"Dear God, dear God, dear God, I melt beneath your
gaze. I'm a poor child. Protect me from the devil and

God. Let me sleep in the shade of your trees, your monasteries, your gardens, behind your walls. Dear God, I have my grief, I'm praying badly, but you know that the position is painful, the straw has left its mark on my knees. . . ."

The priest opened the tabernacle. All the heralds in blazoned velvet jerkins, the standard-bearers and pikemen, the horsemen, the knights, the S.S., the Hitler Youth in short pants paraded through the Führer's bedroom and on into his quarters. Standing near his bed, with his face and body in the shadow and his pale hand leaning on the flounced pillow, he watched them from the depths of his solitude. His castration had cut him off from human beings. His joys are not ours. Out of respect, the parade performed in the deep silence reserved for the sick. Even the footsteps of the stone heroes and the rumbling of the cannons and tanks were deadened by the woolen rugs. At times, a slight rustling of cloth could still be heard, the same sound that is made in the darkness by the stiff, dry cloth of the uniform of American soldiers when they move fast on their rubber soles.

". . . Dear God, forgive me. You see me as I am, simple, naked, tiny."

I was praying spontaneously, from my heart and lips. This attitude estranged me from Jean, whom I was betraying for too lofty a personage. I seized upon this pretext of a delicate sentiment to avoid creasing my trousers. I sat down and thought about Jean with far greater ease. The star of my friendship rose up larger and rounder into my sky. I was pregnant with a feeling that could, without my being surprised, make me give birth to a strange but viable and certainly beautiful being, Jean's being its father vouched for that. This new feeling of friendship was coming into being in an odd way.

The priest said:

"... He died on the field of honor. He died fighting the invader...."

A shudder ran through me and made me realize that my body was feeling friendship for the priest who was making it possible for Jean to leave me with the regrets of the whole world. Since it was impossible for me to bury him alone, in a private ceremony (I could have carried his body, and why don't the public authorities allow it? I could have cut it up in a kitchen and eaten it. Of course, there would be a good deal of refuse: the intestines, the liver, the lungs, the eyes with their hair-rimmed lids in particular, all of which I would dry and burn—I might even mix their ashes with my food—but the flesh could be assimilated into mine), let him depart then with official honors, the glory of which would devolve upon me and thus somewhat stifle my despair.

The flowers on the catafalque grew exhausted from shedding their brightness. The dahlias were drooping with sleep. Their stomachs were glutted when they left the funeral parlor. They were still belching.

I followed the priest's oration:

"... this sacrifice is not wasted. Young Jean died for France...."

If I were told that I was risking death in refusing to cry "Vive la France," I would cry it in order to save my hide, but I would cry it softly. If I had to cry it very loudly, I would do so, but laughingly, without believing in it. And if I had to believe in it, I would; then I would immediately die of shame. It doesn't matter whether this is due to the fact that I'm an abandoned child who knows nothing about his family or country; the attitude exists and is intransigent. And yet, it was nice to know that France was delegating its name so as to be represented at Jean's funeral. I was so overwhelmed with the sumptuousness of it all that my friendship went to my head (as one says: reseda goes to my head). Friendship, which I recognize by my grief at Jean's death, also has the sudden impetuousness of love. I said friendship. I would some-times like it to go away and yet I tremble for fear it will. The only difference between it and love is that it does not know jealousy. Yet I feel a vague anxiety, a weak remorse. I am tormented. It is the birth of memory.

The procession—where could that obscure child have made so many friends?—the procession left the church.

The matchbox in my pocket, the tiny coffin, imposed its presence more and more, obsessed me:

"Jean's coffin could be just as small."

I was carrying his coffin in my pocket. There was no need for the small-scale bier to be a true one. The coffin of the formal funeral had imposed its potency on that little object. I was performing in my pocket, on the box that my hand was stroking, a diminutive funeral cere-mony as efficacious and reasonable as the Masses that are said for the souls of the departed, behind the altar, in a remote chapel, over a fake coffin draped in black. My box was sacred. It did not contain a particle merely of Jean's body but Jean in his entirety. His bones were the size of matches, of tiny pebbles imprisoned in penny whistles. His body was somewhat like the cloth-wrapped wax dolls with which sorcerers cast their spells. The whole gravity of the ceremony was gathered in my pocket, to which the transfer had just taken place. However, it should be noted that the pocket never had any religious character; as for the sacredness of the box, it never prevented me from treating the object familiarly, from kneading it with my fingers, except that once, as I was talking to Erik, my gaze fastened on his fly, which was resting on the chair with the weightiness of the pouch of Florentine costumes that contained the balls, and my hand let go of the matchbox and left my pocket.

Jean's mother had just gone out of the room. I uncrossed my legs and recrossed them in the other direction. I was looking at Erik's torso, which was leaning slightly forward.

"You must miss Berlin," I said.

Very slowly, ponderously, searching for words, he replied:

"Why? I'll go back after the war."

He offered me one of his American cigarettes, which the maid or his mistress must have gone down to buy for him, since he himself never left the small apartment. I gave him a light. He stood up, not straight but leaning slightly forward, so that in drawing himself up he had to throw his torso backward. The movement arched his entire body and made his basket bulge under the cloth of his trousers. He had at that moment, despite his being cloistered, despite that sad, soft captivity among women, the nobility of a whole animal which carries its load between its legs.

"You must get bored."

We exchanged a few more trivialities. I could have hated him, but his sadness made me suddenly believe in his gentleness. His face was slightly lined with very fine wrinkles, like those of twenty-five-year-old blonds. He remained very handsome, very strong, and his sadness itself expressed the lasciviousness of the whole body of this wild animal that was reaching maturity.

He spoke to me very quietly. Perhaps he was afraid I might denounce him to the police. I wondered whether he was carrying a gun. My eyes furtively questioned his blue denim trousers, pausing over every suspect bulk. Though I intended my gaze to be light, it must have

weighed on the fly, for Erik smiled, if I may say so, with
his usual smile. I blushed a little and looked away, trying
to veil my blush by exhaling a cloud of smoke. He took
advantage of this to cross his legs and say in a casual tone:

"Jean was very young. . . ."

He said "Djian," pronouncing the "an" very curtly.

I did not reply. He said:

"*Aber*, you too, you Jean."

"Yes."

I was thinking of the warm, wide, heavy Louis XV bed
covered with Venetian point lace in which Jean's mother
pressed against Erik at night and no doubt during the day,
either in a nightgown or naked. The bed was alive in the
darkness of the bedroom, was emitting its rays, which
reached me despite the walls. It was certain that one day
or another Erik's and Paulo's thighs would constrict me
there, they themselves getting their bellies all raddled
with the maid and the mother, in a room watched over by
the memory of Jean.

At the end of my fourth visit, Erik accompanied me
alone to the entryway. It was late, it was getting dark.
The entryway was very narrow. He pressed against my
back. I felt his breath on my neck, and, close to my ear,
he murmured:

"See you tomorrow, nine o'clock, Jean."

He took my hand and insisted:

"Nine o'clock, yes!"

"Yes."

The gesture of surprise he had just made on realizing
that the two names were the same tightened the trousers
against his buttocks and enhanced them. The outline of
the muscles excited me. I tried to imagine what his relationship had been with Jean, whom he hated and who
hated him. Erik's strength probably enabled him to seem

very mild as he bullied the child. I looked at his eyes and composed in my mind the following sentence:

"So many suns have capsized beneath his hands, in his eyes. . . ."

When I left the apartment after our first meeting, I attempted to retrace the course of his life and, for greater efficiency, I got into his uniform, boots, and skin. Drunk with the somewhat blurry vision of a tall, young Negro behind the windows of the café on the Boulevard de la Villette where he was leaning against a juke box listening to javas and popular waltzes, I wormed my way into his past, gently and hesitantly at first, feeling my way, when the iron toe-plates of one of my shoes accidentally struck the curb. My calf vibrated, then my whole body. I raised my head and took my hands out of my pockets. I put on the German boots.

The fog was thick and so white that it almost lit up the garden. The trees were caught. Motionless, attentive, pale, nude, captured by a net of hair or a singing of harps. A smell of earth and dead leaves gave reason to think that all was not lost. The day would see the reign of God. A swan flapped its wings on a lake. I was eighteen, a young Nazi on duty in the park, where I was sitting at the foot of a tree. Since the seat of my riding breeches (I was preparing for the artillery) was leather-lined, I did not mind the dampness of the grass. Far off, behind me, an automobile drove by in the Siegesallee with its lights off, its noises muffled. Five o'clock was about to strike. I started to get up. A man was coming toward me. He was walking on the grass, ignoring the footpaths. His hands were in his pockets. He was heavy and yet light, for each of his angles was imprecise. He looked like a walking willow, each stump of which is lightened and thinned by an aigrette of young branches. He had a revolver. A force prevented me from getting up. The man was very close. His forehead was narrow, his nose and entire face were flattened, but their muscles were firm, as if wrought by a hammer. He was about thirty-five. He had the face of a brute. As he neared the tree under which I was sitting, he raised his head.

"Why is that man walking on the grass of the lawns?" I thought to myself.

"Say, he oughtn't to be there," thought the man, referring to me. "He's crossed the boundary."

He was smoking. Upon seeing me, he straightened up and threw back his chest with a strong, calm movement of his shoulders. He saw that I was a member of the Hitler Youth.

"You're going to get cold."

"I'm on guard."

"What are you guarding?"

"Nothing."

The man was satisfied with this reply. He was not sad, but indifferent or interested in other things than what he seemed to be. I was watching him. Though he was very close, I still could not see him clearly.

"Here."

He took a cigarette from his trouser pocket and handed it to me. I removed my gloves, took it, and stood up in order to light it from his. I was no stronger standing than sitting. The mere bulk of the man crushed me. I could tell that under his clothes, under his open shirt, was a terrific set of muscles. Despite his bulk and shape, he was lightened by the fog, his outline was blurred. It was also as if the morning mist were a steady emanation from his extraordinarily powerful body, a body strong with such glowing life that the combustion caused that motionless, thick, and yet luminous white smoke to seep out through all its pores. I was caught. I dared not look at him. Germany, stunned and staggering, was just managing to recover from the deep, rich drowsiness, the dizziness, the suffocation fertile in the new prodigies into which it had been plunged by the perfumes and charms emitted slowly and heavily by that strange curly poppy, Dr. Magnus Hirschfeld.

In the triangle of the V-necked shirt, in the middle of a tuft of hair that implied a fleece all over him, I saw, snug and warm, a little gold medallion cuddling in that wool, which was fragrant with the odor of armpits, like a plaster Jesus in the straw and hay dazed by the smell of the droppings of the ox and the ass. I shivered.

"Are you cold?"

"Yes."

The executioner said with a laugh that he had more heat than he needed, and, as if wanting to play, he drew me to him and put his arms around me. I dared not move. My long pale lashes fluttered a bit when the killer grabbed me and looked at me at closer range. A slight quiver ruffled the part of the face which is so sensitive in adolescents: the puffy surface around the mouth, the spot that will be covered by the mustache. The executioner saw the trembling. He was moved by the youngster's timorous flutter. He hugged him more gently, he softened his smile and said:

"What's the matter? Are you scared?"

I was wearing the wristwatch I had stolen the day before from one of the other boys. Was I scared? Why had he asked me that question point-blank?

More out of delicacy than pride, I almost answered no, but immediately, sure of my power over the brute, I wanted to be mean and I said yes.

"Did you recognize me?"

"Why?"

Erik was surprised at hearing slightly hesitant inflec-
tions in his voice which he had not been aware of and,
at times, under the stress of greater anxiety, a slight
trembling over a few notes that were too high for his
usual timbre.

"Don't you recognize me?"

I kept my lips parted. I was still in the embrace of that
unyielding fellow whose smiling face was armed with the
glowing cigarette and bent over mine.

"Well? Can't you see?"

I had recognized him. I dared not say so. I replied:

"It's time for me to be getting back to the barracks."

"Are you scared because I'm the executioner?"

He had spoken until then in a hollow voice, in keeping
with the blurriness of things or perhaps because he feared
a danger might be hidden behind the fog, but when he
uttered those words, he laughed with such violence and
clarity that all the watchful trees suddenly came to attention in the wadding and recorded the laugh. I dared not
move. I looked at him. I inhaled smoke, took the cigarette
from my mouth and said:

"No."

But my "no" betrayed fear.

"No, you mean it, you're not scared?"

Instead of repeating the word no, I shook my head and,
lightly tapping the cigarette twice with my forefinger,
dropped a bit of ash on his foot. The casualness of these
two gestures gave the boy such an air of detachment, of
indifference, that the executioner felt humiliated, as if I
had not deigned even to see him. He hugged me harder,
laughingly, pretending that he wanted to frighten me.

"No?"

He peered into my eyes and dove right in. He blew
the smoke in my face.

"No? Are you sure?"

"Of course I am, why?" And, to mollify the executioner, I added: "I haven't done any harm." The stolen watch on my wrist was punctuating my uneasiness.

It was cold. The dampness was penetrating our clothes. The fog was rather thick. We seemed to be alone, characters without a past or future, composed simply of our respective roles of Hitler Youth and executioner, and united to each other not by a succession of events but by the play of a grave gratuitousness, the gratuitousness of the poetic fact: *We were there,* in the fog of the world.

Still holding me by the waist, the executioner walked a few steps with me. We went down a path and then walked up onto another lawn to reach a clump of trees that made a dark spot in the pale dawn. I could have repeated that my duty obliged me to stay on the footpath. All I wanted was to have a smoke. I said nothing. But my chest was tight with fear and swollen with hope. I was one long, silent moan.

"What will be born of our love-making? What can be born of it?"

Until then I had known only unexciting play with a friend who was too young. Today it is I whom a fellow over thirty, and a headsman, is leading imperiously to love, at an hour when one gets the ax, in the seclusion of a clump of trees, near a lake.

The Berlin executioner was about six feet one. His muscular build was that of an executioner who chops on a block with an ax. His brown hair was cropped very close, so that his completely round head was that of a beheaded man. He was sad despite his smile, which was meant to brave me and tame me. His sadness was profound, its source was deeper than his profession, being, rather, in his strength itself. He lived alone in a comfortable apartment which was tastefully furnished and resembled any other bourgeois apartment in Berlin. Every morning an old woman came to do the cleaning and left in a hurry. He ate in a restaurant. On days when capital punishment was scheduled, he did not go home in the evening. He would stay in a cabaret until daybreak, then wander in the dawn and dew through the lanes and lawns of the Tiergarten. The day before he met Erik and led him beneath the branches of a diamond-studded fir tree, he had detached a murderer's head from its trunk. Our faces were breaking the gossamer.

Now that I was sitting opposite Erik and seeing the beauty of his buttocks and the elegant impatience of his movements, not only was it obvious to me that his adventure had been lived, but, in addition, it fitted him so perfectly that I felt a kind of peace, the deep satisfaction of being present at the revelation of a truth. But my forsaking Jean, or rather granting his enemies such favor, delicately tortured my mind, into which remorse had worked its way and which it then ground, though very gently, with a few gentle writhing movements. I knew that I ought not abandon the boy whose soul had not yet found rest. I ought to have helped him. A few of the crabs he had probably picked up from a whore still clung to me. I was sure that the insects had lived on his body, if not all of them at least one whose brood invaded my bush with a colony that was digging in, multiplying, and dying in the folds of the skin of my balls. I saw to it that they stayed there and in the vicinity. It pleased me to think that they retained a dim memory of that same place on Jean's body, whose blood they had sucked. They were tiny, secret hermits whose duty it was to keep alive in those forests the memory of a young victim. They were truly the living remains of my friend. I took care of them as much as possible by not washing, not even scratching.

At times, I would pluck one of them out and hold it between my nail and skin: I would examine it closely for a moment, with curiosity and tenderness, and then replace it in my curly bush. Perhaps their brothers were still living in Jean's hairs. The morgue keeps bodies for a long time. It has apparatus, refrigerators. Although Jean had been killed on the nineteenth, we did not know of his death until August 29. He was buried on September 3. I had been informed of some of the circumstances of his death by his comrades in the Communist Party, who had also told me where he had been killed. I was forced there by anxiety. On the afternoon of the first of September, I walked to Belleville and then to Ménilmontant, both of which I had forgotten about. The heat of the struggle was still visible on people's faces, but in the few days that had gone by they had lost their vigor. Their faith was slackening. The weather was hot. Although I kept my eyes lowered, I could see the open shops. Wicker baskets, chairs, and mats were being woven in the sky, people were eating fruit in the street, workers were smoking cigarettes made with Virginia tobacco. Nobody was aware of my pilgrimage. A huge sigh congested my chest and throat and might have caused my death. I was on the sunny side of the street. I asked a girl:

"Is this the way to the Boulevard Ménilmontant?"

She seemed not to know about my anguish, and the constipated look on my mug could not tell her the cause of it. Yet she did not seem shocked at my not addressing her more politely. As for me, I felt I was entitled to everything. People, even those who did not know me, owed me the greatest respect, for inside I was in mourning for Jean. Although I had always accepted the costume of widows in deep mourning, nevertheless its reduction to the status of a symbol, the black arm band, the strip of crape on a lapel, the black cockade on the brim of workmen's caps, had previously seemed ridiculous to me. Suddenly I understood their necessity: they advise people to approach you with consideration, to be tactful with you, for you are the repository of a divinized memory.

". . . It's almost at the corner of the Rue de Belleville, opposite number 64, 66, or 68. I know about it from the fellow in the Party. You'll see a delicatessen."

I did not know the flavor of human flesh, but I was sure that all sausages and meat spreads would have a corpse-like taste. I live frightfully alone and desperate, in a voracious society that protects a family of criminal sausage-makers (the father, mother, and probably three kids), mincers of corpses who feed all of France with dead young men and hide at the back of a shop on the Avenue Parmentier. I stepped onto the left-hand sidewalk, where the odd numbers are. I was at 23. It was time to cross. I turned toward the empty gutter, that river of dangerous light which separated me from Hell, and prepared to leave the shore. I was laden, encumbered with a more agonizing pain, with the fear of being alone amidst the passers-by at an invisible theater where death had kidnaped Jean, where the drama—or mystery—had been performed, and the result of which I knew only through its negation. My pain was so great that it sought escape in the form of fiery gestures: kissing a lock of hair, weeping on a breast, pressing an image, hugging a neck, tearing out grass, lying down on the spot and falling asleep in the shade, sun, or rain with my head on my bent arm. What gesture would I make? What sign would be left me? I looked over to the other side of the street. First I saw, directly opposite me, a little girl of about ten who was walking quickly and clenching a stiff bouquet of white carnations in her little hand. I stepped down from the sidewalk, and a car that was going by on the other side, a little way up the street, suddenly exposed a French sailor whom I recognized by his white collar. He bent over toward the foot of a tree where a few people were standing and looking. The sailor's odd movement, which was accompanied by the passing of the girl, made my heart pound. When I reached the middle of the gutter, I could see better: at the foot of the tree were flowers in tin cans. The sailor had straightened up and was no longer a sailor. I had to make an effort to look at the number of the house opposite: 52. I still had a hope: someone else might have been killed there, at the same time as he. I put my hands into my pockets. Let it not be thought that I can be a party to this ridiculous plebeian tribute. Though they looked fresh from a distance and formed a kind of altar, from up close almost all the flowers were seen to be wilted. I was in the heart of China, in Japan, where the dead are honored in the streets, on the roads, on the sides of volcanoes, on the shores of rivers and the sea. I saw a big damp spot and realized immediately it was the water from the flowers that was flowing. Nevertheless, I could not help thinking of all the blood Jean had lost. It was a lot of blood. Hadn't it dried since his death? An idiotic thought. Another: it was his piss. Or maybe the sailor had just relieved himself against the tree. Jean's piss! There's nothing to laugh about. Could he have died of fright? Not at all, one sometimes loses one's urine. No, it's not that. There were holes in the cans. The white shopfront . . . "Delica . . . Oh, God!"

I looked first at the sturdy sailor beaming in the middle of the spreading urine, and my eye took in the whole group: tree, flowers, and people. The sailor was a young fellow who had apparently been in the underground. His face was radiant: brown hair, though discolored by the

sun, a straight nose, hard eyes. In order to put his hands
into his pockets, he pushed back the flaps of a leather coat,
a mackinaw, whose white furry collar—probably sheep-
skin—had misled me, for I had mistaken it for the light
collar of a sailor. The little girl was still squatting in front
of the tree, putting her white carnations into a can with
a red and green label on which the word "Peas" was
printed in black. I tried to recognize her face, but I had
certainly never seen her before. She was alone. She was
probably pretending that she was placing flowers on a
grave. She had found a pretext for performing in everyone's presence the hidden rites of a nature cult and of a
cult of the gods which childhood always discovers, but
which it serves in secret. I was there. What gestures
should I make? I would have liked to lean on the arm of
the husky underground fighter. Does the tree perform
marriages, or what if it records acts of adultery: its trunk
is girdled with an official tricolored ribbon. The tree contains Jean's soul, which took refuge there when the shots
from a machine gun riddled his elegant body. If I approach the fellow in the mackinaw, anger will make the
plane tree shake its plume of leaves angrily. I dared not
think of anyone other than Jean. I was in a cruel light,
beneath the pitiless gaze of things. Since they know how
to read every sign, every secret thought, they would con-
demn me if I had the slightest intention of acting. Yet I
needed love. What to do? What gesture? Too much grief
was pent up within me. If I opened a single thin gate, the
flood would sweep into my gestures and there's no telling
what would happen. Crosses of Lorraine, tricolor cock-
ades, and a few tiny pin-and-paper flags were stuck into
the tree trunk around a sheet of lined note paper pinned
to the bark. And on the sheet, in an awkward hand, was
written the following: "A young patriot fell here. Noble

Parisians, leave a flower and observe a moment of silence."
Perhaps it wasn't he? I don't know yet. But what idiot
wrote the word "young"? Young. I withdrew from the
drama as far as possible. In order to weep, I had descended to the realm of the dead themselves, to their
secret chambers, led by the invisible but soft hands of
birds down stairways which were folded up again as I
advanced. I displayed my grief in the friendly fields of
death, far from men: within myself. No one was likely to
catch me making ridiculous gestures; I was elsewhere.
"Young" had been written in black ink, but it seemed to
me that the certainty of Jean's death should not depend
on a word that can be erased.

"And what if I erased it?" I realized at once that they
wouldn't let me. Even the least hardhearted would prevent me from checking fate. I would be depriving them
of a dead person, and above all a dead person who was
dear to them *by virtue* of his being dead. I thought of an
eraser. The one I had in my pocket was a pencil eraser.
What I needed was a harder, more granular one, an ink
eraser. No. People would slap me. One doesn't try to
resurrect bodies with an eraser.

"He's a Boche!" they would say. "A swine! A rat! A
traitor! He's the one who killed him!" The mob would
lynch me. Its cries welled up within me, rose all the way
from my depths to my ears, which heard them backwards.
The little girl who had been squatting stood up and went
off, probably to her home twenty yards away. Could I be
asleep? Are Belleville and Ménilmontant places in Paris
where people venerate the dead by putting flowers into
rusty old tin cans and placing them at the foot of a dusty
tree? Young! No doubt about it, I said to myself, it's here
. . . I stopped there. The uttering of "here" and, even if
only mentally, of the words meant to follow, "that he

was killed," gave to my pain a physical precision that aggravated it. The words were too cruel. Then I said to myself that the words were words and did not in any way change the facts.

I forced myself to say over and over, inwardly, with the irritating repetitiveness of a saw, He-re, He-re, He-re, He-re.* My mind was being sharpened at the spot designated by "Here." I was no longer even witnessing a drama. No drama could have taken place in an area too narrow for any presence. "He-re, He-re, He-re, He-re. That he was killed, that he was killed, that he was killed, that heels killed, that heels killed . . . " and I mentally composed the following epitaph: "Here that heels killed." People were watching. They no longer saw me, they were unaware of my adventures. An unkempt working-class woman was carrying a shopping bag. With a sigh, she drew from it a very tight little bunch of those ridiculous yellow flowers that are called marigolds. I looked at her. She was somewhat plump, and bold-looking. She bent over and put the bunch of marigolds into a rusty can in which there were wilted red roses. Everyone (five other persons, including the underground fighter, who was at my left) watched her performance. She straightened up and said, as if to herself, but it was meant for all of us: "Poor things. Mustn't ask who it's for."

An old woman wearing a hat nodded. No one else made a gesture or uttered a word. The tree was acquiring an amazing bearing and dignity which heightened with each passing second. If that plane tree had grown on my estate or on the heights where I go to give thanks to love, I could have leaned against it, could have casually

_____

* There is a play here on the words *scie* (saw) and *ici* (here). —*Translator's note.*

carved a heart in its bark, have wept, have sat down on the moss and fallen asleep in an air still blended with Jean's spirit, which had been reduced to powder by a burst of machine-gun fire. I turned around. In the glass of the shopfront were two round, star-shaped holes. As everything was, at the time, a painful sign to me, the glass at once became sacred, forbidden. It semed to be Jean's congealed soul, which, though pierced, retained its eternal transparency and protected the repulsive landscape of his flesh, which had been pounded, chopped, and cut up in the form of sausages and liver paté. I was about to turn around and thought the tree had perhaps lost its ridiculous adornment, the tin cans, the spreading urine, in short what one never sees at the foot of a tree and what could only be the doing of children or dreams. Everything, indeed, might have disappeared. Was it true that philosophers doubted the existence of things that were in back of them? How could one detect the secret of the disappearance of things? By turning around very fast? No. But faster? Faster than anything? I glanced behind me. I was on the watch. I turned my eyes and head, ready to. . . . No, it was pointless. Things can never be caught napping. You would have to spin about with the speed of a propeller. You would then see that things had disappeared, and you with them. I stopped playing. With a feeling of gravity, I turned around. The tree was there. A lady who was going by made the sign of the cross. That little fête, at the foot of a tree that was pissing, was in bad taste. I refused everyone the right to invent such indelicate tributes. Let them stick to the polite, customary rites. The only thing lacking in that indecent spectacle was a wooden bowl draped with a crape ribbon for collecting pennies for the widow and the kids. On a sunny day, with a delicate gesture, they could show that their hearts were in the right place, if they wanted to, though they kept their precious vases at home, and had the nerve to offer a naked hero graceless flowers in empty tins which they had stolen from garbage cans—and they hadn't even bothered to hammer down the sharp edges. While his soul was floating in the air, around the tree, Jean was heartbroken at still having that filthy wound, that damp, flowery canker whose rot stank in my nostrils. The canker was to blame for Jean's being kept on earth. He was unable to dissolve absolutely into the azure.

I looked at the fake sailor. He had put a cigarette into his mouth, no doubt mechanically, but very quickly removed it. Out of respect, I think. Thus, the patriot standing there in the August sun in a fur-lined leather coat open on a flexible waist and a broad chest pure as a banner was not, though I had hoped for a moment that he was, what death had achieved with Jean. He was not Jean transformed, disfigured, and transfigured, sloughing his hide and emerging with a new skin; for Jean, that soldier of the Year II, would not have dared make that inept gesture of respect.

I had never yet seen Jean's half brother. I was sure that it was he, as a matter of fact, whom I saw the following day at the funeral, with his mother.

He went off. For a moment I followed him with my eyes—not that I suspected what linked him to Jean—but because of his splendid bearing, which I shall speak about later. When he entered the room in which I was chatting with Erik for the first time, darkness was setting in. He said:

"Hello."

And he sat down in a corner, near the table. He did not look at either Erik or me. The first thing he did was to take the wristwatch that was lying on the table and put it on. His face expressed nothing in particular.

I was perhaps mistaken in supposing that the two

watches lying back to back on a night table betrayed a
shameful intimate relationship, but I had so often dreamed
fruitlessly of intimate loves that the most desirable of
these loves were signified, written, by things that are
inanimate when alone and they sing—and sing only of
love—as soon as they encounter the beloved, the song,
ornaments of secret states of adornment. Paulo took a
gun from his pocket and began to take it apart. The fact
that he showed so little surprise meant that his mother
must have informed him of my presence. She must have
seen him when he came in. Erik had stopped talking. He
did not look at Paulo. The mother came in by the same
door as her son. She said to me, pointing at him:

"This is Paul, Jean's brother."

"Oh! I see."

The boy did not deign to make a movement. He did
not say a word to me or even look at me.

"Can't you say hello? It's Monsieur Genet, you know,
Jean's friend."

He did deign to stand up and come over to shake hands.
I could tell he had recognized me, but he didn't smile at
me.

"How goes it?"

He looked deep into my eyes. His face was grim, not
because he was tired or out of indifference to my question
or to me, but, I think, out of a violent will to exclude me,
to drive me out. At that moment, Erik, who had left for
twenty seconds, reappeared in the mirror and as he
entered while Paulo was staring at me and gripping the
weapon with one hand, I was seized with fear, a physical
fear, as when one feels the imminence of a brawl. The
grimness of that swarthy little face made me feel immediately that I was entering tragedy. Its hardness and
sternness meant above all that there could be no hope

and that I had to expect the worst. I hardly looked at him, yet I felt him living under very high tension, and on my account. He parted his lips but said nothing. Erik was behind him, ready, I felt, to back him up if, as once happened with a sailor, Paulo said to me, "Come outside," and joined me with a knife in his fist for a fight that would be fatal to me, not because of the blade but because it seemed to me impossible to soften all that hardness. I would have liked the inflexible frame that made Paulo mortally seductive to bend for me. But all I could do was be conscious of his elegant severity, the result of a disheartening failure (for if I can note here this kind of short poem, the reason is that it was not granted me to live a moment of happiness, because a sailor's face in front of me went blank when I asked him for a light). Paulo went to the table and started toying with his gun again. I watched his hands: not a single superfluous gesture. Not one of them that did not do what it was meant to do. That precision created a disturbing impression of indifference to everything that was not the projected act. The machine could not make an error. I think that Paulo's meanness thus called attention to itself by a kind of inhuman severity. I turned to the mother:

"I'll be going."

"But you'll stay and have dinner with us. You're not going off just like that."

"I've got to go home."

"Is it urgent?"

"Yes, I've got to go home."

"But you'll come again. Come and see us again. Erik will be delighted to see you. All this war and killing is so unfortunate."

The maid was in the entryway. She opened the door for me to leave and looked at me without saying anything. In order to open it, she had to lift up a worn hanging that concealed it, and her hand grazed that of Jean's mother, who drew back and said, apropos of so trivial a thing:

"Do watch what you're doing."

She too knew that the father of Juliette's child was not Jean but a former sergeant in the regular army who was now a captain in the Militia.

The maid opened the door. She neither smiled nor said good-by, and I dared not speak to her about Jean.

I left. Jean had hardly spoken to me about his brother, who had gone off to Germany, then Denmark, and then Germany again. Yet, within me, I followed Paulo's adventures very attentively, waiting, so as to record them, in order for them to take on a particular meaning that would make them interesting, that is, capable of expressing me. My despair over Jean's death is a cruel child. It's Paulo. Let the reader not be surprised if in speaking of him the poet goes so far as to say that his flesh was black, or green with the greenness of night. Paulo's presence had the color of a dangerous liquid. The muscles of his arms and legs were long and smooth. One imagined his joints to be perfectly supple. That suppleness and the length and smoothness of his muscles were the sign of his meanness. I mean by "sign" that there was a connection between his meanness and his visible features. His muscles were elegant and distinguished. So was his meanness. His head was small and was set on a massive neck. The fixity of his gaze, which was worse than that of Erik, was that of an implacable judge, of a soldier, of an officer stupid to the point of sublimity. His face never smiled. His hair was smooth, but the locks overlapped. Or to put it another way, he seemed never to comb his hair but only to slick it down with his wet hands. Of all the little guys I like to stick into my books, he's the meanest. Abandoned on my bed, naked, polished, he will be an instrument of torture, a pair of pincers, a serpentine dagger ready to function, functioning by its evil presence alone and springing up, pale and with clenched teeth, from my despair. He is my despair embodied. He made it possible for me to write this book, just as he granted me the strength to be present at all the ceremonies of memory.

That visit to the home of Jean's mother left me in a state of exhaustion. To restore my peace of mind I had to organize and carry on the lives which I had fractured for a moment and integrate them into mine, but I was too weary to do it then. I had dinner in a restaurant, then went to a movie.

Suddenly the audience burst out laughing when the narrator said: "No, indeed, fighting on the rooftops doesn't fill a man's belly," for a militiaman had just appeared on the screen, a kid of sixteen or seventeen, frailer than Paulo. I said to myself: "He's frailer than Paulo," and this reflection proves that the adventure had got off on the right track. The kid was skinny but good-looking. His face had suffered. It was sad. It was trembling. One would have thought it expressionless. His shirt was open at the neck. There were cartridge loops on his belt. He was walking in socks too big for him. His head was down. I felt he was ashamed of his black eye. In order to look more natural, to deceive the paving stones in the street, he ran his tongue over his lips and made a brief gesture with his hand which was so closely related to that of his mouth that it traced his whole body, puckered it with very subtle waves, and immediately made me think the following:

"The gardener is the loveliest rose in his garden."

The screen was then filled by a single arm, which was fitted with a broad, heavy, very beautiful hand, then by a young French soldier who was shouldering the little traitor's rifle. The audience applauded. Then the militia-man reappeared. His face was trembling (particularly the eyelids and lips) from the cuffs he had received a few feet away from the camera. The audience was laugh-ing, whistling, stamping. Neither the world's laughter nor the inelegance of caricaturists will keep me from recog-nizing the sorry grandeur of a French militiaman who, during the insurrection of Paris against the German army in August 1944, took to the rooftops with the Germans and for several days fired to the last bullet—or next-to-last—on the French populace that had mounted the bar-ricades.

In the fierce eyes of the crowd, the disarmed, dirty, bewildered, stumbling, dazed, emptied, cowardly (it's amazing how fast certain words flow from the pen to define certain natures and how happy the author feels at being able to talk that way about his heroes), weary kid was ridiculous. A woman in light-colored rayon was thrash-ing about at my side. She was foaming at the mouth and bouncing her behind on her seat. She yelled:

"The bastards, rip their guts out!"

Confronted with the face of the little traitor (which was luminous just because the film had been shot against the sun), whose youth, caught in a deadly trap, was dazzling the screen, the woman was odious. I thought to myself that little fellows like him were being killed so that Erik might live. The audience was like the woman. It hated evil. My hatred of the militiaman was so in-tense, so beautiful, that it was equivalent to the strongest love. No doubt it was he who had killed Jean. I desired him. I was suffering so because of Jean's death that I was willing to do anything to forget about him. The best trick I could play on that fierce gang known as destiny, which delegates a kid to do its work, and the best I could play on the kid, would be to invest him with the love I felt for his victim. I implored the little fellow's image:

"I'd like you to have killed him!"

If one of my hands holds the lighted cigarette and the other clutches the armrest, they clasp each other even though they do not move. This gesture gives greater vigor to my wish, which is charged with a will and a forceful summons to transform itself into an invocation.

"Kill him, Riton, I'm giving you Jean."

My only gesture was to put my lighted cigarette to my lips, and my clasped fingers clenched each other to the breaking point. Scented with peril, my prayer rises to my head from the pit of my stomach, spreads beneath the vaulted ceiling of my skull, comes down again, emerges from my mouth, and turns my cry into a wail whose value I recognize—I mean something like musical value—and an "I love you, oh" issues from me. I don't hate Jean. I want to love Riton. (I can't tell why I *spontaneously* call the unknown young militiaman Riton.) I plead again as one crawls on one's knees over flagstones.

"Kill him!"

A frightful rending tore out my fibers. I would have liked my suffering to be greater, to rise to the supreme song, to death itself. It was ghastly. I did not love Riton, all my love was still for Jean. On the screen, the militiaman was waiting. He had just been picked up. What can one do to beauty that's so glaringly obvious? One cuts off its head. That's how the fool takes revenge on a rose he has plucked. The cop dares to say of a young thief he brings back in his clutches:

"I just plucked him on the pavement!"

So don't be surprised that I see Riton as a flower of the mountaintops, a gentle edelweiss. A movement of his arm showed that he was wearing a wristwatch, but the movement was rather feeble, unlike those of Jean. However, it might have been one of Paulo's, though more effective. I was going to take off from that idea, and I realized more and more that Riton completed Paulo, but for my work of sorcery I needed perfect attention and had to make use of everything to achieve my end. The audience was whistling and yelling.

"He ought to be torn to bits!"

"Ought to give him another shiner!"

A soldier must have hit the militiaman, for he trembled and seemed to be trying to protect himself. His face clouded over. The beauty of the lily lies similarly in the amazing fragility of the little hood of pollen that trembles at the top of the pistil. A gust of wind, a clumsy finger, a leaf, can break and destroy the delicate equilibrium that holds beauty in balance. That of the child's face wavered a moment. Ruffled as it was, I feared it might not gain its composure. He was haggard. I looked at him closely and more quickly (one can, without taking one's eyes off an object, look very quickly. At that moment, my "gaze" swooped down on the image). In a few seconds he would disappear from the screen. His beauty and his gestures were the opposite of Jean's. I was at once lit up, with an inner light. A bit of love passed over to Riton. I really had the impression that love was flowing from me, from my veins to his. I called out inwardly:

"Riton, Riton, you can kill him, my child! My darling! Kill him!"

He turned his head a little. A colonel in front of me dared to say: "If I get my mitts on him. . . . " Riton's gestures were killing Jean's, were killing Jean. Suddenly the people who were yelling and jeering ceased to be ridiculous. They were ugly with grief. The furious colonel and the woman in tallow who was mad with rage and crimson under her bleached yellow locks were being tracked down by the vengeance that compelled them to honor savagely, though with grandeur, by laughter, the death of a brother or son or lover. Nobody was ridiculous. Their invectives were an additional ovation to Riton's glory. The vise in which I was caught tightened. Another image (a marching army) was on the screen. I closed my eyes. A third silent invocation rose up from me and drew me out of myself:

"Bump him off, I'm letting you have him."

Another wave of love surged from my bent, still body slouching in the seat, and poured first on the face and then on the neck, chest, and entire body of Riton, confined in my closed eyes. I squeezed my eyelids tighter. I attached myself to the captive militiaman's body, which was violent despite its weariness. Beneath his debility, he was hard, fierce, and ever new, like a skillfully made machine. My inner gaze remained fixed on the image of him which I reconstructed in its natural violence, hardness, and ferocity. An unbroken flow of love passed from my body to his, which started living again and regained its suppleness.

I added:

"Go ahead. You can pick him off."

This time the very cast of the formula indicated that my will was going into action all by itself, was refusing the help of invocation. I kept my eyes shut. The same rivers of love poured over Riton, yet not a drop was withdrawn from Jean. I was preserving both youngsters under the double ray of my tenderness. The game of murder in which they will engage is rather a war dance in which the death of one of them will be accidental, almost involuntary. It is an orgy carried to bloodshed. I closed my eyes tighter. My gaze was glued to the militiaman's fly, the image of which was within me, and made it live, gave it weight, filled it with a vigorous monster that was swollen with hatred, and my gaze was the beam on which Riton rose up and returned to the rooftops. I loved him. I was going to marry him. It would perhaps be enough for me to be dressed in white, for the wedding, though with a decoration of large black crape cabbage rosettes at each joint, at the elbows, the knees, the fingers, the ankles, the neck, the waist, the throat, the prick, and the anus. Would Riton accept me dressed that way and in a bedroom decked with irises? For the wedding celebration would then merge with my mourning and all would be saved. Was it necessary that I feel the victor's hardness in my hands? Though he was at the brink of the grave, I knew he was alive. Despite the walls, the streets, the calls, the breathing, the waves, and the automobile headlights, despite his flight to the back of the screen, my mind found him once again. He looked at me. He smiled.

"I killed him, you see. You're not sore at me?"

Had I uttered the words, "You did the right thing," I would have felt so ashamed of myself, of the excessively searing injustice of it all, that I would have rejected the adventure and lost what I'd won in the game. I replied to his image, which was now sharp and almost as firm to my eyes as a muscular body is to one's fingers.

"I gave him to you, Riton. Love him dearly."

I opened my eyes again. The orchestra was playing the national anthem of an ally. A heavier, richer odor was enveloping me. The glands between my thighs and those of my armpits and perhaps my feet had been working intensely. If I so much as stirred, that slightly acrid smell which I had been imprisoning for ten minutes would have escaped and poisoned the audience. I slipped a finger into the opening of my fly; the edges of my thighs were damp with sweat. I had just discovered how and in whose company Erik had spent the first five days of the Paris revolt before being able to shack up with his mistress. Riton will meet Erik, will fight at his side on the rooftops, but he first has to know Paulo. I'm trying to present these characters to you in such a way that you see them lit up by my love, not for their sake but for Jean's, and particularly in such a way that they reflect that love.

After seeing Paulo go off on his bike, I went home. When I got there, darkness had fallen. These early September days are still very warm. I went up to my room. Jean had come to see me there one evening, two months before, to bring me the first pears of the year. The next morning, he left for the provinces with a valise full of guns. We chatted. When he thought of going home, it was late.

"You can stay if you like."

He hesitated, looked at me with a faint smile, and said:

(Until now I have been speaking of one of the dead, that is, of a god or an object, but now that I'm about to repeat his words, to describe his gestures, and recapture the modulations of his voice, I'm seized with terror, not that I'm afraid of remembering incorrectly and betraying Jean but, on the contrary, because I'm sure I'll recall him so accurately that he may come rushing in, in answer to my call. If the fifty foregoing pages are a disquisition on a statue of ice with the feet of an insentient god, the lines that follow are intended to open that god's bosom and that statue and liberate a twenty-year-old youngster. These lines are the key that opens the tabernacle and reveals the Host, and the three raps in the theater which announce the rising of the curtain are the very slightly stylized use of my heartbeats before I make Jean speak.)

He said:

"Oh?"

I realized what he was thinking. There were ten seconds of silence, and he repeated banteringly:

"Oh?"

And again, with the same smile and nodding his head:

"Oh?"

He snorted.

"But if I stay, you'll start fucking around."

"I won't."

I said that in a rough tone. And, with a more detached
air, I added:

"Oh, do as you like."

"Oh?"

But as I spoke he stood up, and I thought he was going
to leave. He sat down on the bed again.

"Well? Are you staying? Or are you going?"

"Will you let me alone?"

"Shit."

"I'll stay."

We talked about other things. From the tone of his
answers, the slight constraint of his voice, his hesitation,
I had been able to tell not only that he was staying but
that he would accept this night what he had hitherto
refused.

"Are you getting undressed?"

It was noticeable that, despite his decision to give himself to me, he was postponing the moment of going to
bed, of getting between the sheets, of pressing his body
against mine. At last, slowly and as if he were sauntering
about the room, he undressed. When he was in bed, I
drew him to me. He already had a hard-on.

"You see, you're not keeping your word. You said
you'd let me alone."

"Oh, come on, I'm just kissing you. I'm not hurting
you."

I kissed him. Then he said, but in a calm voice:

"All right."

This "all right" indicated that he had just reached a decision, that he was casting himself into the irremediable.

"All right."

Then, finally breathing easily:

"What if I wanted to, today?"

"Wanted what?"

He scowled impatiently. He blurted out:

"You know very well, but you want me to say it . . . if I was willing to make love."

The end of the sentence trailed off for want of breath.

"Jean."

I stroked his hand.

"Jean."

I didn't know what to say, or to do. He could feel my happiness. He lay still, stretched out on his back. The position released the muscles of his face, but the eyes remained alert and the lids kept up their regular blinking, which indicated that the kid was on his guard in spite of his excitement. I put out the light. Weary and soft, I lay on his back. A moment later, he whispered:

"Jean, come out."

Anxious to spare him the slightest embarrassment of attending to his personal hygiene in my presence, I ran my hands between his buttocks as if I were caressing him there, and he, out of like modesty, fearing lest my prick be soiled with his shit, cleaned it with his free hand. We performed this double act at the same time, under the covers, with the same innocence, as if my hand met his buttocks and his my prick accidentally in the darkness. It was then that he murmured the well-known words:

"I love you even more than before."

I kissed the back of his neck with a warmth that must have reassured him, for he finally dared sigh the following confession into the folds of the pillow:

"I was afraid you wouldn't love me anymore . . . afterward."

My hand, seeking his hair so as to stroke it, grazed his face and stroked his cheek instead.

Wearing Jean's shirts or his socks wouldn't be enough, nor would loading myself with amulets that he touched, nor weaving bracelets out of his hair or keeping it in lockets. But uttering his name in solitude is somewhat better. If I tried to repeat aloud the words he said, his sentences, the bungling poems he wrote, there would be danger of giving him body within my body.

Language, that language in particular, expresses the soul (I have chosen this word) and speech. (When one yields up one's soul, it seems that it is this physical breath that is the carrier of speech.) The soul appeared to be only the harmonious unfolding, the extension, in fine and shaded scrolls, of secret labor, of the movements of algae and waves, of organs living a strange life in its deep darkness, of those organs themselves, the liver, the spleen, the green coating of the stomach, the humors, the blood, the chyle, the coral canals, a vermilion sea, the blue intestines. Jean's body was a Venetian flask. I was quite certain that a time would come when that wonderful language which was drawn from him would diminish his body, as a ball of yarn is diminished as it is used up, would wear it down to the point of transparency, down to a speck of light. It taught me the secret of the matter that makes up the star which emits it, and that the shit amassed in Jean's intestine, his slow, heavy blood, his sperm, his tears, his mud, were not your shit, your blood, your sperm.

I had gone to bed with my memory of Paulo merging

with that of Jean. Through the open window of my tiny hotel room I saw the Seine. Paris was not yet asleep. What was Erik doing? It was hard for me to imagine his life with Paulo and his mother, but it was comforting to relive at his side—and at times inside him or Riton—the hours he spent on the rooftops with the militiamen.

So, two bare arms stood out at first against the dark sky, on the rooftop. They were bright. Joined at the hands, one of the arms was pulling the other toward it. The almost desperate effort of those arms of strong, muscular men made them stiff as rods, and for three seconds they remained in a state of amazingly light immobility, a mortal moment of indecision. Then a charge of will shot through the less strong of the two. There was a slight click of steel at the edge of the zinc. That poster picture of two outstretched arms knotted together in manly and brotherly aid almost tore the sky apart, almost punctured it. The stars were too dim to light the scene sufficiently. The arm which seemed weaker rose up a little toward the body to which it was attached. Hope brought it an armful of courage. Riton's torso bent forward a bit more, and the whole well-knit body, its shape broken by the movement, withdrew quietly and slowly behind the brick chimney to which the hand of his other arm was clinging. The little militiaman finally managed to draw from the void the German soldier who had lost his footing on the slippery zinc of the roof. Both of them were barefoot and bareheaded. Helping himself with one hand, which was still clutching his harmonica, Erik got back onto the roof, flat on his stomach. When he was in a safe position, his raised head was on a level with Riton's knees. He let go of the boy's hand. Riton, who was as pale as he was, wiped his forehead. He was in a sweat. Then he dropped his hand wearily with a defeated gesture. Erik, who was flat on his stomach, immediately took it and squeezed it.

"*Danke*," he murmured.

Then he stood up. He looked the kid in the eye. He saw a tired, naked face powdered with darkness in which two black eyes were shining. He laid both hands on Riton's shoulders and shook him. A sliver of moon emerged from a cloud. Erik nimbly stepped behind the chimney and blended with the shadow. With equal speed, Riton made the same movement, but, thrown off balance by his harness of cartridges, he botched it. Fatigue and nervousness made him clumsy. With one leg forward and the other bent back, Riton was doing a kind of awkward split on the rooftop. Erik leaned over, grabbed the kid from behind, and locked him in his arms. Their weapons collided. The sound was imperceptible. They stood motionless for a moment, with Riton still locked in the arms of Erik, whose hands were joined by the harmonica. They waited a while, open-mouthed, until the waves of the agitation they had just caused in the darkness subsided. Erik unloosed his embrace and dropped his arms. Riton felt a slight sensation of dampness and coldness on the back of his hand and put his hand to his mouth mechanically. He was not very surprised. He realized that Erik's saliva, which had collected in the holes of the harmonica, had flowed on to his hand. The dark blue wool of the militiaman's breeches and the black wool of the soldier's both held a smell which the sweat of the August days and nights and fatigue and anxiety had accumulated and which that double gesture had freed and blended, and naked black warriors with shiny bodies, wearing scalps on their belts and carrying pikes, emerged from the bamboos. The heart of Africa was throbbing in Riton's closed hand. There was dancing to the sound of a distant and insistent tom-tom. The two kids were staggering, with their eyes popping. Fatigue was pulling and pushing them, was making them whirl and topple.

Erik muttered:

"*Achtung,* watch out, Ritônne!"

They sat down against the chimney among the half-awake Fritzes, and Riton fell asleep. He had escorted six German soldiers and a sergeant, the only one left of the section with which his own militia group had been made to join forces. Thanks to the complicity of Juliette, whom the sergeant had been courting, they were able to reach a building where everyone was asleep, enter by the service window, and get to the roof. The sergeant was twenty; his soldiers were the same age. Keeping the little militiaman with them, they took off their shoes silently to go up to the rafters. They climbed up onto the roof around midnight. For greater security, the little group moved on to another building. Then they chose a post and, tired and despairing, squatted between the chimneys. Precisely because of their despair, they were determined to do everything possible to get out of the fix they were in. Fatigue made them drowsy. Erik, who was less drowsy, took his harmonica from the back pocket of his black breeches and played a tune. He gently ran his mouth over the bee's nest. He was playing very softly, actually in a murmur, "The Blue Java."

> . . . *It's the blue Java*
> *The loveliest Java*
> *The one that bewitches you . . .*

The modulation of the popular waltz was strangling the Boche, was squeezing his throat. He was aware that all the sad sweetness of France was flowing from his eyes. It was then that he fell asleep and rolled down the slope of the roof. Luckily his hand caught on Riton's armor; and Riton managed to get to his feet and pull him back.

Erik was unable to sleep, despite his weariness. He wandered off. It was August, when the sky pours forth showers of stars. As he moved to the edge of the roof, he saw that he was above a narrow balcony with an iron railing that ran along three sixth-floor windows. With a single leap, he jumped down. Sure-eyed and sure-footed, he landed on the balcony, on the tips of his unshod toes, and, as he wavered on his bent calves and thighs, his hands and fingers hesitated in strange positions, but they were quickly used for balancing his whole body. The apartment was empty. When he walked through it, a slight warmth burned his cheeks for the first time. The revolt of the Parisians seemed to him a betrayal. They had tricked him by feigning a four-year sleep. Under cover of the drinking at bars, the friendly slaps on the shoulders, the kindly explanations given with the hands, the girls, women, and boys who were lazily screwed from behind like dogs by men in boots and spurs, a host of deceitful thoughts were preparing vengeance. Erik realized that friendship can be a trap. But after all, what did he care about Germany! He had joined the Hitler Youth in order to have weapons: a knife for show, and a revolver for pillage. He was like the young French militiamen whose souls thrilled at the feel of a loaded revolver under their jackets. He developed his naturally hard muscles. His life had to have the shape of his body, its delicate inner composition. His muscles, all those nervous, vibrant lumps, are the leaping and bounding of his acts. When he rebelled, his revolt had the violence not of the quivering but of the shape of the muscles of his hams, the same curve, the same opulent, unerring fullness, the run-on lines, the swelling of an iron calf directed by a bold upward thrust of the firm flesh. His desertion was as heaving as his shoulders, and any murder he carried out had the actual shape of his neck. When he felt daring and wanted to shake the world, Erik had only to squeeze that unique neck of his with his large, thick hands to feel it was a firm column that supported the world, that held its being and head high, and rose above the world.

His will sometimes had pretty consequences: when he was confronted with an obstacle, his forehead would pucker and the golden curls of his over-brilliantined hair would fall on it; he would frown, charge the obstacle, and be gored by it.

Throughout my youth I viewed the world from under knitted brows, so that above my eyes I saw the hard golden hairs that edged them. I knew I was bearing the burden of a very heavy crop, and even in the brightest moments I felt I was a stalk whose head bristled with grains and whose beard was the hair of my eyebrows.

"He no longer has thirty-two creases. . . . "

This remark, which Erik once heard made about a kid who was suspected by his bunkmates of giving himself to an officer, made him think twice and filled him with a secret fear. And when he heard: " . . . they're going to take a print. They're going to make him sit on flour . . . " he was violently frightened for himself.

"It can be seen," he thought. "Does it change shape as much as that?"

He does not hate the executioner for that. He will think:

"I'm sure the creases come out again. . . . "

I have created within myself an order of knighthood of which I am the originator, founder, and only knight. I award to the Erik who is rising up inside me ideal decorations, crosses, orders, grants. They are my gobs of spit.

I was looking at myself in the wardrobe mirror of my hotel room. The picture of the Führer on the mantelpiece behind me was reflected in the glass. I was stripped to the waist and wearing my wide black breeches, which were tight at the ankles. I was looking at myself, staring into my own eyes, then staring at the Führer's image in the mirror.

What does spit mean? Can you spit on anyone you like?

The most important part of my body is my buttocks. My breeches keep reminding me of them because they contain them and are so tight that I can't forget about them. We constitute a regiment of buttocks.

"What about his cock, what was it like, and how would you like to take it, sideways or crosswise?"

A scurrilous spirit within me asks this question which I dare not answer and obliges me to look away from his rod and turn to Jean, whom I am ashamed of having left. But I am too mired in eroticism to think of Jean without thinking of our love-making. Moreover, those thoughts are forbidden. I feel I am committing an abominable crime if I recall too precisely the parts of him which I loved most and which are now decayed and being gnawed by worms. What shall I think about? The wallpaper doesn't distract me. Every flower, every damp spot, brings me back to Jean. I've got to think about him. I idealize the memory of making love so that I can avoid sacrilege. The liveliest parts of his body become spiritualized, and his rod itself, which takes possession of my mouth, has the transparency of a crystal rod. In fact, what I am holding by the prick with my teeth and pink lips is a fluid, milky body, a luminous fog that rises above my bed or over a wet lawn on which I am lying. It is cold to my lips; I thus avoid pleasure. My love-making continues through this icy fog, which veils it. With our hair light and tousled but damp with the droplets of mist clinging to it, after walking in the dew with our arms still around each other's waist, we came to a grove and stood under a beech with red bark. The executioner pressed me against the tree, but gently, laughing as if it were a game, a kind of friendly bullying. All along the way, which he trod with long, very heavy steps—almost as if he were booted and merging with the equally long and heavy steps of Erik in boots—from the path to the shore of the lake, in the fog, only the executioner spoke. Softening his too clear voice, which with a few blasts might have dispelled all the mist in the woods, he had said, looking at the wet grass:

"Now's the time when mushrooms sprout. We might even find some."

And ten yards farther:

"Won't you have a cigarette?"

Erik's body was pressed against that of the executioner, whose right arm (the ax arm) was squeezing him. As the boy answered merely by pursing his lips and giving an indifferent toss of his head, the man said:

"I'll give you one later."

Erik thought—but did not say—"the last cigarette, the one the executioner gives you." They were under the beech. Their clothes were damp and their feet frozen. They sank into a sodden earth. The executioner put out his arms and held Erik by the shoulders against the tree. He was laughing silently. Despite the power of his muscles—and bones—one could feel that his strength was chiefly passive, that he was able to endure rather than to court danger, to lift heavy sacks, saw wood for days on end, push a truck that had bogged down. It was hard to imagine him fighting. His movements were not swift or dexterous, and his gestures were too mild. He asked again:

"You're not afraid?"

"No. I said I wasn't."

Erik remained calm. He did not even feel angry. His heart was on his wrist. He heard the watch ticking.

"I'll give him the watch," he thought, "and that'll do it." He thought vaguely that by admitting he had the watch he would escape being buggered. Obviously one doesn't send an executioner to execute watch thieves. That's a childish fear.

"If I can get it off. . . . "

He managed to unbuckle the strap. The watch fell to the wet grass. He felt purer. Yet he had no doubt as to the man's intentions. They had walked a few yards farther. Erik leaned against the executioner.

In spite of the cold and dampness and of his anxiety and disgust, Erik was thrilled. He had a hard-on. He shivered, and suddenly, brutally, he pressed against the executioner.

"Ah!"

The man's smile faded, then for three seconds he seemed to hesitate, to wait for an inspiration, and as his eyes met Erik's fleeting gaze, suddenly, at the right corner of his mouth, his smile returned (only to the corner), and became more pronounced, confident, and decisive.

"You're good-looking," he said, freeing Erik's left shoulder from his grip and stroking his cheek with the back of his hand.

Thus the most spiritualized form of Jean was giving fleecy asylum to the love of a Berlin executioner and a young Nazi. Let's see it through. Erik and the executioner

were locked in an embrace, face to face. Erik's underpants were torn. His khaki breeches were falling down
and forming a thick heap of clothes between his legs, and
his buttocks were crushed in the fog against the red
bark, those soft-skinned, amber buttocks, as rich to the
eye as the milky fog whose matter had the luster of a
pearl. Erik hung from the executioner's neck with both
hands. His feet were no longer touching the wet grass,
though his breeches were, having fallen down between
his naked calves and his ankles. The executioner, whose
prick was still stiff and was now between Erik's pressed
thighs, held him up and dug into the rich earth. Their
knees were piercing the mist. The executioner was hugging the boy to him and, at the same time, backing him
up and crushing his ass against the tree. Erik was pulling
the man's head. The executioner realized that the boy
was solidly built and tremendously violent. They stayed
in that position for a few seconds without moving, the two
heads pressing hard against each other, cheek to cheek.
The executioner was the first to break away, for he had
discharged between Erik's golden thighs, which were
velvety with morning mist. The position had lasted only
a brief moment, but long enough to beget in the executioner and the morning's assistant a feeling of simultane-
ous tenderness: Erik for the executioner, whom he was
holding by the neck in such a way that it could mean
only tenderness, and the executioner for the youngster,
for even though the gesture was necessitated by their
difference in height, it was so winning that it would have
made the toughest of men burst into tears. Erik loved
the executioner. He wanted to love him, and little by
little he felt himself being wrapped in the huge folds of
the legendary red cloak inside which he cuddled at the
same time as he took a piece of newspaper from his

pocket and politely handed it to the executioner who took it to wipe his prick.

"I love the executioner and I make love with him, at dawn!"

The same surprise, the same wonderment, made Riton say much the same sort of thing when he realized he was in love with Erik, in the small apartment where he had lain down beside the Boche who was sleeping with his mouth open. Each of his thoughts, which sprang from and were suggested by his excitement, tortured Riton. He was amazed at first at having a hard-on, with no other provocation, because of Erik, who was stronger and older than he:

"All the same, I'm not a queer," he thought. And a moment later:

"All the same, I must be."

This certainty made him feel a bit ashamed, but it was a shame mingled with joy. A radiant shame. The shame in him merged with the joy into a single feeling just as the same color—pink and sometimes bright red—blends them. With a sigh, he added:

"And for a Fritz in the bargain. I'm a real case!"

In the park, crushed by the executioner, Erik thought thus:

"What a great beginning. A real success. He's not good-looking, he's a bruiser, he's hairy, he's thirty-five, and he's the executioner."

Erik said this to himself ironically, but actually he was solemn, he recognized the danger of such a situation, especially if it is accepted. He accepted it.

"I accept it all without a word. I deserve a medal."

When he had pulled up his breeches and buttoned them, the executioner handed him his case and Erik took a cigarette, without saying anything, for he already knew that his gesture meant thank you by virtue of its elegance.

"Are we friends?"

Erik hesitated a second or two, smiled and said:

"Why not?"

"Are we?"

"We are."

The executioner looked at him tenderly.

"You'll be my friend."

Expressed in this form, the sentimentality of the killer's German soul was addressing the German soul of Erik, which was already replying with a kind of spiritual trembling, a kind of hope.

"I will."

The brightness of dawn made it possible to see more clearly in the mist.

"Will you come to see me in my home?"

The executioner's tone of voice became almost feminine at the very moment that he flicked a tiny twig or bit of fluff off the lapel of Erik's windbreaker and pulled it slightly to smooth an imperceptible crease. This first and slightly finical act on his friend's behalf did not make Erik smile until later.

Erik, who was now in the Panzer *divisionen,* was at the top of a Paris building, in a lower-middle-class apartment where the men he had called had cautiously installed themselves, one by one. The last of them, Riton, had jumped nimbly to the balcony, alone, despite the soldiers' offer of help. The straps of three loaded machine guns were wound about his shirt, went around the belt and up across the shoulders, crossed once on the chest and once on the back, and produced a copper tunic from which his arms emerged bare from the elbow almost to the shoulder, where the sleeve of the blue shirt was rolled into a thick wad that made the arm more elegant. It was a carapace, each scale of which was a bullet. This paraphernalia weighed the child down, gave him a monstrous bearing and posture that intoxicated him to the point of nausea. In short, he was carrying the ammunition supply. His uncombed hair was naked in the darkness. His battered thighs bent beneath the weight of his armor and fatigue. He was barefoot. He had jumped with wonderful suppleness and landed on his bent toes, with the barest help from Erik, who had reached out to him from the balcony. He held on to the machine gun, a lean, dark-colored, completely functional instrument. Erik entered the room through the window, and Riton spun around lightly, despite the mass of metal, and, with his mouth agape, found himself at the edge of a starry night on a rickety, ascetically simple iron bridge and confronted with an abyss of darkness that he felt was quivering with chestnut trees, though their leaves barely stirred. It was the Boulevard de Ménilmontant. Ménilmontant, the kid's neighborhood.

A sentence: "My grief in the presence of Jean's grief reveals the force of my love for him!" The more I grieve, the more intense my feeling seems to be. Now, my suffering is often caused and always increased by remembering Jean's blackened corpse in its coffin, with the nostrils probably stuffed and the body slowly decomposing and mingling its smell with that of the flowers. My grief is heightened by the thought of Jean's suffering when he was shot, by his despair when he felt himself lose his footing and leave life for the realm of shades. My daily life is dominated by the memory of the gruesome sights, of the preparations for burial. My contact with the concrete wounds my sensibility cruelly: the black escutcheon adorned with the silver-embroidered "D" that I saw on the hearse waiting at the gate of the hospital, the coffin and the poor quality of the wood, the singing in the church, the *Dies Irae,* the blood-red moiré ribbon on which was inscribed in gold letters: "To our leader, the Communist Youth Movement," the priest's remarks in French, these were all knives that slashed my heart. And all these wounds gave me knowledge of my love. But Jean will live through me. I shall lend him my body. Through me he will act, will think. Through my eyes he will see the stars, the scarves of women and their breasts. I am taking on a very grave role. A soul is in purgatory and I am offering it my body. It is with the same emotion that an actor approaches the character whom he will make visible. My spouse may be less wretched. A sleeping soul hopes for a body; may the one that the actor assumes for an evening be beautiful. This is no small matter. We require the rarest beauty and elegance for that body which is charged with a terrible trust, for those gestures which destroy death, and it is not too much to ask the actors to arm their characters to the point that they inspire fear. The magical operation they perform is the mystery of the Incarnation. The soul, which without them would be a dead letter, will live. Doubtless Jean can have existed momentarily in any form whatever, and I was able, for a span of ten seconds, to contemplate an old beggarwoman bent over her stick, then a garbage can overflowing with refuse, egg shells, rotting flowers, ashes, bones, spotted newspapers; nothing prevented me from seeing in the old woman and the garbage can the momentary and marvelous figure of Jean, and I covered them, in thought, not only with my tenderness but also with a white tulle veil that I would have loved to put on Jean's adorable head, an embroidered veil, and wreaths of flowers. I was officiating simultaneously at a funeral and a wedding; I merged the symbolic encounter of the two processions into a single movement. And even from here, I was able, by fixing my gaze and remaining motionless, or almost, to delegate my powers to the famous actor in Nuremberg who was playing the role in which I was prompting him from my room or from my place beside the coffin. He was strutting, he was gesticulating and roaring before a crowd of spellbound, raving Storm Troopers who were thrilled to feel that they were the necessary extras in a performance that was taking place in the street.

Actually it's hardly possible for a theatrical service to take place in daily life and make the simplest acts participate in that service, but one can realize the beauty of those performances before a hundred thousand spectator-actors when one knows that the sublime officiant was Hitler playing the role of Hitler. He was representing me.

Curled up inside my grief, I nevertheless paid close attention to the performance, in which there was not the slightest hitch. I dispatched my orders from beside the coffin. The entire German nation was entering a state of trance at the celebration of my own mystery. The real Führer was standing beside a dead boy, but a high priest was performing magnificent rites for me at a kind of gigantic fair.

If my feelings are real only through my consciousness of them, ought I to say that I would have loved Jean less if he had been born in China? And that neither the living Jean nor the charming, handsome Jean of my memory would have been able to reveal to me one of the most painful, most intense feelings I have ever had, whereas Jean *seems* to me to be the sole cause of it? In short, all that grief of mine—hence the consciousness of that beautiful love, hence that love—would not have existed if I had not seen Jean in a state of horror. If I am told he was tortured, if I see him in a newsreel being mutilated by a German, I shall suffer more and my love will be exalted. In like manner, Christians love more when they suffer more. And the sentence, "My grief at Jean's death revealed to me the force of my love for him," can be replaced by "My grief at the death of my virtue revealed to me the force of my love for it." The desire for solitude, which I spoke of briefly a few pages back, is *pride*. I want to say a few words about the admirable solitude that accompanied the militiamen in their relations with Frenchmen and with each other and finally in death. They were considered to be worse than whores, worse than thieves and scavengers, sorcerers, homosexuals, worse than a man who, inadvertently or out of choice, ate human flesh. They were not only hated, but loathed. I love them. No comradeship was possible between them, except in the very rare case when two boys had enough confidence in each other not to fear that the other might inform on him in their marginal world where informing was a matter of course, for, loathed like reptiles, they had assumed the morals of reptiles and made no bones about it. Thus, any friendship between them was uneasy, for each of them wondered: "What does he think of me?" It was impossible for them to pretend that they were acting out of idealism. Who would have believed it? They had to admit: "It's because I was hungry; it's because I'll have a gun and may be able to plunder; it's because I like to squeal, because I like the ways of reptiles; in short, it's in order to find the grimmest solitude." I love those little fellows whose laughter was never bright. I love the militiamen. I think of their mothers, their families, their friends, all of whom they all lost in joining the Militia. Their deaths are precious to me.

Members of the Militia were recruited mainly from among hoodlums, since they had to brave the contempt of public opinion, which a bourgeois would have feared. They had to run the risk of being murdered at night on a lonely street, but what attracted us most was the fact that they were armed. So for three years I had the delicate pleasure of seeing France terrorized by kids between sixteen and twenty.

I loved those tough kids who didn't give a damn about the blighted hopes of a nation, whose distress in the heart of everyone, as soon as he spoke about it, merged systematically with the most beloved being of flesh and blood. And the armed youngsters were perhaps thrilled at moving in the halo of shame with which their treason surrounded them, but there was enough grace in their gazes and gestures for them to seem indifferent to it. I was happy to see France terrorized by children in arms, but even more so because they were crooks and little rats. Had I been young, I would have joined the Militia. I often caressed the handsomest of them, and I secretly recognized them as envoys of mine who had been delegated to operate among the bourgeois and carry out the crimes that prudence forbade me to commit myself.

At a time when the death of Jean D. ravages me, destroying everything within me or leaving undamaged only the images that enable me to pursue doomed adventures, I want to derive incomparable joy from the spectacle of the love of a militiaman and a German soldier. It was no doubt natural for me to couple a warrior, whom I want to be as subtly cruel as possible, with the person whose moral nature is vilest in the eyes of the world—and sometimes in mine—but how could I justify that with respect to the friend I loved most who had died fighting against my two heroes, fighting against what my two heroes defended? You can't have any doubt about the pain that his death causes me. For a few days my despair made me fear for my life. I was so grief-stricken at the thought that Jean had been lying in a narrow grave for four days, with his body decomposing in a wooden coffin, that I was on the point of asking a scientist:

"Are you sure he can't be brought back to life?"

I don't see the folly of that question even now, because it's not my reason that asks it but my love. Not having a scientist at hand, I put the question to myself. I waited for the answer, quivering with hope. In fact, hope made everything in and around me quiver. I was waiting for an invention that only hope could devise.

That quivering was the flapping of wings which is the prelude to flying. I know that a resurrection isn't possible and wasn't then, but I won't allow the order of the world not to be *disturbed* for my sake. I thought for a moment of paying a man, a gravedigger, to unearth what remained of the child in order to hold in my hands a bone, a tooth, so that I could still realize that a wonder like Jean had been possible. My poor Jean-in-the-earth. I would even have allowed him to return to us in any form: that of two pieces of veneered black wood streaked with white lead, glued together, like a fantastic silent guitar lying in a bed of dry grass in a shelter made of boards, far from the world, which he would never leave, not even to get air, not even at night, not even during the day. What would his life be like in the form of a crude, stringless guitar without a pick, which could hardly talk and complain of its lot through a crack in the board? It doesn't matter. He would live and be present. He would be in the world and I would clothe him in white linen every day. The fact is that my grief, which made me rave, invents this riot of blossoms, the sight of which gives me joy. The more Jean changes into fertilizer, the more the flowers growing on his grave will perfume me.

The appetite for *singularity* and the attraction of the forbidden in concert delivered me up to evil. Evil, like good, is attained gradually by means of an inspired insight that makes you glide vertically away from human beings, but most often by daily, careful, slow, disappointing labor. I shall give a few examples. Of the tasks involved in this particular ascesis, it was betrayal that was hardest for me. However, I had the admirable courage to move further away from human beings by a greater fall, to turn my most tormented friend over to the police. I myself brought the detectives to the apartment in which he was hiding, and I made a point of being paid off for my betrayal before his very eyes. Of course, that betrayal causes me tremendous suffering, which reveals to me my friendship for my victim and an even deeper love for man; but in the midst of that suffering it seemed to me, when shame had burned me through and through, that there remained amidst the flames or rather the fumes of shame a kind of imperishable diamond with sharp clean lines, rightly called a solitaire. I think it is also called pride, and humility too, and knowledge too. I had performed a free act. In any case, refusing to let my act be magnified by disinterestedness, to let it be purely gratuitous, an act performed for the fun of it, I completed my ignominy. I required that my betrayal be paid for. I wanted to strip my acts of anything beautiful that might be involved in them despite everything. However, the most heinous crimes are embellished with a bit of light when they are committed by a handsome person who lives in the sun and is bronzed by the sea, and I had to rely on a little physical beauty in order to attain evil. May I be forgiven for doing so. Because I envisage theft, murder, and even betrayal as emanating from a bronzed, muscular, and always naked body that moves in the sun and waves, they transcend this ignominious tone (which was an attraction for me) and find a nobler one, which is more closely related to solar sacrifice. But despite my life in the sun and my live body—the sort of life which I have been living since Jean's death—I am still attracted by so-called somber people, those in whom something reveals darkness, those who are wrapped in darkness (even if it is the darkness that is also the brilliance they radiate), those who are dark or fair with dark eyes, or with a tense face, an evil smile, nasty teeth, a large member, a thick bush. I feel they have dangerous souls.

"What is the soul?"

"It is that which emerges from the eyes, from tossed hair, from the mouth, from the curls, from the torso, from the member."

It has only two qualities: it is good or it is bad. Erik's soul was bad. He killed whenever it was bad to kill, because it was bad. At first, in order to be worthy of the fate betokened by the strange sign of that nation of pirates. The swastika contains not only the particular exaltation of dangerous banners, but also devastation and death. No doubt he had got over the first shudders of disgust and little by little grown used to the idea of being the executioner's friend. In the small Berlin apartment where he spent his time when he was away from the barracks, Erik became accustomed to certain comforts of which his working-class youth had dreamed. His friend treated him with motherly concern (contained entirely in the gesture of flicking Erik's lapel) rather than with that of a lover, and each day, Erik's arrogance quickened. It was intensified by the fact that he wore boots (he liked to hear the clack of their heels). And the executioner had him play the male role in bed. Pressed against the older man, clinging to his neck as in the Tiergarten, but with his hands now clasped on the Adam's apple rather than on the back of his neck, Erik knew he was a kind of quickening excrescence of a beautiful monster. It was not that he himself would have tried to play the male. In fact, he was greatly surprised one night when the executioner rolled over onto his belly and asked to be reamed.

Some time after his arrival in Paris, Erik, who was on his way to a brothel all by himself, caught sight of the militiaman at a crossing of four streets. The boy was walking toward him. Erik, in order to see him at closer range and enjoy the sight of his face, stepped away from a group of soldiers. He was willing to lose sight of him for a second, but suddenly the kid committed the discourtesy of turning to the left and vanishing in a colonnade before Erik could get a look at him.

Riton had spotted the soldier, but out of discretion he walked in another direction. He did not realize the pleasure he would have given. Erik felt like a fool in the suddenly empty crowd that was rushing ridiculously toward the useless. No presence had ever been so present to him as the child's absence. He felt insulted, for he had a sense of his individuality. Usually the world unfolded around him reverently, the houses drew aside, the trees shook, the sky grew overcast. You sometimes feel a respect that things owe you or a respect that you owe them.

When I saw him in front of me, the sun was warming the forest. He was carrying neither a gun nor a knife. It was by his smile that I could tell he was a hunter. My hair quivered. I took his hand. But at that very instant the following prayer rose up within me:

"Don't let me touch you. Never speak to me. . . ."

The image of him within me was astonished. Its forehead, its eyebrows, each of which was as strange, but naturally so, as those of clowns (a mouse whose head is the eye, a cherry leaf whose eye is the cherry . . .), its eyebrows contracted. The image clenched its fist in order to strike. Yet I kept talking to it:

". . . for one mustn't touch beauty. Stay quite far away from me. . . . "

My hand was in his, but mine was four inches away from the hand of the image. Although it was impossible for me to dare live such a scene (for nobody—including him—would have understood what my respect meant) I had a right to want to. And whenever I was near an object that he had touched, my hand would move toward it but stay four inches away, so that things, being outlined by my gestures, seemed to be extraordinarily inflated, bristling with invisible rays, or enlarged by their metaphysical double, which I could at last feel with my fingers.

What a demonstration of geometrical force there was in the angle of light, the mobile yet rigorously immobile legs of the compass which his legs were when he walked! I sometimes moved my hand close to the edge of him, careful not to touch him, for I was afraid that he might dissolve or drop dead or rather that I might die; that is: either I would realize I was suddenly naked in a crowd that saw my nakedness; or my hands would grow covered with leaves and I would have to live with them, lace my shoes with them, hold my cigarette, open the door, scratch myself with them, or he himself would know spontaneously who I really was and would laugh at the knowledge; or I would shit out my guts in his presence, dragging them far behind me in the dust, where they would pick up bits of straw and wilted flowers (black and green flies would alight on them and he would shoo them off with his flabby white hand, and he would brush them away with disgust as they swirled about him); or I would see and feel my penis being eternally devoured by fish; or a sudden friendship would allow me to stroke toads and corpses to the point of orgasm; for evoking these torments—and others—my death may well be the knowledge of my shame appearing in the play of those manifestations most dreaded in the presence of the loved one. I therefore kept him at a distance.

Once, however, I touched his hair.

In the camp at Rouillée, Paulo was the victim of a mock execution. One morning he was taken to the yard and stood against the wall. Twelve soldiers took aim. The officer cried: "Fire!" Shots. A cloud in Paulo's eyes. When he was untied and started to walk, he thought he was walking in death. Twenty-four hours after touching Jean's hair, I thought I was walking in death. Rather, I was flying, flying lightly over fields of asphodels.

These encounters, which were never perfect, exasperated Riton, distressed him, made him feel queasy. Paulo was in the jug, and he himself could not summon up courage to steal. He hardly ever left his room.

He withdrew from society, and his withdrawal was helped along by hunger. For a long time he suffered from it, and from the cold, in a small room he didn't pay for. One night he couldn't stand it any more. His hunger was so great that it could have nourished him. He felt it in his stomach as if it had the consistency of food about to be assimilated. It rose in waves from his stomach to his mouth, where it expired from exhaustion at being only a desire. He rolled over in bed and tried to think about Paulo, who had given him the scarf that was hanging from a nail on the wall. Friendship did not resist the thought that he might get enough money for that faded silk rag to buy bread. To whom could he sell it? It was a souvenir, but Paulo would not mind if his scarf helped to ease his friend's hunger.

"If I cut my leg, he'd think it was natural for me to stop the blood, even if the scarf was spoiled after that."

An appeal was made in his body, as if an organ were being slightly twisted by a delicate hand. He got up. As the room was small, he was at the door immediately, and he went out. These few movements and those he made to go down the stairs caused him to forget his hunger, but as soon as he was on the boulevard and was wondering whether to turn left or right, it rushed at him with the speed of a galloping horse, that is, he had the sensation of being knocked down by a victorious animal that would trample him till doomsday. He turned to the right. The boulevard was dark. The trees were living in glory, in an infernal joy. The very darkness was cruel. Riton walked. He had to rely on a miracle. On a ground-floor window sill—the concierge's—he saw a cat. Riton stopped and took the animal in his arms without even stroking it. The cat did not stir, but joy was already giving the boy wings. He headed for home, transported by hope and an already satisfied belly. The tom was big and fat. The murder was ghastly.

Riton first tried to kill it with a hammer. He had an obscure feeling that one who murders is less guilty if the blow does not involve direct and continuous participation in the murder by approving it every second, and so he threw the hammer. Only the cat's fur was touched. The cat hid under the bed, but the room was so small Riton caught it quickly. The trapped animal tried to scratch him. It struggled. Riton wrapped his left hand in a towel, grabbed the cat by the tail, and bashed the head with the hammer with his right hand, but the animal's spine was so flexible that the creature squirmed like a hanging reptile. It miaowed. It felt death coming, knew it was inevitable. Riton tried to whack it again. He missed. The instrument hammered the air. He whacked. He kept whacking wildly and missing.

"The bastard."

The scene was silent from beginning to end. Riton struggled in silence against the silence which was also teeming with the desperate, criminal thoughts of the child and the terror of the cat, which seemed to become the Enemy because of its furious will to live, despite everything, the skill with which its body avoided the blows, its fur, which was full of animal softness and tenderness that protected the animal but were also ra-diated outward by the fur and reached Riton's very soul. The sea was filling the room, the roar of the waves was making the boy dizzy. The cat was a big gray tom that he would have liked to stroke. I can very well see the kid picking up the cat, which would climb to his shoulder and keep mournful vigil beside his face. It would sit and purr.

The thought of strangling the cat, which was born at the same time as that of murdering it with the hammer, grew more precise, but Riton did not want to let go of the animal and look for a rope. He unbuckled his belt, pulled it through the loops of his trousers, and, using only one hand, he made a running loop. The cat waited in silence. Riton put his foot on the little head and pulled the end of the belt, but he did not strangle the animal, which was as supple and lively as ever. Riton was wrapped in the folds of a repulsively soft sleep. He attached the belt to a nail and hanged the cat, which, getting its strength back, clawed the wall, trying to climb up it. Suddenly a great shudder shook the boy's body, a shudder that deepened and grew more definite, as the thought dawned on him that the neighbors were standing at the door, listening through the walls, aware of the murder not because they heard the cries and moans and prayers of the victim, but because murder itself charged the room, like a Crookes tube, with subtle emanations that pierced the walls better than X rays. Then he realized the absurdity of the thought and continued to hammer away with one hand while holding up his falling trousers with the other. The cat was living more intensely, its life was exalted by danger, suffering, and fear. There was no blood yet, and Riton was pooped. Then he was worried again that the animal might be the devil, who sometimes changes into a cat, in order to enter people's homes more easily.

"If it's the devil, I'm a goner!"

He thought of taking it down, but he was afraid the devil might stand up and slit open his belly with a hooked finger. Stories have it that if you throw three drops of holy water on the cat, the devil will assume his human form. There was no holy water in the room, not even a branch of box, not even a first communion photo. What if he made the sign of the cross? The devil would remain hanging and perhaps retain, though assuming human form, the cat's size. What was to be done with the corpse of a devil of such dimensions? So Riton didn't dare make a gesture lest he involuntarily make the sign of the cross over the cat.

He heard a merry-go-round in the distance, on the boulevard.

"It's the caterpillar."

The noise seemed to be going on in the child's head.

The movement of the merry-go-round passed its climax and slowed down perceptibly, then slowed down more. It seemed utterly exhausted, as a hand is by long drawn-out masturbation that is about to end in orgasm. The merry-go-round discharged like a vigorous boy.

On the balcony, his gestures were hindered only slightly by his equipment, for though the straps of the machine gun had been tied around his chest tightly, his breathing had quickly eased the strain a little and freed his thorax. He reached into the pocket of his breeches for a cigarette. He found only a few butts, and his disappointment restored the lucidity that fatigue and adventure had swept away. Fatigue was numbing his anxiety so that he could rest.

"No question about it, they're the last butts. And the Fritzes don't have a damn thing. Not much grub left. Nothin' to smoke. Nothin' to eat. Not even shoes."

He felt his barefootedness on the iron of the balcony. His stomach was rumbling. The bareness of his feet and their delicacy and the flesh of his arms made the German soldiers green with jealousy as they watched him, made them think of an animal with an extremely fragile body that emerges from a few holes in its protective shell. He was in Ménilmontant, on the hill, not far from his own street, entwined from his belt to his neck in the mutely glittering coils that the Fritzes made him wear. When they left the cellar of the house, which until the insurrection had been used as barracks by the decimated platoon, the Boche sergeant had decided that the militiaman would not do any shooting. They wrapped him in bullets. His bare arms and legs were suddenly clad with sovereign gentleness and elegance, that is, the elegance and gentleness of a sovereign when he emerges for a moment from armor that is only slightly more glittering than his majesty. He insisted on keeping his machine gun.

"Come on, sarge, lemme keep my putt-putt."

He looked at the German out of the corner of his eye, and, though he was joking, his whorish gaze was so imploring—one sees that look in the gaze of certain dogs when the gravity of the circumstances, the proximity of death or danger, impart to their eyes a gleam of appeal (a signal light)—that the sergeant smiled with amusement at the contrast between the eyes and the mouth. Like a shot, Riton's legs carried him back two yards, near the wall where the machine gun was lying, but the torso, from which two bare arms emerged, like cabin boys emerging from the hatchways of a battleship, responded to the agility of the legs with lordly slowness and heaviness, and it was then that it occurred to Riton to look at himself in the mirror. He turned to the wall instinctively: there was no mirror. Then he felt his body. He ran his hands over the surface of the metal, grazing the shudder of the bullets. Projectiles were raining all around the house and bursting against the wall, fragments of which could at times be heard falling to the ground. In the cellar, the seven German soldiers were busily preparing their escape. (It was impossible to defend the house. They had to beat a retreat, to try to get to the roofs. What was left of the platoon had escaped by the sewers.) They were continually obsessed by the secret thought of a danger greater than the combat of which they were the center. They spoke very little among themselves and hardly ever helped one another. As Riton saw them, they were seven young men whose only fault was cocksuredness.

Standing motionless in front of the soldiers, he was as fragile, and elegant too, as a hazel stick that has been placed—and abandoned by the hand of a young cowherd who has just entered a cabaret—against the horns and slobbery muzzles of a pair of motionless, *subjugated* oxen.

The sergeant had told him to take off his shoes. Since

then, he has been barefoot. And that night on the balcony, at sea in Ménilmontant, with his machine gun lying beside him, he thought:

"All the same, it's gorgeous."

Had he been the target of a whole army of soldiers, he would have loved to show himself to them at dawn, standing on a roof in that gleaming array that the Boches had tied around him. He took his machine gun and sat for a few seconds without moving. A shot rang out, perhaps from a roof, perhaps from below.

"What if it was someone alone? It would be pretty lousy. Poor guy."

He thought fleetingly of the militiaman alone on a roof, but alone with his weapon. Alone, one is only one's self. With a weapon, solitude is shared. One is one's self and one's duty. Self and . . . another character who is invisible but present and who changes name depending on the case. Self and . . . triumph or death. Alone, one manages. Either one surrenders or one gets away without being bothered since one is unarmed. The enemy pursues not so much the warrior as what makes the warrior: his weapon. It's not true that one can easily throw away one's rifle, machine gun, or knife and slip off. If the exchange of charms between the weapon and the warrior has taken place in accordance with the rites, if it was consecrated by combat and the prestige of a chief, bonds are formed between the weapon and the warrior, bonds that it is harder for a man to cut if he is valorous himself, and his valor—I'm so glad—leads him to his death.

"Who can it be? Maybe it's a guy I know. No way of telling. The hell with it. He's doing what I'm doing, he's in the shit and doing what he can."

Riton was going from one painful idea to another idea, like a monk who, at night, near a torrent that runs along the stations of the cross, rushes from station to station and kneels before the rocks that shimmer in the faint light of a lantern. The landscapes in which Riton and the monk are moving are identical: stones through which the barrel of a rifle may be peering, black thorns gleaming with black eyeballs, the devastating roar of a torrent.

In order to be sure of himself and the better to shake off his flabby thoughts, he put a fist on his hip and tried to arch his calf, but he was standing on bare heels. However, his fist struck his carapace and that was enough to make him more keenly aware of the value of the moment. He felt that beneath the armor he had a heart of bronze, and he wanted to die, for bronze is immortal. This time he was handsomer than the fellow in the underground whom he and his captain had arrested. In the darkness, looking out on the city that was palpitating with such a beautiful day but was still uncertain of the consequences of the victory, he had an extraordinary consciousness of his transformation into one of those terrifying, sharp-eyed characters whose gestures have long been prepared for combat and whose knees and elbows bristle with blades. A dragon. A chimera. His hair was poisonous. His stomach surged with repressed farts which he dared not unleash, for he heard the soldiers who were nearby in the darkness organizing for the night. He smiled over Paris as he thought that he would have driven mothers mad with terror by stroking a child's cheek.

"I'd like to be the one who makes mothers cry!"

That remark had once been made to him by the former *bataillonnaire,* Paulo's friend, who had brought it back from Africa. He was alone on that sixth-floor balcony despite the presence of the German soldiers. He felt a slight itching between his legs and was obliged to scratch. As his exceptional situation distorted the slightest circumstance, his member and its surrounding bush suddenly seemed to him to be a kind of stone at the bottom of the sea, encrusted, among the algae, with tiny shellfish that made it even harder, and his mind went back to the sight of Erik making the same gesture, then to Erik's tool in the black breeches which he assumed was another mossy megalithic monument studded with gray, hard-shelled parasites.

"When the shootin' starts, there'll be hell to pay," he thought, in a slightly somnolent state that unsteadied him. He woke up in surprise. He got his bearings in the twinkling of an eye.

"Sure thing, I'm in a hole," he said to himself.

He realized his sorry state. Down below, beneath his feet, beneath the spit—he spat on the trees—was the ground where Frenchmen could circulate, though they had to be somewhat careful.

"All the same, they're my brothers."

In order to think, he used the word "brothers," which belongs to the sentimental language of hoodlums. He felt that this thought was the center, the ideal point of his solitude. Although it lost some precision in revolving, it remained at the origin of his discouraging situation.

The following took shape around it: "I've abandoned my brothers, my family, my friends. I run around. I run in the streets. I escape to the roofs. I kill Frenchmen whenever I can. They try to kill me. I shoot at everything that served me. This evening I ought to serve for love's sake. I've sided with the monsters, with the Kings. I'm going to be killed, I'm a traitor. I'm already an outcast and condemned. I'm alone on the bridge of a sinking ship. The whole city hates me. The stones, the walls, the railing on which I'm leaning can come loose and kill me. I'm at home in a foreign country. This apartment is an enemy's, the home of a Frenchman with whom I went to school. I'm losing the benefit of all the games, of all the girls. I'm alone. My mother wants to pick me off. She's aiming at one of my eyes. I'm fighting for Germany." As a result of revolving and thereby showing all its sides, which the speed blurred, the initial remark had become as dim as a top, light as a trail of mist, and, as the speed of the whirling made it disappear, Riton was conscious for a moment only of his solitude, of his height on the balcony. His right arm pressed his black, intelligent, crafty machine gun against his hip. He was holding it with one hand. With the other he stroked his torso, which felt lithe and fragile under its copper breastplate.

One morning, when the captain entered the militia-men's barracks before they were up, he held his nose and shouted:

"It reeks of modesty here!"

Riton thought, blushing:

"Maybe the modesty's me."

"Eh!"

He jumped. He had thought someone was talking to him.

"I'm hearing voices. I'm like Joan of Arc."

A girl may be a Maid, but she nevertheless has her periods. The evening before her execution, Joan put on the white robe of the doomed. The blood ran down her joined thighs. In the darkness of her cell, she washed herself gropingly in the bucket from which she drank. Having no other linen, she tore her shift to make a kind of pad, which she attached between her legs. While the left hand pulled up her white robe, the other one wrote sacred signs on the darkness, signs of the cross that merged with pentacles (or continued with them), with sketches of exorcisms. Weary, exhausted, panic-stricken by the blood that had been shed in the course of a tragedy in which the murderer and the victim remain invisible, she lay down on the straw. She modestly covered her legs with her robe and prayed, interspersing her invocations to God, Mary, and her saints with magical phrases addressed to the infernal spirits as she had been advised to do by the witches of Lorraine. She lay still, but as the pad did not stop the blood, the robe, which was already spotted with more or less definite stains and which sagged in the hollow of the prudently joined legs, was adorned in the middle with an enormous bloodstain. The following day, in the presence of the gilded bishops and the men-at-arms carrying satin banners and steel lances, Joan of Arc mounted the stake through a narrow opening between the faggots and stood exposed with that rusty rose at cunt level.

At eight o'clock, exactly when her mistress was waking up under the flowers, the little housemaid walked out by the freezing hospital amphitheater and into radiant sunlight. She walked behind the hearse. The priest had come running up. He was late, but he had come, for in villages the priest is always present at the removal of the body. If the deceased lives too far away from the rectory, the clergy contents itself with going halfway. The family and he, who are ambassadors of two equally illustrious rival kings, choose a place on the road, amidst the fields, where death and God meet. The priest was accompanied that morning by two choirboys who were walking in front of the hearse that contained the tiny coffin, which was adorned with the wreath of artificial pearls in the form of a blue and white star. You have gathered that the younger of the two choirboys, who are in black cassocks and white surplices trimmed with a broad band of old lace, will have the face of Riton and the other that of Erik. Behind the hearse walked the housemaid, who was followed by an undertaker's assistant.

"A hearse is a basket.* I'm behind a basket."

She had gone to the hospital very early, and when she crossed the porch which was opened for her by a sleepy porter, she found herself in the most flowery of gardens plumed with dawn (it was seven o'clock when she arrived). She saw the hearse of the poor, which seemed to her to be the skeleton of the hearse of the rich; she was not hurt by this. It was drawn by a hairless, non-descript horse and was waiting at the door of the amphi-theater. The maid entered. The amphitheater attendant greeted her very quietly. He was chatting with the driver and the undertaker's assistant. The driver said to the maid:

"We're a little early. We pick up at half-past seven."

The maid thought: "They bury by mail." Though it was a silent reflection, the driver heard it, for he added: "I'm talking of picking up the body, of course." He sniffled and with his sleeve wiped off the drop that was hanging from his nose. At the summit of the maid's soul, in the noblest part of her, the one that did not yield to grief, a nervous voice lost patience and cried: "Be qui-et. Be qui-et." But the poor girl herself could only hear a murmuring and did not understand what it meant. With her heavy hands, which were chapped from doing laun-dry, she tightened Madame's crape veils as one tightens a shawl around one's shoulders. She walked very lightly, in silence.

"I'm walking very light, and in the king's flower beds."

Her poverty and meager salary obliged her to wear

---

* A play on the words *corbillard* (hearse) and *corbeille* (basket). —*Translator's note.*

rubber-soled shoes. In that stark white room, the electric bulb was set in the angle of the wall and ceiling, which the inordinately large shadow of the little maid in mourning touched on the opposite wall. The little coffin in which her baby daughter lay, rested on two rather low black trestles.

"She's sleeping, the poor little dear."

There was enough silence to hear around her the croaking of the frogs that were jumping and diving into the water of the misty swamp in which she was still standing. The coffin was covered with a white sheet on which the nurses had laid the little star-shaped blue and white wreath of pearls that Madame had had delivered the day before. A plump, pink china cherub that trembled at the end of a brass wire floated amidst the artificial pearls. After muttering a brief Hail Mary, the maid leaned against the wall to be more comfortable while waiting for the priest. He came. When the procession reached the church, it had to wait in a corner until the end of the religious ceremony of the funeral of eleven German soldiers who had been killed the day before. It had to wait three hours. Juliette had been unable to cry.

"They'll think I'm not sad," she thought.

"They'll think I didn't love my little girl."

"People'll think I killed her, who knows."

The soldiers of the squad accompanying their dead comrades looked at the little woman in mourning who was standing near the hanging ropes that passed through a hole in the belfry. Finally, the eleven coffins were carried out and taken to the station so that they could rest on the other side of the Rhine. In the church, the prayers of intercession were run off rapidly. The black cassocks, which were too short and had buttons missing (buttons round as boot buttons), exposed the choirboys' legs, which were bare and hairy in the kind of rubber boots that were often worn by men in the Resistance, and the white lace surplice detracted not a bit from their vigor. They served the priest as one serves a piece of artillery. The servant is the one who passes the ammunition. They served with the same faith, the same devotion, the same promptness: whether it was the incense, the holy water, or the responses. Then, when the ceremony in church was over, they marched out first, preceding the priest, the two undertaker's assistants, and the mourning housemaid. A sexton closed the church door behind them. And on that interminable day began the long night of the maid's journey from the church to the grave and from the grave to her room.

I would have liked to say more about the hero Jean D. in a particular tone, to give an account of him, with facts and dates. But such a procedure is quite pointless and deceptive. Song alone can give some notion of what he meant to me, but the register of poets is limited. Although the novelist can deal with any subject, can speak of any character in precise detail, and can achieve variety, the poet is subject to the demands of his heart, which attracts to him all human beings who have been marked obliquely by evil and misfortune, and the characters in my books all resemble each other. They live, with minor variations, the same moments, the same perils, and when I speak of them, my language, which is inspired by them, repeats the same poems in the same tone.

When Jean was alive he made me suffer terribly, and his death now does the same. His life was a miracle of purity which his death in combat continues to illuminate. During the funeral ceremony, the priest said a few words, including the following: "He died on the field of honor." On any other occasion, the formula would have made me shrug and smile, but the priest made this statement about Jean. Apart from the fact that it magnified him by granting him the honors that are at men's disposal (the field of honor is a long, wide vacant lot behind the home of my foster-parents where a few heroes who have come a great distance, sometimes from Japan, go at night to die), the velvet and gold fringe, that statement, coming from a Christian, whose role is to pacify, to shed further light on the figure of Jean, made it stand out more sharply, and showed him as a hero of the just cause against evil, like the pure-hearted knight confronting the beast. That purity impresses me. I now understand the value of symbols, since I wanted to toss a flower on his grave and since the priest's statement produced a kind of physical steadying during my grief, a tension of the thighs and buttocks that enables me to say I am proud of Jean. It was to that purity, to the grandeur of that death, to my child's calm, silent courage that I wanted to dedicate the story which best expresses the secret iridescences of my heart, but the characters I find in it are what I adored in the past, what I still love, but what I want to mutilate hatefully.

Though all these spirited characters have not yet made their exit, nevertheless it is not possible for me to see them in the same lighting. Am I going to love uprightness, nobleness? The more Jean's soul inhabits me—the more Jean himself inhabits me—the fonder I shall be of cowards, traitors, and petty no-goods.

I shall speak first of his presence within me. As soon as he was covered with earth at the cemetery, when the little mound was finished and I took my first step away from the grave, I had the distinct feeling that I was detaching myself from the corpse which for four days, plus a good quarter of an hour before they locked the coffin, had taken Jean's place, from the corpse into which Jean had been transformed by the prodigy of a well-aimed bullet. Then immediately, not the memory, Jean himself took a place in what I am really obliged to call my heart. I recognize his presence by the following: I dare not do or say or think a thing that might hurt or anger him. And here is another proof of his presence within me: if anyone were to make a remark about him, a remark inoffensive in itself but vulgarly worded, for example: "He's dead, he won't fart any more," I would consider it an insult and more than an insult, a profanation, and I would kill the insulter who insults not only my grief but Jean himself, who can hear, for he is inside me and I hear the insult. I would kill him because Jean has only my arms—which are his—with which to defend himself. I would have put up with his being insulted when he was alive, if he couldn't hear. And if he did hear, let him defend himself! He was young and strong. But he now hears with my ears and fights with the help of my fists. I therefore cannot doubt my love when this book which I am writing while he inhabits me is the eager quest for the hoodlums he despises. But I do not feel that I am committing a sacrilege in offering him monstrous stories. My earlier books were written in prison. In order to rest, I put my arm around Jean's neck in my imagination and spoke to him quietly about the latest chapters. As for the present book, whenever I stop writing I see myself alone at the foot of his open coffin in the amphitheater and I relate my tale to him sternly. He makes no comments, but I know that his body which has been disfigured by the bullets, blood, and an overlong stay in the refrigerator hears me and, though it may not approve of me, accepts me.

It is raining this morning, and it grieves me to think

that he is in damp earth. I sit down, and my movement tells me that he can no longer sit. I beg of you, God:

*Palace of my memory where the sea coils*
*Miraculous and wingèd, herds grazing on fear*
*God of mingled plaster and night gospel of fingers*
*Frozen by gold weak buttons harmony of woodwinds*
*Red cap black ark and blue gaze of Spanish wells*
*God of heaven and bare arms product*
*Of fear and fire peaceful pillow*
*Where I dream secret object malaise swarm*
*Of lost fans end of time god alone*
*And only house shutter sweet lime-blossom*
*Refuge god of evening or of sorrowful woods*
*White tortured bones gift of a happy prince*
*Palace of my memory where fear coils.*
*The guard who watches at your door, and these*
                    *spear flowers*
*And that sponge, O my God, I am here.*
*I offer you my song that is drawn by your weary eye*
*Like a thread wound off through the eye, and my body*
*All hollowed out by that light golden thread*
*Will be thread of your dreams, reserve of piety,*
*Clear recording for your summer harps.*
*Precious spool, O God, your machines*
*Have so deep a need for love. Keep nights and my sleep*
*So that he may sleep, hear me Lord*
*A tale of nailed bones, of pierced bones, from elsewhere*
*Paradises closed over twisted boughs,*
*Shepherdess without echo, moonlight stretched*
*On the wires of the dryer, walk, walk through*
*The lost churches of the marbles of the sea.*

The boy I carry about inside me smiles and is sadly amused at my being concerned with things of this world.

"Why buy dozens of handkerchiefs?"

Since my life no longer has meaning, since a gesture denotes nothing, I want to stop living. Even if this decision is nullified and renewed every single moment, it prevents me from using the future. Everything must be done within the moment, since the next moment I shall be among the dead, squatting in the field of honor and talking to Jean. Every empty gesture that makes me think life will continue either betrays my wish to die or gives offense to Jean, whose death should lead to mine by means of love. That is how I lace my shoes, and the gesture quickens him. One doesn't wear shoes among the dead. I am therefore as detached from things as the condemned men I used to see in prison.

The only image of Jean I preserve within me is the one which shows him lying in his coffin, where he was still only a man condemned to death since his body had a more terrible and frightening presence than that of a boy who stopped breathing while awaiting the verdict. Although I knew he was dead, I saw him only as a condemned man who cares a little less about things and persists in his game of sleep. He had a haughty contempt in my presence, and his true death occurred only after the ceremony in church.

. . . . . . . . . . . . . . . . . . . . . . . . . . . . . . . . . . . . . . . . . . . . . . .

Erik, who dressed like a prince, was the executioner's lover for two years. They would meet in the killer's small apartment on the Kronprinzenufer. The windows, like those of a Venetian palace, overlooked a canal. From behind the colored panes one could feel a thick fog rise up from the river. The fog might have set the house adrift had the building not been anchored to rock by the executioner's presence. But the house was firmer than a light-house lashed by storms. It was inhabited by a quiet killer, a man who indulged in guilty but peaceful love affairs.

The two rooms were dark because of the leaded windows. They were simply furnished in middle-class style: oak furniture, a radio, a bed. The walls were adorned with a photograph of the executioner and one of Erik. They led a domestic existence that enabled Erik to do his job in the Hitler Youth and the other to perform his morning murders. Erik played the harmonica. He would sometimes ask for details about an execution. He would insist on being told the victim's last words, on getting an account of his cries, gestures, and grimaces. He was becoming callous. And the executioner, in emptying himself a little into the ears of a boy who loved him, was becoming gentler. He would take long naps on the cushions. He would stroke an old dog whose rheumy eyes moved him to pity, just as he was moved by children's snot, the gum of a cherry tree, the juice of poppies and lettuce, the tears of gonorrhea.

Erik had been transformed. He cropped his hair less closely. What had been too soft in his expression had hardened. His cheeks had grown hollow. He had a growth of beard which he shaved every day. Marching, exercise, and physical training had strengthened his muscles even more. But his eyes still had a bland, faraway look, and his mouth, which was sharply outlined and amazingly sinuous, was as sad as ever. His voice finally now had assurance when he spoke to the executioner. It no longer had shrill notes and the trembling that accompanied them, notes that will come back when he is a prisoner in the apartment of Jean's mother.

Yet there were times when he would have liked to be the executioner so as to be able to contemplate himself and enjoy from without the beauty he emitted: to receive it. As for me, I would have loved to perform a single one of those gestures so as to have been caught, if only fleetingly, in a moment of beauty. When a speeding train gives me a glimpse of a boy standing in a fog amidst wet leaves and dead branches, a boy whose shoulder supports the weight of a big fellow whose breath mingles with his friend's, I no doubt envy his beauty, his ragged grace, and his luck in serving a happy minute. I console myself with the thought that he can't enjoy the moment because he is unaware of its charm and is waiting to get it over with.

I said earlier that Pierrot was willful and gentle. A word about his will: as a child, he spent the summer in the country. He would often fish in a stream and bait his line with the long worms called earthworms. He would look for them in loose ground and cram them into a pocket of his kneepants. The habit of biting one's nails is often accompanied by a corollary of putting into the mouth whatever the hand happens upon. Pierrot would mechanically pick from his pocket the dried bread crumbs of his four o'clock snack and eat them. One evening, he took from his pocket something hard and dry and put it into his mouth. The warmth and moisture quickly restored the softness of the shriveled worm which had remained in the pocket where it had dried and which the darkness had prevented the boy from recognizing. He found himself caught between fainting with disgust or mastering his situation by willing it. He willed it. He made his tongue and palate knowingly and patiently suffer the hideous contact. This willfulness was his first poet's attitude, an attitude governed by pride. He was ten years old.

Other and more generally practiced concerns were

going to direct Erik as he pursued his individual destiny. Although the theft of the watch had delivered that proud young brute to the executioner, pride had led him to Russia where at times he still suffered at the memory of two years of humiliation. As shame assured him that not a single bond remained between him and human beings, he was ready for anything. In short, since circumstances —then judged unfortunate—had set him on a path that leads to the renunciation of honor, he would take advantage of them to rebuild his life on the basis of that terrible failing, not so as to erect it with abjection as its foundation but rather to allow the abject to make it achieve power.

I still do not know why it is necessary for Erik to commit a murder at this point. The explanations I shall give will not seem valid at first. However, if the murder of the child is out of place, that is, not in accordance with a logical order that justifies its presence in the novel, I must state that this act of Erik's comes in here, at this particular point, because it forces itself on me. It may shed light on what happens later in the story.

If the only sin—evil according to the world—is to take life, it is not surprising that murder is the symbolic act of evil and that one instinctively recoils from it. The reader will therefore not be surprised that I wanted to be helped in my first murder. The declaration of war thrilled me. My hour had struck. I could kill a man without danger, I would know what one kills in oneself, and what remorse after killing is like. But without danger, I mean without danger of social reprobation, without incurring the prison sentence of the person who destroys life. At last I was going to strike out for my freedom.

One evening when I was strolling outside a small French village that had recently been taken, a stone grazed the bottom of my trousers. I thought it was an attack or insult. My hand flew to my revolver. I was immediately on guard, that is, I bent one knee and spun around. I was on a small dune in the deserted countryside. Sixty feet away I saw a kid of about fifteen playing with a puppy, throwing stones which the animal retrieved. One of the carelessly thrown stones had grazed me. Fear and then anger of having been afraid and reacting with fear in sight of a child's innocent eyes, and the fact of having been a Frenchman's target, plus the nervousness of all my gestures, made me grab the grip of my revolver and tear it from its holster. In any other circumstance, I would have come to my senses. I would have sheathed my weapon, but I was alone and felt I was. Immediately, on looking at the child's delicate face, which delicacy made ironic, I realized that the moment had come to know murder. The swift, shoreless rivers of green anger were flowing within me, from north to south, from one hand to the other, mingling their boiling, impetuous waves and their calm, flat ones. My gaze was fixed in a set, grim, and yet sparkling face, for rays from all the features converged around the bridge of the nose. A cry might have saved me from the mute, blurred rattle that rose up, without emerging, from my stomach to my mouth. The child bent down in the twilight to take the slobbery stone from the dog's mouth. He straightened up with a laugh. Snow fell. Before my eyes, such gentleness descended upon the woebegone landscape to soften the ridges of things, the angles of gestures, the thorny crown of the stones, a snow so light that my hand with the gun lowered a little. The joyous black puppy yelped twice as it frisked about the child. The twilight soothed bleeding Europe. The boy's lips were parted, and I parted mine in the same way, but without smiling, for I inhaled not air but more hatred. The dog was leaping about its bare-kneed master without a sound.

The green waves, which had grown calm for a moment, rolled through me faster and faster. The cataracts set electrical machines going, turbines, something like that, dynamos which emitted a terrible current that escaped through the gauze, piercing the veil of snow, splitting the muslins that the sweetness of the child's face spread like a twilight of milk over the countryside which had been frightened by the anger of the offended soldier.

"Violence calms storms, the time has come."

I felt my weapon in my right hand. A column of dark-ness or pure water, contained by the shape of our lips, circulated from my open mouth to the open mouth of the child sixty feet away and linked us down as far as our stomachs. But my periwinkle gaze was destroying the strict appearances and seeking the secret of death. My black police cap, which had been too far down over my eye, was displaced by my brusque about-face, fell on my shoulder and to the ground.

"I'm shedding my leaves" was a thought that flashed through my mind, barely grazing me. My left hand made a very subtle gesture to snatch up the fallen cap. A faint green vapor rose up over my subsided rivers. A touch of humanity brought thought back to me, slowly, though only three seconds had elapsed between the brusque about-face and the gesture of aiming. My more human glances were even graver, more bent on melting the gen-tleness that the boy's smile had snowed over the stunned countryside, which had fallen on its ass without daring to complain. In order to aim, I had only to shift the gun imperceptibly, to right the muzzle, whose cunning black mouth, though it had been humiliated for a moment at watching the earth laugh below, suddenly became strong in the assurance that it was expressing an eternal, obvious truth: a tiny fraction of an inch in the new aim was sufficient. Nevertheless, my hand moved slowly and solemnly as I readjusted my aim. The black-sleeved arm holding the gun strayed a huge distance away, moved the hand into the darkness, passed behind the mound over which the child towered, enveloped him several times, bent back, returned, passed behind me, and tied me to the child, who was still linked to me by the column of darkness. Then, getting still longer and suppler, the arm enclosed the countryside, seized the darkness, compressed it, fastened it in that slow but sovereign movement of encircling the moment and turned it into a repulsive block traversed by the blue ray of Erik's increasingly human gaze. The arm made a few more loops, grabbing and strangling every living thing it encountered, and brought back in front of me, waist-high—a bit higher— and slightly more to the right, the resolute revolver. The first stroke of seven rang out from the invisible belfry. Stars in the sky, maybe one or two. I felt that the gun was becoming an organ of my body, an essential organ whose black orifice, which was marked by a more gleaming little circle, was, for the time being, my own mouth, which at last was having its say. My finger on the trigger. The highest moment of freedom was attained. To fire on God, to wound him and make him a deadly enemy. I fired. I fired three shots.

"A boy as pretty as that can make me shoot three times."

Anyway, the first shot was the only one that mattered. The child fell as one does in such cases, giving way at the knees and with his face against the ground. I immediately looked at the gun and knew I was truly a murderer, with the muzzle of my revolver like that of the

gangsters, the killers, in the comic books of my childhood.
The dramatic moment and movement were fortunately
not over, for contact with life would have killed me.
Everything that bore on the drama continued it. The
smoke and the black muzzle, shadowed by the powder,
were the main things that riveted my attention on the
drama. With my eyes still fixed on them, I lowered my
body, not by stooping, but by bending my knees, and,
with my left hand, picked up my cap, which lay at my
feet. I kept it in my hand and stood up, without losing
sight of the muzzle. I knew that my return to earth would
be frightful. The last stroke of seven rang out. From the
dryness that coated my lips and palate, I realized that my
mouth was still open, and I felt the horror of having a
physical and magical relationship with a warm corpse.
The child must have clenched his teeth, must have cut
the column of darkness that was traversed by starlit waves
with his incisors; it had probably been broken by the
body's falling on the face. Nevertheless, I closed my
mouth so as to cut off all contact with the child. Then, I
tried to turn around and leave without seeing the result
of my first murder. I felt somewhat ashamed of my
cowardice. The German columns were on the lookout all
around.

"I will. Why not? Maybe he's only wounded. No, he'd
scream. No, they don't always scream. The executioner
used to tell me about his ax jobs."

"He taught me courage. I will."

I shifted my eyes to the outstretched child, but at the
same time I raised the revolver so that my gaze would
cross and register the muzzle, which was still warm, and
include it in the game that had been bagged, where it
would perform the function of establishing the continuity
of the drama, thus keeping me on a nervous pinnacle of

calm and silence where men's fear and their cries and their indignation could not reach me. I looked at my outstretched victim. The astonished dog sniffed at his feet and head. I was surprised that the black puppy did not begin a clever funeral ceremony worthy of a prince by a secret process known to black dogs, that it did not summon a band of angels to come and bring its master back to life or carry him up to heaven. The dog was still sniffing.

"Luckily it's not howling, it's not wailing. If it wailed, all the angels would come running." I thought that very fast, as my left foot was simultaneously stepping back. The ground was soft. I sank a little into a small hole and immediately felt I was supported at the waist by the executioner with whom I had been mired in the Tiergarten. Then the thought of my boots occurred to me, and the boots reminded me that I was a German soldier.

"I'm a German soldier," I thought. Then, with my eyes still on the scene of the corpse and the dog, I lowered my left arm; the gun, which was both executant and sign of the drama, disappeared from the scene, which I saw in its cold nakedness, in its commonplace abandon, even more lonely in that lovely twilight of peace, as a foul murder discovered at dawn near the slums. Feeling a little stronger and more sure of myself, I noted the details: the child's round behind, his curly head on his bent arm, his bare calves, the surprised black dog, a vague clump of trees. I took a second step back. Suddenly, I was afraid of having that murder at my heels pursuing me through the night. Finally I dared to turn around. Holding my black cap in my left hand, which hung motionless against my body, and the revolver at the end of my outstretched right arm, rather far from my body, I slowly went down into the night in my German boots and my black trousers, which were swollen with sweaty effluvia and curly vapors, and began moving toward the dreadful and comforting life of all men, followed by a procession of helmeted, powdered, flower-bedecked, fragrant warriors, some of them laughing and some severe, some of them naked and some clad in leather, iron, and copper, emerging in a body from the gaping chest of the murdered kid. They were carrying red oriflammes with black symbols and were being led by the solemn march of the world's silence. Trampling on the bleeding vanquished, frightened not by remorse or possible punishment but by his glory, Erik Seiler returned to barracks. He went by roads that ran along a torrent whose roaring filled the darkness. His curls were damp. At the roots of the hair above the forehead were delicate beads of sweat. He felt he was borne up by fear itself and that if it stopped he would not only collapse but be annihilated, for he realized he was now only a very fragile framework of salt that was supporting the undamaged head, with its eyes and hair and its mass of brain that secreted fear. The flesh of his body had all melted away. Only the white, very light frame was left. (Do you know the amusing physical experiment in which a ring that hangs from a thread is supported after the thread is burned? The thread is soaked in very salty water. The ring is then tied to it. Then you burn the thread with a match. The ring stays up, supported by the delicate cord of salt.) Erik felt he was composed of a skeleton as breakable and white as that cord, which was traversed by a shudder from one particle of salt to the next, also like a chain composed of doddering old men. If a shock occurred, if fear itself were lacking, he would crumble beneath the great weight of his head, which was needed to preserve his consciousness of fear. He was walking at the edge of the torrent and heard its

roar. The big shadow of the executioner was walking at
his right, supported by the bulkier and slightly paler mass
of Hitler, who loomed against the starry background of the
night as a block of blacker darkness in which one felt there
were sharp rocks, and also caverns whose silent call was
a danger to Erik who—had he heeded their wailing ever so
little—would have been willing to lie down in them and
sleep and die, that is, to let himself be caught in the
austere reins of remorse and oblivion. The torrent was
booming at his left. The noise became almost visible. The
soldier's blue scarf shivered in the wind. He thought he
recognized a man's breath, the caress of a lock of blond
hair, of a finger of light and ivory. His skeleton of salt
shuddered. Then calm and flesh returned to him when
he realized it was the silk and the wind. I could make
out in the darkness a tangle of stiff, mournful branches
that loomed against the sky like black Chantilly lace. Its
strangeness exceeded ugliness to the point of the most
evil intent. I kept walking, though without hesitation. In
that nocturnal landscape, near an abbey where I was
recopying this idiotic and sacred book, reliving Erik's
anguish and giving it life by means of my own, I thought
I recognized the dangerous spots where the fellows in
the Resistance were on the lookout, and among them, just
behind that rock, ready to pick me off, was Paulo, who
was enveloped in shadow, silence, and hatred. I also
imagined him in the midday sun observing from a distance the funeral of the maid's daughter as the procession
very slowly made its way to the cemetery by the white
motionless roads of a rocky countryside. The horse that
was drawing the hearse was weary. The two choirboys,
one of whom was holding a holy-water basin, were
whistling a java under their breath. The priest was en-
gaged in a monologue with God. The little maid was

perspiring in her black clothes under her veils. She tried for a while to keep up with the procession, but she was soon tired and the hearse outdistanced her. Her shoes hurt her. One of them became unlaced and she dared not tie it, for she was not supple enough to bend down, and on the day of her child's funeral it would not have been proper for her to put her foot on a stone during the procession, for such a gesture, in addition to immobilizing you in the jaunty posture of a very proud lady going up a flight of stairs, distracts you from your grief (or from everything that should signify it, which is even more serious) by interesting you in the things of this world. The rites allow only a few gestures; drying one's tears with a handkerchief. (One can know that one has a handkerchief, although not to know it and to let the tears flow is proof of greater sorrow, but the maid was too weary to weep.) You can also wrap yourself in your crape. On the way from the hospital to the church she let the veil fall over her face, and as she was looking at the world through the transparent black cloth, it seemed to her that the world was grieved, mourning her sadness, and that touched her. In addition, the veil, by isolating her, endowed her with a dignity she had never known, and the great heroine of the drama was herself. She herself was the dead person who was solemnly walking the road of the living, for the last time exposing herself to everyone's respect, a dead yet living person on the way to the grave. From the hospital to the church, she was that dead person, taking it upon herself to allow—conscious that she was doing so—her daughter to tread the everyday road for the last time. But when she left the city to go to the cemetery in the country, she put the veil behind her by simply turning that fantastically winged hat around her head. Walking then became an act of drudgery, which she piously wanted to perform but the difficulty of which exhausted her. She undid a hook of her corset, and then, a hundred yards farther, another. The procession drew away from her. She was surprised, however, to recognize the fields, the groves, the dry stone walls. "After all, I'm going to the cemetery," she said to herself, "and now that I'm so far away from my daughter (for she thought she would never catch up with the hearse) I could take a short cut." She didn't dare. Her shoe was hurting her more and more. Soldiers, using a slang expression, sometimes say during forced marches: "My dogs are barking." "My dogs are barking," thought the little maid, but she reproached herself for the thought, which recalled too precisely her relations with a private in an eastern city. She turned her mind to her daughter and, immediately raising her eyes, saw her so far away that she tried to catch up by walking faster: "It's walk or croak." She thought of the soldiers again and again felt ashamed. All these inner incidents were exhausting her.

"It's awful to lose a child. And they make me bury her. At least my kid's *someone,* she's a colonel's daughter."

"Is it still far to the cemetery, sir?" She put this question to the wind, to the sun, to the stones, to nothing. There was nobody around her. The procession was going down a hill which hid it from us. The maid was alone.

"They're at table. No one's waiting on them. Oh, I'm so, so tired! It's annoying that kids die and have to be buried. Why not make soup of them? It would boil down into stock and make a nice meat soup."

The maid was telling her beads, each black pellet of which was vermiculated. The markings in relief made the object look like a toy, like the least serious of toys. Is it quite certain that grief is greater if one is more conscious of it? One is conscious of grief when the mind is focused on it, when one examines it with unflagging tension: it then withers you like a sun that you look in the face, its fire so devours you that for a long time I felt my eyelids burning. But grief can also disintegrate the faculties, tear the mind apart. The fellows from those parts also have an expression to designate a man who has gone to pieces under too great a suffering: "He's turning into a pair of balls." We suffer at being unable to look at our grief steadily; our acts are wrapped in an aura of weariness and regret that makes the acts seem false—only a tiny bit false, true on the whole, but false since they do not fully satisfy us. An uneasiness accompanies them all. A slight shift could, we feel, we think, destroy the uneasiness and make everything hang together. All that is needed is that they be performed—or that we see them performed—in the world where the person for whom they are performed lives, the person without whom they no longer have meaning if love did not oblige you one day to dedicate them to him secretly. Grief caused the maid to fall apart. She rarely thought of her daughter, but she suffered at being unable to make a gesture that would satisfy her completely. She walked by a farmhouse, the gate of which was ajar. The dog took her for a beggar or a tramp, for she was limping. He came up and sniffed at her and then barked.

"If the dog throws a stone at me," she said to herself, "I'll bring it back in my mouth."

Spinning around, she made a sweeping gesture with her arms, frightening the dog which ran off yelping even louder. This first violent attempt to fit into life almost mechanically entailed the gesture of catching her veil, which had risen from her bosom and bellied like a sail during her spin. Her whole body was somehow comforted by the effort. She extended her calf, and felt like taking off her hat to relax. As she walked, she put her hand to

it, removed it, and was immediately overcome by a wave
of fatigue, for, without further thought on that account
of her daughter's death or her own sorrow, she had the
sudden feeling that these acts were false. They had been
performed in the normal, physical, everyday world,
whereas she was moving in, of course, that same world,
but that world corrected by grief. And, in such cases,
only certain symbolic gestures afford us the plenitude of
which all others deprive us. The poor thing could no
longer think about her baby, which had never been anything but a kind of excrescence of foul ruddy flesh detached from its mother's body. It had died at the age of
two weeks. . . . She had not lived for it. A housemaid does
not make plans for her daughter. Her grief was mostly
physical, it had been caused by that loathsome amputa-
tion: the death which tore from your breast the burden
of flesh attached to it by the mouth. Her mind brushed
away the memory of her child, who appeared to her as a
small, shriveled corpse clinging monstrously to one of her
boobs by its nails and dead mouth. Thus do I meditate
during the walk in the sun to the cemetery, on the road
along which a maid who is going to bury her little girl is
trudging.

Paulo had watched her calvary without turning a hair.

It was regrettable that the little girl had died no
sooner than she was born. The maid would later have
taught her the art of two-part singing so as to beg in
the street, just as she herself had been taught by her
mother. In their little room, near a window that looked
out on the yard, they would have gravely learned to sing,
in strict time, the touching and bewitching songs that
open hearts and purses. Art. Great art.

. . . . . . . . . . . . . . . . . . . . . . . . . . . . . . . . . . . . . . . . . . . . . . . . . .

Standing on the balcony, with his elbow leaning on the night, Riton waited. Far off, intermittently, the cannon boomed.

"That's the big works. Go to it. I know all about it!"

The disorder in his intestines, the bubbles of gas he heard fizzing inside him added to his monstrousness. The awareness, in the midst of that infernal solitude, of what that solitude had made of him—a barbaric divinity of all-out war looking down at the city it condemns—filled him with an evil joy, the joy of being joyous and handsome in a desperate situation which he had evilly got himself into, out of hatred for France (which he rightly confused with Society), the day he signed up for the Militia, the day his contempt for his "brothers" impelled him to choose gestures more beautiful than anything.

I have the soul of Riton. It is natural for the piracy, the ultra-mad banditry of Hitler's adventure, to arouse hatred in decent people but deep admiration and sympathy in me. One day, when I saw German soldiers firing at Frenchmen from behind a parapet, I was suddenly ashamed of not being with the former, shouldering my rifle, and dying at their side. I mention also that at the center of the whirlwind that precedes—and almost envelops—the moment of orgasm, a whirlwind more intoxicating at times than the orgasm itself, the loveliest, the gravest erotic image, that toward which everything tended, an image prepared by a kind of inner fête, was offered me by a German soldier in the black uniform of the tank driver. But though, in the depths of the eye of Gabès, Erik was sustained by grim music and the fragrance of dawn as he galloped on his horse of light (with an ax, swathed in crape, at the side of his saddle), the sweating executioner was naked, having arrived from Germany after crossing rivers, forests, and towns in a single day: dark, hairy, and muscular, in trim, spangled tights, the sky-blue jersey of which delicately molded the detail of the soft, heavy prick and balls. The ridges of my brow were crushed against Jean's behind, and a momentary but severe headache sharpened my vision, exacerbated it. The delights there where the iron soldier was entwining himself with the azure executioner came swarming in. My tongue burrowed more deeply. My eyes were devoured by suns, by the steel teeth of a circular saw. My temples were throbbing. Riton was standing on the footbridge.

Not far away, a shot rang out from the Belleville area. A voice whispered in Riton's ear:

"*Komm schlafen, Ritône.*" Someone gently took hold of his right arm. He turned around in terror. The ship had gone down. Without realizing it, he had just sunk to the bottom of the sea and was already hearing the language that is spoken there. He could not break away. He was the prisoner of an emotional tangle, which is worse than a mechanism of locks or laws. In that darkness, at the end of his reverie, he thought he was hearing, close to his ear, his own voice for the first time. It was attached to no human branch and seemed to be uttering the words of a language that can be spoken only in the depths of what is a fabulous element, namely any enemy family and people. He turned his head to the right. Erik was at his left, and his arm was around the boy's shoulder.

Erik felt strong, and tender. The thought that all was lost impelled him to kindness for the first time.

His beauty dictated his proud attitudes, and he would have died standing, offering himself, without witnesses, to the bullets—not in order to compose an image of gallantry for the final hour, but because his physical beauty, being proud, allowed him only such gestures as: raising his head or torso, crying no, tossing a grenade or a stone as a last projectile, crushing a face beneath his heel, etc., gestures which were in keeping with his gaze and also with the harmonious model of his whole body and of his features. His heroism was not a pose, nor was it assumed so that he would be worthy of his beauty—so as to heighten it, for example—for he forgot about it in action. Rather, he was heroic because that beauty (of the face and body) acted, without his realizing it, in all his acts, commanded them, filled them.

Though he tried to take advantage of the war to break away from the executioner, in moments of sadness—that is, when he was resting in the rear lines or immobilized in snow and mud—a great need for tenderness and protection made him turn toward his friend, who would then appear to him (so far away, in the center of the capital) in the role of an imperturbable dispenser of justice whose life and function were becoming more and more of a mystery to him.

He plundered France, shipped to Germany furniture stolen from museums, and paintings, carpets, cloth, gold. He wanted his destiny to be carried out quickly and death to take him without his regretting anything. With icy cruelty, he was pursuing his ascesis. For the same reason that made him choose his linen with great care and buy leather goods and English cloth, that is, in order to keep his feet on the ground, with desperate eagerness he sought a pretext that would justify his social life— and found it. In short, he had given himself an aim, and a most frivolous one, for he had no faith that might have enabled him to choose serious ones.

"That's all I can do, be a pivot (which is what I am) and surround myself with the rarest ornaments in the world so that I don't covet anything. With luxury and

money I'll be free." He had to fulfill himself in the
easiest way. And to see himself for only one day. To know
for only one day that he was complete would be enough
for him. There is a book entitled *I'll Have a Fine Funeral.*
We are acting with a view to a fine funeral, to formal
obsequies. They will be the masterpiece, in the strict
sense of the word, the major work, quite rightly the
crowning glory of our life. I must die in an apotheosis,
and it doesn't matter whether I know glory before or
after my death as long as I *know* that I'll have it, and I
shall have it if I sign a contract with a firm of undertakers
that will attend to fulfilling my destiny, to rounding it
off.

"*Komm, mein Ritône.*"

Perhaps because he had to muffle his voice, he uttered
the words so tenderly that Riton was flooded with disgust. He was being torn from his proud solitude. No doubt
he knew he could never maintain it, but they could at
least let him enjoy that beautiful moment which he
thought he had artfully prepared a long time before. Let
him and the moment remain alone together, in a sublimity
that would end only with daylight.

With the speed of a man falling, he again became a
fleeing soldier who runs off exhausted. He said:

"Yes yes, I'm coming." But he did not move. An added
gush of bitterness sickened him. While trying so cleverly
to pride himself on having accepted, alone and light-
heartedly, the fact of being abandoned by an entire
people, he was secretly hoping for the faint excuse of
a threat, of pressure exerted by the Germans, for one
does not escape as easily as one thinks from a country
that sticks to you, that clings to your hands and feet, if
you pull them, in cables of molasses impossible to break.
Threats and blows would have helped Riton break free.

Instead of gripping him firmly, the German, his comrade-in-arms, spoke to him in the tone in which one speaks to the dying. Anyway, Riton had a right to count on the Germans' disgust with a Frenchman who goes over to the enemy. By increasing his solitude, such disgust would have made him stronger, harder, more capable of putting up with it. Since the first day's fighting he had lost all hope of saving himself. Perhaps a few more flights over the rooftops, a few bursts of machine-gun fire, but there was little chance of getting out of it, since the sergeant and his men refused to surrender. If he himself surrendered, he would be shot. In any case, barring a miracle, he had little time left. A whole lifetime would be too long for him to take the risk of accepting it with utter contempt, but at least let them not diminish his sacrifice by offering him ridiculous tenderness.

Riton thought of the German soldiers and his friends who had escaped by the sewers. They were leading, in another darkness, a life which was the subterranean replica of his life up in the sky. They were somewhat like our reflections at the bottom of muddy ponds when we are on the shore. "The poor guys, they must be with the rats. I ate cat and they're eating rat. If we see each other again, we'll start fighting. . . ." He felt in his flesh the presence of a cat, a cat so well assimilated that at times he was afraid it could be heard miaowing and purring. He was also afraid that it might emerge from him and go off in its new form (of cat or devil) with part of his flesh. He kept peering into the darkness with his hand on his gun, and Erik thought he was aiming at something. He himself looked around suspiciously and whispered:

"You, want shoot?"

He stopped talking.

A deep modesty suddenly prevented him from wanting to know any more or say any more about himself. He saw himself in an iron darkness, in the presence of a strange, barefoot creature on the balcony, a creature with arms of flesh who was emerging from a heavy, dripping corset and was dressed in a complete weapon as if he had dwelt in the barrel of the machine gun and bullets had shot from his mouth. We know the power of the muzzle of a gun. When I heard that Jean had gone to a party despite his oath, I put my gun into my pocket and left with the kid. We went down to the Seine. It was dark. There was nobody around. We were near the parapet, under the trees. My arm was around his neck.

"My darling."

My mouth was on his ear, and my tongue and lips got busy. He shuddered with pleasure. I got a hard-on. I put my right hand into my pocket and very cautiously took out my gun. My anger was softened by my excitement and loosened its hold. The air was mild. The most serene music descended from the sky to the water and from the trees to us. I whispered in Jean's ear:

"You little bitch, you gave yourself, eh?"

He thought I was using a lover's language, he smiled. My gun was in my hand and was being caressed by the night air. I pressed the muzzle against the kid's hip and said, in an implacable tone:

"My finger's on the trigger. If you move, you'll drop."

He understood. He murmured, facing the river:

"Jean!"

"Don't say a word."

We stood there motionless. The water was flowing with such solemnity that one would have thought it had been delegated by the gods to make the slow course of the drama visible. I said:

"Wait."

I withdrew the muzzle that was buried in the cloth of the jacket. At no time did I feel that I was preparing a murder. I added, softly:

"Do as I tell you. Do it or I'll shoot. Here. Now suck."

I placed the muzzle of my gun on his parted lips, which he brought together.

"I'm telling you it's loaded. Suck."

He opened his mouth and I inserted the tip of the weapon in it. I whispered in his ear:

"Go on, suck it, you little bitch."

His pride hardened him. He was motionless, unperturbed.

"Well?"

I heard the click of his teeth on the steel. He was watching the Seine flow by. His whole body must have been waiting for the lightning that would kill us, the hummed love song that would distract me, the eagle that had been instructed to carry off me, the cop, the child, the dog.

"Suck or I'll shoot."

I said it in such a tone that he sucked. My body was pressed against his. With my free hand I stroked his behind.

"That must give you a hard-on since you like that."

I delicately contrived to slip my hand into his fly, which I opened. I stroked him, I kneaded him. Little by little he got excited, though not as stiff as I pride myself that I can make someone if I care to.

"Go on, suck it till it shoots."

I tremble with shame at the memory of that moment, for it was I who gave in. I withdrew the muzzle of the gun from that beautifully curved mouth and moved it to Jean's ribs, at heart level. The Seine kept flowing quietly.

Above us, the still foliage of the plane trees was animated by the very spirit of tragic expectation. Things around us dropped their defenses.

"You're lucky, you bitch."

He turned his head slightly toward me. His eyes were shining. He was holding back his tears.

"You can talk now. You're lucky I don't have the guts to blast your dirty bitchy little mug."

He looked at me for a second, then turned his eyes away.

"Beat it!"

He looked at me again and walked off. I went home with my weapon lowered. Early next morning he knocked at the door of my room. He took advantage of my usual morning torpor to bring about the reconciliation I longed for.

. . . . . . . . . . . . . . . . . . . . . . . . . . . . . . . . . . . . . . . . . . . . . . .

The winded hearse had come to a stop, for the road was going uphill through pine woods. The horse stopped to rest. The familiarity of death with nature was nobility itself. The maid, who was ready to drop, caught up with the procession, but no sooner was she under the pines and stirred by the smell of resin and life when the funereal machine got under way again. A hundred yards farther, the horse's shoes rang out on the king's highway. The procession was going through a suburb. The maid looked up. The first thing she saw was the police station, which is always at the entrance of villages. The policemen were sleeping on cots. The dark uniforms lay strewn on the worn, mud-stained bedside rugs or drooped on chairs above empty boots. The muscular bodies were naked, chastely stretched out in the summer humidity. Black flies alighted on them. The men's sleep was dreamless. Making one's rounds against petty theft in the country- side is tiring. But had one of them seen the maid go by as he stood at the window with shirt half unbuttoned and his belt loosely buckled, he would not have recog- nized the wiliest of hoodlums under that extravagant grief and mourning. A little farther off was the prison. In the façade, behind the outer wall, were seventeen sky- lights, and through the bars of one of them hung a huge and tiny hand frozen in a gesture of farewell, the un- happy hand of a condemned woman. Finally we reached the town. All the windows were decked with flags, and tricolored bunting hung in the sun. The stone balconies were decorated in Roman fashion with sheets, rugs, garlands, and ivy monograms. The whole village was at the window to see the royal procession go by. People were waving their arms, applauding, laughing, shouting for joy. The maid was so weary that she felt smaller than a stone, fit at most for blocking the wheels of the hearse. She was as weary as a soldier back from a parade, but she held herself together, supported at each step by the na- tional anthems which were playing a victory march for her alone.

That day will be a long one. Perhaps the sun set and rose several times, but a kind of fixity—which was chiefly in the gaze—made people, animals, plants, and objects stand out with flawless lucidity. Every object maintained within itself a motionless time from which sleep was banished. It is not by exceeding twenty-four hours that this day is lengthened: it stretches the moments, and each thing observes them with such fixed attention that one feels nothing will pass unnoticed. The trees in partic- ular want to catch you in the act; their immobility in- furiates me. The day of Jean's funeral thus acquired a

living personality which seemed to me to be marked by
the contents of Jean's death, or rather by the contents
of Jean dead, wrapped in cloth, a precious and life-giving
nucleus, a soft, compact almond around which the day
wound itself, worked at its thread, spun its cocoon in
which the dead boy lived; around which life and its
characters—and I, exceptionally, along with them, whereas
usually I am that nucleus—wound and unwound themselves spirally in all directions. From the moment I saw
Jean displayed in his coffin (at four in the afternoon)
until midnight of the following day, this day, which was
strange on account of its position in time and frightening
on account of the very presence in its heart of a corpse
that in the end filled it completely since it was its essence,
rendered painful and made difficult because of my friendship for Jean, and violently revealed to me by his death,
could end, despite two evenings, two dead suns, two or
three lunches, two or three dinners, only after I had
slept. When I woke up, I felt a little less horror, but for
forty hours had lived, had flowed on, within a living day
whose life was emitted, like dawn around the manger,
by the luminous corpse of a twenty-year-old child that
had the shape and consistency of a milk-almond in its
cloths and wrappings. A similar day is going to flow by.
Every single object is very attentive and is making an
effort to note it by noticing it. Things are on the watch.
The colonel's tooth-glass makes its crystal maintain a
deeper state of pensiveness. It listens. It records. The trees
can toss about, shake their feathers in the wind, they can
growl, fight, sing, but their agitation is deceptive: they
are on the watch. One of them in particular disturbs me.
As for the characters, they are poisoned. All these pages
will be pallid, for moonlight flows in their veins instead
of blood.

On each side of the street stood three- and four-story middle-class sandstone houses. Faces were smiling at the doorsteps. People were throwing kisses to the Prussian tank that was covered with foliage. The top of the turret was crowned with the motionless torso of Erik. He was fascinating because of the color of his outfit, the severity of his gaze, the beauty of his face. The people were delirious. All the bands of heaven were blaring their music. Hitler appeared on the balcony of a very simple house. He looked at the maid. She was following the tank, which was accompanied by the noise of cannon and churchbells. He saluted, in his fashion, with his arm extended and hand open, but he did not smile. Erik did not see the Führer. Sharp-eyed, evil-eyed, he was driving his tank.

"Hitler surely recognized me," thought the maid, and her grief eased a little, for her daughter's death was serving the Führer's glory. The souls of these cherubim and the fragrance of their innocence were enough to destroy the world. The people were still cheering the tank as it went by. Hitler left the balcony, and, after dismissing the dignitaries of the Air Force and of the Army and Navy, who had accompanied him at a respectful distance, he retired to his room.

Jewelers call a good-sized, well-cut diamond a solitaire. One speaks of its "water," that is, its limpidness, which is also its brilliance. Hitler's solitude made him sparkle. In one of his recent speeches (I am writing this in September 1944), he cried:

(It may be noted that his public life was no more than a raging torrent of cries. A gushing. A fountain whose limpidness is free of any thought other than the physical movement of the voice) he cried:

". . . I shall withdraw, if necessary, to the top of the

Spitzberg!" But did I ever leave it? My castration forces me to a white, icy solitude. The bullet that tore off both my balls in 1917 subjected me to the harsh discipline of the dry masturbator, but also to the sweet pleasures of pride.

Gérard, who was the master of my secret revels, had the right to enter immediately when I was alone. He therefore entered, pushing in front of him a pale, young French hoodlum with a cap in his hand. The boy was not particularly surprised at finding himself in the presence of the most powerful man of the age. Hitler stood up, for he knew that the politeness of kings is exquisite, and put out his hand to Paulo, whose amazement and horror began that very moment. The seated wax effigy came to life on his behalf. Despite having done so, it retained the damp lock of hair across the forehead, the two long wrinkles, the mustache, the cross-belt, all the attributes by which the most obscure of men had suddenly become the most illustrious, and the only one Paulo had really looked at in the waxworks museum in Paris when he was sixteen. However, he had already been dragged to so many orgies, in Paris and Berlin, where he had honestly thought that all the tired queers at those parties were infantes, princes, and kings that he was not intimidated. The Führer looked at him. He had weighed the thigh muscles in the trousers with wrinkles at the knees as soon as the door opened. The sculpture of the neck and head seemed fine to him. He smiled and looked at Gérard.

"*Wunderschön,*" he said. And to Paulo:

"*Wie heissen sie?*"

"*Er ist Franzose,*" said Gérard.

"Ah, you are French?" Hitler's smile broadened.

"Yes, sir," said Paulo, who was about to add . . . "and

from Paname,"* but he checked himself in time. This
time he had the feeling that he was at the very heart of
one of the world's gravest moments. The ambassadors,
the general staffs, the ministers, the whole world, who
were unaware of this interview and still arranging for
it, had to wait for it to come to an end. Paulo hardly
breathed. The room was rather large but had commonplace printed drapes and was furnished with Tyrolese
chairs. In that room was the world's pivot, the diamond
axis on which, according to certain Hindu cosmographies,
the world turns. The bronze doors of the moment were
closed. Paulo thought very fast, and with such fright that
he squeezed his cap against his chest with both hands:
"Even though Hitler acts so charming, he won't be able
to let me leave the palace, for there are secrets it's mortally
dangerous to know." And while all this agitation, which
lasted the rest of his life, was taking shape, Paulo barely
noticed that the Führer was beckoning to Gérard and
saying good-by to him.

"This way."

Hitler gently pushed the terrified hoodlum into a room
without a window, actually a kind of alcove which a
movable panel had opened in the wall. The alcove contained only a huge unmade bed, the covers of which were
pulled back like a turned-up eyelid, and some bottles and
glasses on a small table. The child's heart was thumping
so erratically that it realized its own agitation. The secret
alcove which the panel revealed to him was where Hitler
loved and killed his victims. The bottles were poisoned.
Paulo found himself in the presence of death. He was
surprised at its having the familiar face of an alcove prepared for love, and because death used such simple objects, it seemed to him inevitable. What filled him at first

---

* French slang for Paris. —*Translator's note.*

was not the sadness of losing his life but the horror of
entering death, that is, entering the solemn stiffness that
causes you to be respectfully referred to as: his remains.
He felt that Hitler, by touching him amorously, would be
profaning his corpse. I haven't said that the little hoodlum thought all these things. He felt the emotions which
I experience in transcribing them as they occur to me,
and I think they are suggested to me by the following
feeling that has not left me for two days and that I
merely reflect: the feeling of being somewhat ashamed
to think of the gestures of sensual pleasure when one is
in mourning. I thrust aside the images of them when I
go walking, and I had to do violence to myself to write
out the preceding erotic scenes, though my soul was full
of them. I mean that, after getting over the unpleasant
feeling of having profaned a corpse, this game, for which
a corpse is the pretext, gives me great freedom. There
was an appeal for air in my suffering. Not that I dare
laugh, but I am assimilating Jean, I am digesting him.

No doubt Paulo was afraid. Yet he felt assured of
eternal life. One experiences this certainty in the most
desperate moments.

"He can't do anything to me."

Although the very stuff of Paulo was meanness and so
suggested crystal and its fragility, it gave the lie to any
idea of destruction.

The third time I went back to the apartment of Jean's
mother, the street fighting had stopped. It was no easier
to get food, and up there they were almost in a state of
famine. When I entered after knocking three times, as
agreed, Erik came to me with his hand out and his lips
pursed in such a way that, though it was not quite a
smile, I regarded it as a sign of his counting on me, of
confidence in my arrival.

"How goes it?"

"And you?"

When he shook my hand, I had a feeling of uneasiness which made me realize that he was slightly less tall than usual. I looked down: he was in his stocking feet. Before I found it necessary to be surprised at this (which I could ascribe to the heat), Jean's mother came in. She smiled when she saw me, and I felt her face was relaxing from too long a tension.

"Ah!" she said.

She was holding a small handkerchief and rolling it into a little ball to mop her forehead. She took my hand and said, "It's so hot!" Whereupon she leaned on Erik's shoulder. He turned his head and looked at her with a tender smile.

I had sat down. I took a bar of American chocolate from my pocket and handed it to them, but instead of moving toward Jean's mother, my arm went in Erik's direction.

"I was able to get this. . . ."

Erik took it.

"Oh, that's awfully nice of you! We. . . ." And suddenly, as her back was to the half-open window, she spun around, pushing Erik aside. "It's mad," she exclaimed in a choked voice.

It was then that I realized why Erik was not wearing shoes, why they spoke in a low tone, why the room was dark and fear was in the air.

"You're the only one we trust."

Erik glanced at me, then at her, then at the bar of chocolate he was holding, and finally at her again, and there was more tenderness in his gaze than there had been a little while before.

"You don't know the kind of life we live here. I tell Juliette to say that I'm not well, and I don't go out any more. She does the shopping. Paulo too. If only we can run away some night. He (she pointed to Erik) would like to leave. He really feels he's in danger. But where can he go? They're arresting everyone. Have you been to the cemetery?"

"I have. The grave is all right."

"Is it? My poor little Jean!"

She turned to the photograph of Jean which was on the buffet, and looked at it for quite a while.

"I'll have to make arrangements for the winter. Winter will be coming with all its sadness."

Jean didn't give a damn about having a well-tended grave, about even having a grave. I think he would have preferred a nonreligious funeral.

"Of course, I know that very well, but a mother's a mother."

Although her manner at the moment was very simple, a pathetic veil inflated the last word: "mother."

"And besides, there's the family. There had to be a funeral."

I thought to myself: "Why not bedbugs," for the word funeral is used the same way the word is by the people of Marseilles, who exclaim: "Ugh! A funeral," or, in the same tone: "A bedbug."

I had already stopped a feeling that I was profaning his memory and ventured a grim joke with regard to him.

"What has to be has to be."

"What has to be?"

She looked at me with a touch of surprise.

"Well . . . there had to be a Mass . . . the emblem. . . ."

The escutcheon with a capital D embroidered in silver had been, for a day, the family's coat of arms.

"That would have given him a laugh."

"You think so? Yes, you're right. He wasn't a believer."

She hesitated a second and said, "He didn't like money."
Jean did not believe. He did not believe enough. Yet his
mind, which submitted to Marxist disciplines, could not
keep from trembling a little about the very things he
mocked.

"Is Paulo in?"

"No, he went to get groceries. I wonder what he'll
bring. If only they don't kill him, him too!"

"Oh, why would they?"

It was Erik who asked the question as he shrugged
slightly and put down the chocolate beside a glass on the
table. It was then I felt that Paulo could not die, for
nothing could destroy the kind of hardness he was made
of. The sight of the wine glass reminded me of him. The
last time I had seen him in that same room, he was removing four wine glasses from the table—the kind of
glass that's called a "snifter." He picked them all up with
only one hand, but in such a way that three of them in
a triangle were the only ones touched by his fingers, while
in the middle the fourth was supported simply by the
edges of the three others. It was chance that arranged
them in that way, and also the fortuitous precision of
the hand that took away the four glasses being carried
by three stems. For a second or two, Paulo achieved the
state of balance, but in order to maintain it he had to
summon up extraordinary skill, which itself required un-
divided attention. Tight-lipped and with fixed gaze, he
looked at that light, fragile crystal rose. Sitting upright
at the table, rigid as a bar of iron, attempting to get
my balance, I was amazed to see that essentially evil
nature refuse the help of its other hand but, with exquisite
skill, maintain the transparent flower of air and water
in two fingers and carry it very carefully from the table
to the sink before the eyes of the smiling Erik. One of

those glasses was there in front of me and reminded me that it was more than anything the youngster's elegance that had made me aware of his inviolable hardness and endurance.

Puny, ridiculous little fellow that I was, I emitted upon the world a power extracted from the pure, sheer beauty of athletes and hoodlums. For only beauty could have occasioned such an impulse of love as that which, every day for seven years, caused the death of strong and fierce young creatures. Beauty alone warrants such improper things as hearing the music of the spheres, raising the dead, understanding the unhappiness of stones. In the secrecy of my night I took upon myself—the right way of putting it if one bears in mind the homage paid to my body—the beauty of Gérard in particular and then that of all the lads in the Reich: the sailors with a girl's ribbon, the tank crews, the artillerymen, the aces of the Luft-waffe, and the beauty that my love had appropriated was retransmitted by my hands, by my poor puffy, ridiculous face, by my hoarse, spunk-filled mouth to the loveliest armies in the world. Carrying such a charge, which had come from them and returned to them, drunk with themselves and with me, what else could those youngsters do but go out and die? I put my arm around Paulo and turned my body so that we faced each other, and I smiled. I was a man. The text of my stern gaze was inscribed on Paulo. That sternness of gaze corresponded to an inner vision, an amorous preoccupation; it signified attention to a kind of constant desire, in short to covetousness, in accordance with our arrangements straight out of a novel, it indicated that this little fellow never left to itself the living, gesticulating image of its double that stood at the tribune in Nuremberg. Paulo's teeth were clean. My mustache was now near him, and he could see

it hair by hair. It was not only a sign—harmless or dangerous—of the pale, nocturnal blazon of a race of pirates, it
was a mustache. Paulo was frightened by it. Could it be
that a simple mustache composed of black hair—and
dyed perhaps—meant: cruelty, despotism, violence, rage,
foam, asps, strangulation, death, forced marches, ostenta-
tion, prison, daggers?

"Are you scared?"

With his whole inner being trembling, that being which
vainly sought, by fleeing, to drag along the flesh-and-
blood being whose prisoner it was, Paulo replied, with a
lump in his throat, "No."

The sonority of the word and the strange sound of his
own voice made him more aware of the danger that lies
in daring to enter dreams with one's actual flesh and
blood, to have a private conversation with the creatures
of night—a night of the heart that was poured out over
Europe—with the monsters of nightmares. He felt a very
slight throbbing at his temples—which I saw—a throbbing
as clear as the vibration of crystal, and he yearned for an
awakening, that is, for France. Then, the remoteness of
France immediately gave him the same feeling of being
abandoned that he would have felt had his mother died.
Ramparts or rifles, cannons, trenches, electric currents,
separated him from the world in which he was loved.
Cunning and treacherous radios were lulling his friends
to sleep, were denying the rumor of his death, were turning off his appeal, were consoling France for her loss.
He felt he was a prisoner, that is, alone with destiny. He
was sorry for France, and his sorrow included the following more particular regret: "I won't be able to tell the
boys that I saw Hitler," and the inner fluttering that
accompanied this regret was the finest tribute, the most
touching poem addressed to the Fatherland.

Nevertheless, I smiled. I was awaiting death. I knew
it was bound to come, in violent form, at the end of my
adventure. For what could I desire in the end? There is
no rest from conquest; one enters immortality standing
up. I have already considered every possible kind of
death, from the death by poison that an intimate friend
pours into my coffee to being hanged by my people,
crucifixion by my best friends, to say nothing of natural
death amidst honors, brass bands, flowers, speeches, and
statues, death in combat, by stabbing, bullets, but above
all I dream of a disappearance that will astound the
world. I shall go off to live quietly on another continent,
observing the progress of, and the harm done by, the
legend of my reappearance among my people. I have
chosen every sort of death. None of them will surprise
me. I have already died often, and always in splendor.

I sensed the child's distress, and, despite my delicacy,
I could think of nothing to say that would reassure him.

"You're very good-looking," I said.

Paulo smiled wanly, with that extremely weary smile
in which the teeth are not even bared. He did not take
his eyes off mine, which had grown gentle. The gentleness that he could see in my gaze thrust me deeper into
the region of foulness. I was a figure emerging from a
silent cave. I seemed unhappy in the open, and it was
evident from my attitude that I wanted to go back to
my darkness. I think of that lair, the eye of Gabès.

"You're very good-looking," I repeated.

But I felt that the sentence did not have the amorous
ring that would shatter the youngster's fear. And my
graciousness found the following: I placed my two hands
on his eyes, obliging his eyelids to close. I waited ten
seconds, then I said, "Are you less afraid?"

I was laughing wildly, and at the same time my left

hand was pressing Paulo's shoulder, forcing him to sit down on the bed. I paused to contemplate the folds of his ear, the head part of which was shiny, polished. My laughter widened his smile and made him show his teeth. That wider smile in which the teeth got a breath of air and the light infused a bit of intelligence into Paulo, banished his fear and some of the mortal beauty with which that fear covered up his fate. He was less close to death, less dominated by the rites that the heart devises for the killing, but his body thereby gained a little well-being, a slight relief. Anyway, the first gesture of a man and not of a shadow that he made—laying his cap on the rug—led him a little farther into the light. The deep silence in the room, which was no doubt insulated by cork, reassured him, for the slightest noise, even that of an alarm clock or of water dripping from a tap, would have been suspect to him and have meant invisible, hence supernatural, dangers. I took him by the neck, and our faces were against each other. I kissed him on the corner of his mouth. An anxiety of another order—though brief—came over him: although respect naturally froze him, advised him not to venture any intimate gesture, any caress, or even a too tender abandon, a quivering of the muscles or a contraction that would have brought his thighs close to mine, he wondered whether too tense an attitude might not wound the Master of the World. This thought made his smile, which saddened slightly, close slowly over his teeth and thereby take on the gentleness contained in all sadness. A touch of trust melted him, and he responded to my stroking his hair with an equally gentle caress on my shoulder, which, squeezed by the gabardine tunic, suddenly seemed to him as strong as a counterfort of the Bavarian Alps. Meanwhile he was thinking, word for word:

"But this bimbo's just a little old guy of fifty, after all."

However, he dared not continue the caress or the thought. He withdrew his hand, and this single shy token of kindness magnified my gratitude. I eagerly kissed his throat, temples, and the back of his neck—having made him turn around, with, for the first time, sovereign authority and self-assurance on my part. As we had been sitting on the edge of the bed, this movement left Paulo with his belly on the same edge, his face against the velvet, and his back supporting the German pasha. He found himself in that posture for the first time in his life. No longer supported or directed by my gaze, he was panting with unsatisfied pleasure. Like that of a drowning man, his whole life passed before his eyes. The sacred thought of his mother flashed upon him. But he realized the impropriety of such a posture for meditating upon a mother, father, or love affair. He thought of Paris, of the cafés, of the automobiles. The presence above him was total and tumultuous: his thighs, his legs had their exact burden of thighs and legs. His limbs accepted the domination, they rested in it. His body was compressed by the soft ridge of the bed. In an attempt to disengage himself he made a slight movement that raised his rump, and I responded to the summons with greater pressure. A new pain forced Paulo to repeat his movement, to relieve his stomach, and I shoved harder. He did the same thing again, and I squeezed him tighter. Then sharper and cleaner thrusts unleashed the surge that had been aroused by a misunderstanding. I went at him again ten times, and, though his stomach was being crushed, Paulo stopped. He had a hard-on, and when, a second later, I grabbed his hand and squeezed it tenderly, that big, broad, thick hand became tiny, docile, and quiet and murmured, "Thank you." My hand and I understood that language, for no sooner did I hear the words than I detached myself from the child's back. He had a feeling of relief because his guts had calmed down and were at ease again, but he suffered at being confronted with his regained wholeness, his free and lonely personality, the solitude of which was revealed to him by the detachment of God himself. Then and there he felt a pang that could be translated by the following question, which I ask in his stead: "What can you do now, without Him?"

His anguish was quickly destroyed by amazement. I gave him a push and roughly laid him down on his back. Paulo smiled at my smile. The mustache, the wrinkles, and the lock of hair suddenly took on human proportions, and, by the grace of an unequalled generosity, the fabulous emblem of Satan's chosen people descended to inhabit that simple dwelling, the puny body of an old queen, a "faggot."

I was about to—I mean that there was no visible sign of my intention, though the latter had already made me more masterful by describing the movement from beginning to end within me and thus making me feel a lightness that would have enabled me to go backward in time —as I was saying, I was about to jump on the bed, but I immediately checked myself and, very deliberately, I lay down beside Paulo. I had made that brisk movement, which had remained an inner one and which I had and had not controlled, because my soul had meant to put itself on the level of Paulo's and my gestures to be those of someone his age. It was then that, in order to free my buttonholes, I had to turn my body slightly toward Paulo and push up his belly and then that my forelock, which was mysteriously composed of hair, grazed the nose of Paulo, who dared to raise the lock delicately with his fingertip, which had a black, bitten nail. Hitler was resplendent.

It was a rough-and-tumble—or rather a systematic labor—in which I tried in every possible way to return to the larval form by virtue of which one goes back to limbo. Paulo's behind was just a bit hairy. The hairs were blond and curly. I stuck my tongue in and burrowed as far as I could. I was enraptured with the foul smell. My mustache brought back, to my tongue's delight, a little of the muck that sweat and shit formed among Paulo's blond curls. I poked about with my snout, I got stuck in the muck, I even bit—I wanted to tear the muscles of the orifice to shreds and get all the way in, like the rat in the famous torture, like the rats in the Paris sewers which devoured my finest soldiers. And suddenly my breath withdrew, my head rolled and, for a moment, lay still on one buttock as on a white pillow.

I was sure of my strength. Yet I felt that that naked part of me in the room was vulnerable. I was being spied upon from all sides, and the enemy spies might worm their way in through that orifice. The Parisian youngster was doing his job valiantly. At first, he was afraid of hurting the Führer. The essential part of Paulo the torture-machine was the penis. It had the perfection of clockwork, of a precision-tooled connecting rod. Its metal was solid, flawless, imperishable, polished by the work and the hard use it was put to: it was a hammer and a miner's bar. It was also without tenderness, without gentleness, without the trembling that often makes even the most violent ones quiver delicately. Paulo was overjoyed to feel the thrill of happiness and to hear the happy moan of Madame. The recognition of the beauty of his work made him proud and more ardent. The Führer was now lingering over it with veneration rather than simple respect. Being the object of such a cult, Paulo's rod was never more beautiful. It quivered with insolence, was set apart for deification, while, at the end of it, Paulo, now shy and simple, watched the ceremony without curiosity and was bored. Finally, Hitler gave it a more devout kiss. Then he put his right arm around it and cuddled it in the hollow, in the fold formed by the inner side of the elbow. Such a gesture would have made anyone other than Paulo let his prick be transformed into a babe in arms to be cuddled. He didn't bat an eyelash. Boredom made him flee the place, but the wheedling movement of my head brought him back. He did not put down his arms. He did not allow his naughty tool to lose any of its hardness, and I remained a poor fellow, a poor abandoned kid whom life sweeps up in a nausea of happiness and sadness.

"He's going to kill me," Paulo thought. "Since he won't be able to accuse me openly, I'll be poisoned. Or shot. They'll give me the works in a hurry, in a garden."

. . . . . . . . . . . . . . . . . . . . . . . . . . . . . . . . . . . . . . . . . . . . . . . . . .

For a moment, hope welled up in Paulo, he had a feeling of confidence, of peace. Then suddenly, because upon turning around to button himself he saw on the wall a photograph of the Führer, who was so like the man whose death rattle he had just heard, with a hop, skip, and jump, fear came from the end of the world and sat on his shoulders. He took a step on the rug. Hitler was behind him, ready to intervene. Paulo was slowly buttoning himself up and waiting. His lips were parted and his eyes staring. He looked at the white porcelain bidet, the wallpaper, the cheap furniture. In the silence he could hear the earth rotating on its axis and revolving about the sun. He was filled with fear. He oozed fear. He was not trembling. From all his pores, traversing the cloth of his mechanic's overalls, seeped a very light but luminous vapor which enveloped his whole body and which he seemed to be emitting (as ships do their artificial fogs at sea) in order to camouflage himself, to disappear. Fear assured him invisibility. In the thickness of light in which he was shrinking to the size of a twig, he felt quite safe. His entire skin was pleating, like an accordion, and if, with a kind of superhuman courage (no doubt impossible amidst those milky and too blindingly bright jitters), he had dared to make the gesture of putting his hand to his fly, he would have seen his prick, which usually stuck such a long way out of his foreskin, withdraw into itself, as on cold days, completely covered by the skin. The piteous thing barely dangled. He walked to the window slowly and lifted the lace curtain where I watched the Seine flow slowly by.

. . . . . . . . . . . . . . . . . . . . . . . . . . . . . . . . . . . . . . . . . . . . . . . . . . . .

Riton, who was constipated and whose whole digestive system had been upset by fatigue, felt a fart coming. He squeezed his buttocks, he tried to make it flow upward so that it would explode inside him, but his armor was too tight, and for several moments the gases which he was holding in for the sake of decency could no longer be controlled. He farted. This made a muffled and rather brief sound in the darkness, a sound which was quickly checked. The soldiers were behind him, in the room.

"They're Germans," he thought to himself. "Maybe they don't realize."

He hoped so. The soldiers weren't shy in his presence. For three days he had been at war, and close contact revealed that the sternest-looking warriors probably were rotten inside. In spite of their example, he dared not forget himself in their presence, dared not relieve himself openly, but his discomfort was too great that evening. Erik whispered "Sh!" as he rolled his eyes and pointed with his finger to indicate that the darkness could hear the slightest noise. Then he smiled a little. Riton felt his humanity more keenly. He was still in a world where one dared not fart. Death was not with us. The ears of the two friends were full of the crickets of silence. A shot rang out in the distance. Riton trembled. That fatal contraption was surmounted by a very beautiful head of curly hair. Erik recognized and did not recognize the little fellow in the subway. The picture he had of him and the sight of him that evening in battle dress made him compare Riton to an unhappy, new-born snail that he might have first met without its shell. A hermit without the cave in the rocks who is living out his fate. The kid of the subway and of all the encounters had not yet donned his tough-mindeness or parade dress to confront death, glory, and shame. The charming little creature of the past was perhaps a gentler sister of his. We know nothing about the prodigies that transform a passing child who sings and whistles into a delicate instrument of death whose slightest movement, even a frown, the too elegant play of an invisible fan, reveals a will to destruction. Erik had before him what, to a German, is the most amazing creation that there can be: a youngster betraying his country, but a madly courageous and bold little traitor. At that moment, he was on the alert so as to kill like a murderer.

"No, there's nothing," mumbled Riton.

"*Wie?* Nothing? *Nichts?*"

"*Nichts.*"

In order to utter this last word, which he pronounced "nix," distorting it the way Paris street boys did, Riton turned his head all the way around and smiled. His smile

reached Erik, who returned it. The sky above them was
studded with stars. The shagginess of Riton's curls gave
him an even crueler look, which the smile did not dispel.
The darkness was working away on Erik's tired face. It
was furrowing the eyebrows and hardening the fleshy
parts, which seemed made of stone. It cast the shadow of
the nose very low, and from the four-day growth of beard
a very soft, blond light flowed. Separated by Riton's
machine gun, they looked at each other in silence. The
sergeant, who was behind them, approached in his stocking feet. His silence added, for a moment, to that of the
other two. He asked Erik softly whether he had noticed
anything suspect. There was nothing. He told him to go
in, and, taking Riton by the hand, he succeeded in saying,
talking to him very slowly: "You . . . should . . . take off
. . . the bullets."

Riton tried to explain silently that he wanted to keep
his coat of mail on, but the sergeant insisted. Riton
turned around so as to go in behind the sergeant, and it
was at that moment that his eyes spotted a strange thing
which he had not yet noticed, a kind of rag hanging from
a window of the house at the left. Leaning forward, he
recognized the broad-striped American flag. He hardly
thought it was on display, but rather that it was a secret
signal. He went in. With infinite care Erik and the sergeant undid his metal bands. As they had just been
operating in silence with cautious movements, the three
of them had kept their mouths open. They needed a bit
of water to moisten their dry palates.

"*Wasser*. . . ."

Riton whispered, inverting his thumb above his mouth
as if it were a faucet run dry, "*Wasser*, sergeant . . . I'm
thirsty. . . ."

"No."

"A drink. . . ."

"No water. . . ."

"In the kitchen?"

The sergeant made a broader grimace as his lips silently formed the word *Nicht*, and he moved his forefinger back and forth in front of Riton's face. Riton was about to insist, not understanding why he was being refused water, but the sergeant went to the bedroom. He silently opened the wardrobe, took two armfuls of linen, carried it to the bathroom, where he made a kind of mattress of it in the bathtub, then went back to get Riton, whom he wanted to sleep there. Riton refused. A touch of pride bade him do so, as did the respect for German hierarchy which he had already acquired after two days of life in common with the Fritzes. The sergeant insisted.

"You are very little . . . very young."

In the darkness, clinging to the sergeant's arm so as to put his mouth against the other's ear, the kid tried to sound firm.

"No, sergeant," he whispered, "me a private, you a noncom."

And he added, beating his chest with broad silent slaps, "Me strong, me hefty."

But though the sergeant was worried for a few seconds about allowing him to be at liberty among the weapons (his plan was to lock him in the bathroom), he remembered how devoted Riton had been on the Rue de Belleville, and that reassured him. Finally, his own fatigue made him want the little bed he had just prepared in the bathtub. He went back to the dining room, again very quietly, to shut the windows. Riton looked for a glass in the darkness, found one on the shelf above the washbowl, and turned on the faucet. There was no water. He finally realized why the sergeant had refused. In desperation, fuming like a kid who feels his thirst more acutely, he went back to the dining room. The sergeant had already had time to mumble in German to Erik, who was sitting in a chair with his elbows on his knees and his head in his hand, "I'm leaving you with the Frenchman. So keep your eyes open."

He shook hands with Riton and went quietly back to the bathroom. For a few seconds the kid remained standing silently beside the table. Erik, who was at the back of the room, saw him outlined against the light background of the window. Disencumbered of his metal garment and his weapon, Riton realized how tired he was. Everything drained out of him at the same time—his pride, his shame, his hatred, his despair. All that remained was a poor, exhausted child's body overcome with weariness, and a mind disintegrating with fatigue. With minute attention to his movements, he moved forward to Erik's chair. He groped for a few seconds, grazed the hair, the collar, the shoulder. When he recognized the feel of the German insignia, he felt a discharge in his arm, in his shoulder, in his entire body. The monstrousness of his situation was more keenly apparent to him in the deep darkness. He was the prey of the insignia which, when he was a kid of twelve just before the war, had been the mark of the devil. No movement of withdrawal betrayed his anguish. At the first touch of a hand on his hair, Erik started as he recognized the little militiaman. He waited without moving so as to know the boy's intention. The hand seeking in the darkness found one of Erik's and squeezed it. As Riton bent forward until his breath lightly stroked the Fritz's neck, he murmured with a gentleness that more and more became his tone of voice, *"Gute nacht,* Erik."

*"Gute nacht,* good night, Riton."

"Good night."

With the same caution Riton moved back to the window and lay down on the rug very quietly with his hands clasped behind his head. A very slight excitement had swollen his prick when he was next to Erik, but no sooner did he stretch out than he felt only the bliss of being in that position. Peace had entered him, and in order to prolong the enjoyment of it he kept his eyes open in the darkness and refused to fall asleep. His limbs and outstretched body grew heavier with fatigue; his bulk lay heavy on the rug, which was becoming the very stuff of his life, for the entire day had been one long fall. The feeling of certainty of his presence assembled his body from all parts of the horizon, sent out a call to arms toward an ideal point in the middle of himself by carrying to it, on a blissful surge, from the outermost tips of his fingers and toes to that imprecise point of the body (it is not the heart) where the lines of force converged, a message of peace and orderliness of the limbs, of the extremities, of the head itself. In exchange, that certainty of presence relieved the limbs of their function; it discharged them of all responsibility. Only his presence was awake, his muscles no longer existed. The goal of that day, to stretch out on the rug, had just been attained. That makeshift berth was more restful to the boy than a soft bed would have been. He felt secure in it. Every point of his body found a reassuring support in it. And also, the silence, the darkness, and the presence of the sleeping Erik, who was mightier by virtue of his sleep, protected his rest by thick walls, behind which, unfortunately, was enclosed, without anyone's being able to drive it away, a frightful anxiety: who was the tenant of that empty dwelling at the top of a house that was mined with the presence, on every floor, of hate-ridden French-

men bent on the greatest evil, who would blow up or
set fire to the building in order to kill the pack of Boches,
the swarm of wasps clinging to its summit? They wouldn't
get out of the scrap unscathed. The only refuge was his
trust in Erik. The breadth and strength of the dark chest,
the hair of which Riton had seen through the opening of
the shirt, was apparent to his mind's eye. Riton also
hoped, for the space of one brief reverie, that all the
tenants would be Germanophiles and that the flag at the
window was there only to put people off. He even hoped
that they would be decent and would not denounce him
to the insurgents. He dared imagine that they had a
greatness of soul larger than life. But no sooner did these
hopes light up than they went out.

"No crap about it, we're done for. If we don't get the
works tomorrow, we'll get it the next day."

Twenty seconds later, Erik, who was too uncomfortable
in his chair, silently lay down beside Riton. Erik was
dropping with sleep. As he bent down to lie at the right
of the kid, over whose body he had just stepped, the
leather of his new belt creaked slightly.

"Pretty supple," thought Riton, not knowing whether
he was thinking the word about the leather or the
athlete's torso. The creaking, which evoked muscular
strength, the power of lithe and sturdy haunches, the perfect play of the joints, both reassured and disturbed him.
Erik stretched out and turned slightly onto his right side
because his pistol was in the holster on the left and
would have been in the way, but he kept his legs straight
and parallel. He was in his stocking feet. His right arm
was pinned down, was being crushed on the floor by his
body, and his left hand became aware, in his half-sleep,
of its strength as it stroked his terrifying neck, which it
circled, as if to polish it, though it was careful to be aware

of what it was doing and remained conscious of that
muscular neck beneath its palm and took pleasure in
the back of it. It stroked his hardened face, which was
softened by his blond beard. Then it returned and laid
itself on his chest, where it remained, spread flat, with a
few fingertips in the opening of the jacket and shirt
touching his skin and golden hairs. Two fingers inspected
the quality of the granite of that cellar flagstone. Erik,
soothed by the slight contact with this body, fell into a
deep sleep. He could die the next day since he had
acknowledged his beauty that evening. He hardly realized that he had turned to Riton, and it was in the position which I have just described that he fell asleep almost
immediately. In the darkness, some blond hairs on the
top of his raised toes caused the black waves of sleep
and silence to break over the dead soldier. The bodies of
the two boys were touching. Riton, lying on his back,
was on Erik's shore. If he had a dizzy spell, he would fall
into him and drown in the deep eddies that he sensed
were rolling from the chest to the thighs, which were the
more mysterious for being alive beneath that funereal
cloth which also concealed a paraphernalia (such as is
no doubt hidden behind a black curtain in special houses)
of straps, belts, steel buckles, teamster's whips, boots,
which the sound of the leather had conjured up, thighs
whose strength derived from a fascination with death.
He lay still on his back, looking straight ahead at the
far end of the room whose darkness his eyes were getting
used to. He was seized with fright, for he was unable to
see anything of Erik, though his whole body registered
the other's presence. He stiffened with anxiety. Had he
been lying on his right side, that is, with his back to the
soldier and not grazed by him, it would not have been
the same (his curled-up position would have made it

possible for him to keep his usual Erik within himself).
Had he lain on his back, he would have seen him in
detail and been able at the same time to remain deep
within himself, but apart from the fact that the power of
that presence was too great for him not to be excited by
it, his position left him exposed, defenseless, before the
driving waves that rolled up to him from Erik's body and
thrilled him to the point of dizziness. He got a hard-on.
Not with a sudden swiftness, but slowly. It started the
moment when he was most deeply conscious of his
anxiety, that is, when Erik, whose clothes touched his,
lay quite still. Then when the first thrill, the first thrust
of extreme violence shook him, he became aware of his
desire. A half-hour went by before Riton came to a decision or began the first movement, though his face had
turned to Erik's. Suddenly the true meaning of his treason
became apparent to him. If French rifles had been aiming
at him for days, it was in order to prevent him from
isolating himself at the top of the rock which all eyes had
seen him climb to with that extraordinary mountaineer.

"So what?"

He was in love with a man. He quivered with pleasure
at the thought of being so near the goal.

"I love him mad. . . . "

Even in thought he did not complete the word
"madly." The passion, born in the words "I love him,"
continued, increasing with wild speed and leaving him
breathless halfway through that dizzying word which
ended with the very shudder that quickened the beginning of it, shaking Riton's whole body as he mused, for
the first time, but then greedily, with a kind of despair,
on Erik's organ. He was too excited to imagine it precisely. The swollen crotch of the dark trousers was all
he saw. Then he suddenly feared that Erik might know

what he was thinking and be revolted at such a thought, but almost immediately his pride in his beauty restored his confidence.

"Since there're no girls around, maybe I'll be doing him a favor. He could find worse-looking guys than me."

By that thought alone he was bestowing his body on the soldier. He realized it, and, sweetly, naively too, he was willing to assume any posture to please him. Suddenly, he thought of the danger of such an adventure: he was afraid that all the soldiers might want to go down on him. They were German, squareheads, rough-hewn, and he, the youngest and weakest, alone and French.

He tried to conjure up Erik's prick more precisely. He imagined it huge and heavy in his closed hand. He made a slight movement to extend his arm, but he left his hand lying on his thigh. This venturing of a first gesture took his breath away. Behind the simple door that one opens perhaps there awakes a dragon whose body coils round itself several times. If you look a dog in the eye too intently, it may recite an astounding poem to you. You might have been mad for a long time and have realized it only at that moment. Is there perhaps a snake in the bag hanging from the coatrack? Beware. From the slightest patch of shadow, from a spot of darkness, there rise up prowlers armed to the teeth who tie you up and carry you off. Riton waited a bit in order to catch his breath. Erik's whole body from head to foot was lying against his. The fact that his love had been revealed to him at the moment of its greatest danger imparted such great strength that Riton felt he was brawny enough to crush dragons. The peril lay not in death but in love. He had the wit to feign sleep. He breathed noisily. The thought of Erik's prick became obsessive, and, with tears at the rims of his eyes, he wanted to extend his left hand, but, before making the movement, he realized, while executing it mentally, that it would be difficult for him to open the fly. He turned a bit on his left side.

"The fly, that's all I needed!"

So what! What did reproval of that love matter to Riton since he would be dead the following day, and what did life matter since he loved Erik! Very skillfully he pretended to be shifting in his sleep and put his right foot, on which was a soft, gray sock, across Erik's foot. He made the gesture very naturally, without any fear, but he felt it was the first phase of an embrace that could tighten to closest intimacy, when, with bated breath, he stretched out his right hand and laid it, hardly touching, on Erik's thigh.

"If he realizes, there'll be hell to pay!"

So what? We'll be killed tomorrow! A day of torture would be nothing. He pressed down with his hand gently, then a little harder. Unable to see the spot, he tried to figure out where it was. On the basis of the folds of the cloth and his own position he thought it was the middle of the thigh. If Erik woke up at that moment, he might think that sleep alone was responsible. Mad with fear and boldness, he moved lightly over the cloth, or rather he flew over the area. Erik slept on.

"You don't get a hard-on when you're asleep."

The hand moved upward with the same delicacy. It reached the fly and recognized it. Riton had difficulty breathing. The treasure was found. His light, fearful hand remained as if suspended for a moment. Not a sound in the room. He heard another shot, far away.

"It's fighting on the Rue de Buenos Aires," he thought. "It's a hell of a way off." His hand assumed greater authority and it was blessing or was on the lookout for the nest below. The hearts of the seven German soldiers must have been beating. Riton would surely be killed the next day, but before that he would bump off quite a lot of Frenchmen. He was in love.

"Those damn jerks. What the hell are they to me, they're just a bunch of idiots. I'm going to bump a few of them off. . . ."

With, as it happens, that same right hand. He made the movement, despite himself, of pulling a trigger with his forefinger. His pinky struck the cloth—to have done so was to knock at the door of darkness and see that darkness open onto death, and it was with a closed fist that he remained there, first making its pressure light and then gradually letting it sink by its own weight into the moss.

The building was doomed. A face, a destiny, a boy, are said to be doomed. A sign of misfortune must have been inscribed somewhere, an invisible sign, for perhaps it was at the bottom of a door in the left corner, or on a window pane, or in the twitching of a tenant. Perhaps it was an object that at first sight was harmless—that a second look does not enable you to detect—it was a spider's web on the chandelier (there was a chandelier in the living room) or the chandelier itself. The house smelled of death. It was drifting toward an abyss. If that's what death is, it's sweet. Riton no longer belonged to anyone, not even to Erik. The fingers of his hand spread like the folioles of a sensitive plant in the sun. His hand was resting. He had placed his head under his left arm, and the graciousness of that posture was entering his soul. He had not killed enough Frenchmen, that is, not paid dearly enough for that moment. If the house blows up, that means it is thoroughly mined. If it burns, love is what fires it. With infinite delicacy Riton took his handkerchief from his pocket, wet it silently with saliva, and slipped it through his fly and between his legs, which were slightly drawn up so that he could clean his "bronze eye" properly.

"You think he'll stick it up me? Oh well, you never know." He wanted less to be ready for the act than to be ready for love. He rubbed a little, then took out the handkerchief so as to wet it again, happy to smell beneath his nostrils and on his lips the odor of sweat and shit. This discreet and careful grooming enchanted him.

Around the building and in the building itself, which was being undermined by mysterious insects, the nation was busying itself, as he would have desired. Multi-colored paper garlands were being nailed to windows, flowers were being hooked on to electric wires, streamers and lanterns were strung from window to window, cloth was being dyed in the darkness, women were sewing flags, children were preparing powder and bullets for the salvos. People were building up around the apartment a catafalque that was caught in the childish combinations of tricolored ribbons with more complicated intertwining than the arabesques of bindings which are called "fanfares." In the darkness, half of Paris was silently constructing the new funeral pyre of the seven males and the kid. The other half was on the lookout.

His hand opened. A harder fold made Riton think he was touching the prick. His chest collapsed. "If he's got a hard-on, it means he's not sleeping. In that case, I'm in the shit."

He decided to let his hand play dead. Its being there was no small joy, but the fingers had a life of their own and kept seeking, despite the rough cloth and the stiff edge of the fly where the buttons were. Finally they felt a warm, soft mass. Riton parted his lips. He stayed that way for a few seconds, straining his mind so as to be fully aware of his joy.

"He's got an octopus there between his legs."

"I'll just stay this way."

But the fingers wanted full particulars. They very delicately tried to distinguish the various parts of that mass whose abandon in his hands gratified him. All of Erik's power was contained in that little heap, which, though quiet and trusting, radiated despite its death. And all the might of Germany was contained in those sacred and peaceful though heavy and sleeping repositories which were capable of the most dangerous awakenings. They were watchful repositories which millions of soldiers carried preciously in freezing and scorching regions in order to impose themselves by rape. With the skill of a lacemaker, the hand above the dark cloth was able to sort out the confusion of the treasure which lay there all jumbled up. I prejudged its splendor in action and imprisoned it, sleeping little girl that it was, in my big ogre's paw. I was protecting her. I weighed her in my hand and thought, "There's hidden treasure in there." My cock stiffened out of pure friendliness. I was worthy of her. My fingers squeezed her a little more, with greater tenderness. They stroked her again. A slight movement of Erik's leg disturbed his immobility. I was filled with terrible fear, then immediately with hope, but first with fear. A mass of cries of fear rising from my belly tried to force open my throat and mouth, where my strong, clenched teeth were on the alert. Finding no outlets, those cries punctured my neck, which suddenly let flow the twenty white streams of my fear through twenty purple ulcers in the shape of roses and carnations. I kept the prick in my hand. If Erik awoke, I would take my chance. I even hoped he would. I squeezed a bit harder, and as soon as I did, I was astounded to feel the Fritz's cock swell between my fingers, harden, and quickly fill my hand. I stopped moving, but I left my hand there dead and dancing. Since my stroking had just given Erik such a violent hard-on, he was awake, and he did not rebel. I waited wonderful seconds, and it's amazing that there was not born of that waiting, from the moment that begins with the prick's awakening to happiness, the most fabulous of heroes, as Chrysaor sprang from the blood of Medusa, or new rivers, valleys, chimeras, in a leap on a bed of violets, hope itself in a white silk doublet with a feathered cap, a royal breast, a necklace of golden thorns, or tongues of flame, a new gospel, an aurora borealis over London or Frisco, a perfect sonata, or amazing that death itself did not make a fulgurant appearance between the two lovers. My hand squeezed the cock a second time; it seemed monstrously big.

"If he sticks the whole caboodle up my cornhole he'll wreck the works."

I squeezed a little harder. Erik did not stir, but I was sure he wasn't sleeping, because the regular sound of his breathing had stopped. Then I ventured a stroke over the cloth, and then another, and each time my gesture was more precise. Erik didn't make a move, he didn't say a word. Hope filled me with a boldness that amazed even me. I slipped the tip of my forefinger into one of the little interstices between the buttons. Erik was wearing neither jockey shorts nor boxer shorts. My finger first felt the hairs. It moved over them, then over the cock, which was as hard as wood, but alive. The contact thrilled me. In the state of ecstasy there is also an element of fear with respect to the divinity or his angels. The prick I was touching with my finger was not only my lover's but also that of a warrior, of the most brutal, most formidable of warriors, of the lord of war, of the demon, of the exterminating angel. I was committing a sacrilege and was conscious of it. That prick was also the angel's weapon, his dart, a part of those terrible devices with which he is armed. It was his secret weapon, the V-1 on which the Führer relies. It was the ultimate and major treasure of the Germans. The prick was fiery. I wanted to stroke it, but my finger was not free enough. I feared lest my nail hurt it if I pressed. Erik had not moved. In order to make me think he was sleeping, he resumed his regular breathing. Motionless at the center of a state of perfect lucidity —so extraordinary that he feared for a moment lest the purity of his vision radiate outside him and illuminate Riton—he let the kid alone and was amused by his playing. I withdrew my finger and very skillfully succeeded in undoing two buttons. This time I put my whole hand in. I squeezed, and Erik recognized, I don't know how, that I was squeezing tenderly. He didn't stir.

The moon was veiled. Barefoot, I first walked on tiptoe, then I ran, I went up steps, I scaled houses so as to reach the most dangerous crossroad of the Albaïcin. Everybody in Granada was asleep. The few Gypsies who were prowling about in the darkness could not catch a glimpse of me. I was still swept up in my course, but as there was no way out of the square my movement continued in a silent whirl, on tiptoe. I felt, however, that a Gypsy had just awakened: ten houses away perhaps, beneath a porch. His big sleeping body had stirred in the brown woolen blanket. He was crawling. He grazed walls, went through alleys, stood up, walked over to meet me, finally leaped into the darkness. We were alone on the square. The moon was still veiled, but very thinly so. The Gypsy seized me by the waist, broke me, tossed me up, and then caught me smoothly and silently in his arms. The embroidery and white lace of my petticoats whirled in the darkness. With a flip of his cock the Gypsy tossed me up into the sky. From the whole land of

Andalusia, from every ornament, from every lock there welled up a music that caressed me. It all took place in the morning. A few streaks of dawn kept watch on the hills. Their blue songs were still sleeping rolled up in the throats of the herdsmen. I fell astride the Gypsy's prick. The flounces of my skirts spread over the countryside like moss. It was April, and the moon lit up a vast stretch of flowering almond trees around Granada.

Anyway, completely reassured by Erik's immobility, I jerked him off quickly. He was no doubt thinking of that girl's head which surmounted the strong and delicate body that held a tunic of bullets suspended over the frightened city. He beguiled the time by reconstructing her face in his imagination. The greatest happiness was granted him, since it was the kid himself who answered his secret call and came running up to impale himself. The old hallucination of my childhood obtruded itself, and I can render it only by the following image: *still rivers that do not mingle,* though they have a single source, rush into his mouth, which they spread and fill. One of the soldiers made a slight noise. Fearing that Riton might remove his hand, Erik took hold of it, pressed it down, and made it stay. There was another noise. They waited a moment.

I have killed, pillaged, stolen, betrayed. What glory I've attained! But let no run-of-the-mill murderer, thief, or traitor take advantage of my reasons. I have gone to too great pains to win them. They are valid only for me. That justification cannot be used by every Tom, Dick, and Harry. I don't like people who have no conscience.

The Führer sent his finest-looking men to death. It was his only way to possess them all. How often I have wanted to kill those handsome boys who annoyed me because I didn't have enough cocks to ream them all at one time, not enough sperm to cram them with! A pistol shot would, I feel, have calmed my desire-ridden, jealousy-ridden heart and body. Germany was a fiery stake that had been set up for Riton, a stake more beautiful than one of flames, cloth, and paper. In fits and snatches, without regularity, the flames, embers, and brands were earning their living and their death, were biting, here and there, were menacing Hitler. A very slight displacement —ridding it of irony by means of words—is sufficient for humor to reveal the tragedy and beauty of a fact or of a soul. The poet is tempted by the game. Before the war, cartoonists caricatured Hitler as a Maid with clownish features and a movie comedian's mustache. "He hears voices," said the captions. . . . Did the cartoonists feel that Hitler was Joan of Arc? They had been aware of the resemblance, and they noted it. Thus, the starting point of the features they gave him was that great similarity, since they had thought of it, whether clearly or confusedly, in making their drawings and comments. I regard that recognition as more of a tribute than a mockery. Their irony was the laughter you force for its arrow in order to puncture the agitation that would make you weep in certain moments of overpowering emotion. Hitler will perish by fire if he has identified himself with Germany, as his enemies recognize. He has a bleeding wound at the same level as Joan's on her prisoner's robe.

Like all the other boys of the Reich, Erik's face had retained something of the spatters of a royal sperm—a kind of shame, of deflowering, and at the same time a luster both bright and cloudy (like that of the pearl), precious and triumphant, opaline, the memory of which I thought I discerned in the beads of sweat on his forehead, which I took for tears of transparent sperm. No doubt it was owing to Nazism that Erik wore that thin veil of shame and light, but the executioner once actually did discharge in his face, and Erik was already overcome with dizziness and was sinking into the idea whose pressure was drowning him:

"He's darkening my sky!"

We were in bed. At the sight of the jet a very brief admiration coursed through him, perhaps with a bit of fear in regard to me whose oak, instead of being struck by lightning, issued the lightning, but when the drops, which were still warm, touched his cheek and torso, I saw a gleam of hatred in his eyes.

. . . . . . . . . . . . . . . . . . . . . . . . . . . . . . . . . . . . . . . . . . . .

The usual image appeared in the Führer's eyes: a fancy white cradle. But at the very moment that he saw the lace and the muslin puffs, he noticed, around the pillow and covering it, the garland of white roses and ivy with which it had been adorned, since it contained a dead child. Hitler stood up. He wiped his fingers on his handkerchief. As always when he finished playing, he thought of his executioner, who must not be confused with the criminal executioner, the headsman, for we are referring to his private executioner, a killer with a revolver. It was by this male, who was, in short, the natural excrescence of a cruel animal, the poison-gland and the dart, that he had had most of his victims executed—whether political victims or others—but every time that he had dealings with him, and even more often, he thought with anguish that there perhaps existed a list or a notebook with baffling information which this killer, in order to kill time, kept up to date.

After buttoning his fly, the Führer went to the conference room, where the generals, the admiral, and the cabinet ministers were waiting for him. Hitler's gracious and simple life was going to unleash terrible acts on the world, acts that would give rise to the most prodigious flowering of nightmares that a man has ever generated all by himself. High dignitaries, very noble ones, whose heads and shoulders were covered with gold, surrounded him, preserved him as priests preserve the gold of a relic. Hitler had secrets. Master magician that he was, he could float on carpets through several rooms whose walls were pierced by holes for the barrels of rifles.

"I'm just an old fossil," he thought, on his way back from the conference. He felt himself being a dusty fossil. Love-making had drained him. He dared not wipe his nose or even put a finger into it. Am I quite sure I *command* the world?

Riton will not kill himself . . . unless. . . . We shall see. I am keen on his continuing until the last fraction of a second, by destruction, murder—in short, evil according to you—to exhaust, and for an ever greater exaltation—which means elevation—the social being or gangue from which the most glittering diamond will emerge; solitude, or saintliness, which is also to say the unverifiable, sparkling, unbearable play of his freedom. To anyone who may point out that Riton is not alone since he is in love, I wish to say that were it not for that love he would not have gone freely to the very top. It was necessity itself that made the militiamen—and especially our militiaman —fire on Frenchmen, but the only thing that counts is this: solitude being given and accepted. Rejection of it when it is inevitable is despair, a sin which is in conflict, I believe, with the second theological virtue. In any case, I am writing this book and proposing these things, and I

climb limpingly and often tumble on my way up to my
rock of solitude when, along with my eroticism, my friendship for the purest and most upright of adolescents, a
saint according to men, conjures up the image of a haloed
traitor. It is under the sway of the still-young death of
Jean, red with that death and with the emblem of his
party, that I am writing this book. The flowers that I
wanted to be in profusion on his little grave which was
lost in the fog are perhaps not faded, and I already
recognize that the most important character glorified by
the account of my grief and of my love for him will be
that luminous monster who is exposed to the most splendid solitude, the one in whose presence I experience a
kind of ecstasy *because* he discharged a burst of machine-
gun fire into his body.

Riton continued his unhappy destiny which will never
bring him out of a frightful misery contained in a very
beautiful vase. When he joined up, he was still good-
looking, and yet his life was ugly. Bear in mind that,
weary, sweating, and livid, he took down the cat and
put it into a canvas bag, which he closed; then, with all
his might, he hammered away at that grotesque, mysterious, and plaintive mass. The cat was still alive. When
Riton assumed that the head was smashed, he removed
the still quivering animal. Finally, he attached it to the
nail in the wall that I mentioned earlier and cut it up.
The work took a long time. Hunger, which had disappeared for a moment, returned to Riton's stomach. The
cat was still warm and steaming when he cut off the two
legs and boiled them in a pot. With the mutilated remains before him, the skin of which was turned inside
out like a glove and covered with blood, he ate a few
pieces which were almost raw, and which were insipid,
for he had no salt, and ever since that day Riton has been

aware of the presence within him of a feline that marks
his body and, to be more precise, his stomach, like the
gold-embroidered animals on the gowns of ladies of
former times. Either because the tom was sick, or had
become sick—and had gone almost mad—as it was being
tortured, or because its meat had not yet cooled, or also
because the battle had unsettled the kid, Riton had pains
during the night in his stomach and head. He thought he
had been poisoned, and he offered up ardent prayers to the
cat. The next day he joined the Militia. It pleases me to
know that he is marked thus, in his inmost flesh, with
the royal seal of hunger. His movements were so nimble
and sometimes so nonchalant that he himself thought oc-
casionally that he was actuated by the cat he carried
within him, and was already carrying when Erik met him.
Later, Erik will confess to me that in Berlin the dogs
growled at him when he was in a state of restrained or
manifest anger.

"Dogs come sniffing at me. They jump all around me
and try to bite me."

If, because of his anger, Erik became as disturbing an
animal to dogs as the hedgehog or toad, the cat's presence
in Riton could make him think he had been transformed,
deformed, that he exuded a feline smell.

"The guy," he thought, when he felt Erik's chest
against his back, "the guy must realize. . . . His eyes were
so bright that they looked black."

. . . . . . . . . . . . . . . . . . . . . . . . . . . . . . . . . . . . . . . . . . . . . . . . . .

The funeral procession continued on its way. When it
reached the open grave, the priest said a few more
prayers, and the choirboys made the responses. Then the
gravediggers lowered the little coffin. The hole was filled

quickly. The hearse left with the priest. The choirboys withdrew a bit and sat down in the grass behind a granite vault to eat a ham sandwich. The only ones who stayed on were the two gravediggers and the little maid. She stood for a moment facing the grave in the same posture as the warbler when it remains suspended in mid-air, supported by the rapid flutter of its wings, with its body motionless in the strange flight that immobilizes it on a level with the branch and facing the nest where its young are chirping away as it watches them. A great tenderness startles it. "It could be caught by a bird of prey." Thus thought the little maid. She was flying. She was teaching to fly. A quivering prayer shook her soul and transported her "on the wings of prayer," as they say. She was sweetly advising her daughter to be bold, was calling her to the edge of the nest. She broke up the movements of her wings, thus giving the dead child the first lesson. Then she took off her hat, laid it on the ground, and sat down on the tombstone next to the grave. As she was not crying, the gravediggers did not think that she was the mother. One of them said:

"It's pretty hot even for July, eh? You'd think we were in Algeria."

He had turned naively to his fellow worker, but his tone of voice indicated that he was addressing the maid. With both hands in his pockets and his chest thrown back, he stamped with his heel, which clacked on the dry earth.

"It sure is warm," said the other. And he winked at his colleague in such a way that one would have thought he had just uttered a remark charged with weighty implications.

"What we need now is rain. It's hot enough for vegetables."

"And us, we need wine, don't you think?"

They both roared with laughter, and the one who had spoken first, a tall brown-haired chap of about thirty with rolled shirtsleeves, laughing eyes, and flashing teeth, pushed away the star-shaped wreath that was lying on the tombstone and sat down beside the maid.

"You look tired, girly."

She seemed to be smiling, since fatigue made her grimace. Unlike Paulo, who was always grim, Riton was smiling. His was a joyous nature. When he made gestures such as getting on a bicycle and driving off fast with his body bent over the handle bars, or leaning against a railing, or watching girls in a casual way, or hitching up his trousers, men in the street would look at him with astonishment. And when he knew he was being observed, he would smile good-humoredly. With a smile on his face, he would accentuate the pose and thus succeed in being all coquetry. But let us go back to the maid. This book is true and it's bunk. I shall publish it so that it may serve Jean's glory, but which Jean? Like a silk flag armed with a golden eagle crowning darkness, I brandish above my head the death of a hero. Tears have stopped flowing from my eyes. In fact, I see my former grief behind a mirror in which my heart cannot be deeply wounded, even though it is moved. But it's a good thing that my sorrow, after having been so pitiful, triumphs in great state. May it enable me to write a cruel and beautiful story in which I keep torturing the mother of Jean's daughter.

Every grimace, if observed minutely, proves to be composed of a host of smiles, just as the color of certain painted faces contains a host of shades, and it was one of those puckers that the gravediggers saw. The maid did not answer. A kind of murmur continued inside her, though thought was foreign to her: that her foot hurt, and that Madame was, at that very moment, clearing the table.

"You can see she's sad," said the other man.

"Not at all, death's never serious, young lady. We see it every day."

He put his grimy, though broad and shapely, hand on the maid's knees, which were covered by the black dress. She was paralyzed with such indifference that she would have let her throat be slit without thinking of any reproach but the following:

"Well, well, so my time has come."

The man grew bolder. He put his arm around her waist. She made no movement to shake him off. In view of what seemed to be willingness on her part, the second gravedigger regretted not being in on the fun, and he sat down on the stone on the other side of the maid.

"Ah, she's a very nice little girl," he said laughingly. And he put his arm around the maid's neck and pulled her to him, against his chest. No doubt an entreaty arose within her, but she found no word to formulate it. The sudden boldness of his mate excited the first fellow, who leaned over and kissed her on the cheek. Both men laughed, grew still bolder, and kept pawing her. Beside her little daughter's fresh grave, she allowed them to mistreat her, to open her dress, to stroke and fondle her poor, indifferent pussy. Grief made her insensitive to everything, to her grief itself. She saw herself at the end of her rope, that is, on the point of flying away from the earth once and for all. And that grief which transcended itself was due not only to her daughter's death, it was the sum of all her miseries as a woman and her miseries as a housemaid, of all the human miseries that overwhelmed her that day because a ceremony, which, moreover, was meant to do so, had extracted all those miseries from her

person in which they were scattered. The magical ceremony, which lies in polarizing around its paraphernalia
all the reasons one has for being in mourning, was now
delivering her up to death. She thought a little about her
daughter and a little about her wretched lot. The men's
hands met under her dress. They were laughing very
loudly, and often their laughter was carved by a kind of
death rattle, when desire was too great. But they did not
particularly want to screw her. Rather, they were playing with her as with a docile animal, and in their play,
in order to complete it, they placed on her head the
wreath of glass beads which the tall one pushed down
with a tap of his fist, while his friend, with another tap,
knocked it down over her ear, where it remained until
that evening, at the cocky angle at which militiamen and
sailors sometimes wear their berets, pimps their caps, and
Fritzes their black forage caps.

. . . . . . . . . . . . . . . . . . . . . . . . . . . . . . . . . . . . . . . . . . . . . . . .

Flowers amaze me because of the glamor with which
I invest them in grave matters and, particularly, in grief
over death. I do not think they symbolize anything. If
I wanted to cover Jean's coffin with flowers, it was perhaps simply as a gesture of adoration, for flowers are
what one can offer the dead without danger, and if the
practice did not already exist, a poet could invent this
offering. The lavishing of flowers gives me a little rest
from my grief. Though the youngster has now been dead
for some time, the notes on which I base this book—which
is meant to be a tribute to his glory—bring back the sadness of the early days, but the memory of flowers is sweet
to me. As soon as I left the icy amphitheater, when I no
longer saw his pale, narrow, terrifying face with the bands

around it and his body with other linen, but in their stead
the embellished, stylized, perfumed, and moving image
of that spectacle, no sooner did I feel amazed and in-
dignant at the wretched dryness and poverty of those
remains, and suffer thereby, when I saw them and then
wanted them to be covered with flowers. With my eyes
still full of tears, I rushed to the nearest florist and
ordered huge bouquets.

"They'll be delivered tomorrow," I thought, feeling
calmer, "and they'll be laid all around his body and face."

The memory of those funeral flowers, furnishing a
helmet for the soldiers who flee amidst the laughter of
girls, cluttering the amphitheater, gives shape to the most
beautiful expression of my love. If they adorn Jean, they
will always adorn him in my mind. They bear witness
to my tenderness, which made them spring from Erik's
splendid whang. Dawn was breaking, what a dawn that
haloed whang breaking out of the hoodlum's pants was,
what a gloomy dawn!

I have no right to be joyful. Laughter desecrates my
suffering. Beauty takes my mind off Jean, to whom the
sight of vileness brings me back. Is it true that evil has
intimate relations with death and that it is with the intention of fathoming the secrets of death that I ponder
so intently the secrets of evil? But all these evils do not
help me reason. Let us try in another key: is it possible,
to begin with, if my grief diminishes when I contemplate
evil (which I am willing, for the moment, to call evil
according to conventional morality) that it does so because the distance is less great between this world which
is decomposed by evil and Jean who is decomposed by
death? Beauty, which is organization that has attained
the height of perfection, turns me away from Jean. Better
a fine living creature than a fine object, and my suffering

increases. And I weep if I do not bind Jean to this world in which beauty lives.

Yet, though I take pleasure in the sight of so many ugly things which I make even uglier by writing about them, in that which Jean's death inspires me to write, there is an order to do no evil. Is it because life orders me to set off a death with a life, that is, with good (a word also employed in its usual sense), to balance death with life? But if I delight in examining evil and dead or dying things, how could I be implementing life? And as for the homage which I think I am rendering Jean when I grieve, when I weep, isn't it because I bring my state a little nearer his, because everything within me grows desolate and his solitude less great, a solitude that death accords with a suddenness that may chill the dead person's heart? That world without gaiety or beauty which I draw from myself slowly with the intention of organizing it as a poem that I offer to Jean's memory, that world lived within me, in a sunless, skyless, starless landscape. It does not date from today. My deep disgust and sadness have been wanting to express themselves for a long time, and Jean's death has finally given my bitterness a chance to flow out. Jean's death has made it possible for me, by virtue of the words that enable me to talk about it, to become more sharply aware of my shame about the following error: my thinking that the realms of evil were fewer than those of good and that I would be alone there. A few pages hence, Jean's death will continue to confront me with relations that seem to exist between, on the one hand, evil and death and, on the other, life and good. We know the command contained in my grief: do what is good. My taste for solitude impelled me to seek the most virgin lands. After my disappointing setback in sight of the fabulous shores of evil this taste obliges me to turn back and devote myself to good. I am disturbed by the encounter with these two pretexts that are offered me for departing from a path I had taken out of pride, out of a preference for singularity, but this book is not finished.

. . . . . . . . . . . . . . . . . . . . . . . . . . . . . . . . . . . . . . . . . . . . . . . . . .

Ever since I began writing this book, which is completely devoted to the cult of a dead person with whom I am living on intimate terms, I have been feeling a kind of excitement which, cloaked by the alibi of Jean's glory, has been plunging me into a more and more intense and more and more desperate life, that has been impelling me to greater boldness. And I feel I have the strength not only to commit bolder burglaries but also to affront fearlessly the noblest human institutions in order to destroy them. I'm drunk with life, with violence, with despair.

. . . . . . . . . . . . . . . . . . . . . . . . . . . . . . . . . . . . . . . . . . . . . . . . . .

The age has accustomed us to such rapid transformations of gangsters into policemen and vice versa that the reader will not be surprised to learn that one of the gravediggers, after coming, took a gun from his pocket and aimed it at the girl, while the other, who had been playing for some moments with the pair of handcuffs, slapped them on her wrists. The maid felt no fear. She thought that everything that was happening to her was what usually happens in cemeteries and was reserved for persons in mourning who stayed behind after the burial and sat down on tombstones. All she said was:

"May I lace my shoe, sir?"

But the two bandits pushed her along and insulted her. They called her a cheap whore and a little hypocrite.

They kept poking and punching her until they reached the door of one of those miniature temples, little chapels whose architecture recalls (at least the architecture of this one did) that of the Law Court, on a very reduced scale. It was the vault of the Chemelats-Rateau family. The two men made the girl go inside and then they shut the door. She was a prisoner. She realized it. Before sitting down on the tombstone she should have looked at the cap of one of the gravediggers. On it was the silver star of prison guards. She had not thought of taking her hat, but she was still wearing the star-shaped wreath set at an angle on her head. Informing was a familiar practice at the time. This comment prompts me to say a few words about myself in the middle of the period. I love Parisians, who look deliriously beautiful as they deliver themselves from the Boches. Man is beautiful when he delivers himself (I'm substituting the word "beautiful" for "great," which I wrote first). This beauty lasted only a very brief moment, for a few days of danger and faith during which love prevailed. The Germans had already legalized informing, and when General Koenig drove them out, he recommended it in posters that were stuck up all over Paris. It's impossible for this frame of mind not to correspond to the propensities of an entire age. One rather likes "to squeal" and "sell out." One puts an honest hand on one's heart and talks. Speech kills, poisons, mutilates, distorts, dirties. I would not complain about it if I had decided to accept honesty for myself, but having chosen to remain outside a social and moral world whose code of honor seemed to me to require rectitude, politeness, in short the precepts taught in school, it was by raising to the level of virtue, for my own use, the opposite of the common virtues that I thought I could attain a moral solitude where I would never be joined. I chose to be a traitor, thief, looter, informer, hater, destroyer, despiser, coward. With ax and cries I cut the bonds that held me to the world of customary morality. At times I undid the knots methodically. I monstrously departed from you, your world, your towns, your institutions. After being subjected to your legal banishment, your prisons, your interdicts I discovered more forsaken regions where my pride felt more at ease. After that labor—still only half-finished—which required so many sacrifices as I persisted more and more in the sublimation of a world that is the underside of yours, I now know the shame of being approached painfully, by people lame and bleeding, on a shore more populous than Death. And the people I meet there came easily, without danger, without cutting anything. They are as at home in infamy as a fish is in water, and all I can do to attain solitude is turn back and adorn myself with the virtues of your books. In the face of such misfortune there remain tears or anger. The maid was a captive.

. . . . . . . . . . . . . . . . . . . . . . . . . . . . . . . . . . . . . . . . . . . . . . . . . . . .

But that life in the apartment to which I was admitted had its drawbacks. The day I was invited, Jean's mother dressed and preened with the slovenly precision of women who are too stout and well-to-do. Her hatred for the maid had not left her by noon. She was waiting for Erik, who was dawdling in his room.

"A maid! A maid!" she muttered. "After all, damn it, what's it to me if Jean knocked her up? I'm Madame."

She had set the table with a white cloth on which were placed white porcelain plates with a thin gold edging and, in front of the plates, wine glasses with flowers cut into the crystal. She was now placing the silverware. She

heard a knock at the door of the kitchen. It was the boy
from Gaillard's. Before he set down his two baskets on
the white wooden table, she screamed at him, "What
about bread? You never bring bread. Go get it." She was
frightened by her own voice. A rage against a dead son
that immobilized her for ten seconds, that made her as
cutting as glass, took possession of her: it was rage at
not having the power to give the storekeepers a week in
jail. She pulled herself together little by little.

"I'm going to be nervous at the table," she said to
herself.

She went back to the bedroom, the window of which
she had not opened all morning, and she was lying in bed
a few moments, in her lace, freeing all her winds, which
spread, forming thicker and thicker layers and changing
their smell as they aged. Suddenly she heard someone
walking in the dining room and footsteps approaching
the bedroom. In a twinkling she realized that her lover
had found the door open. She was panic-stricken at the
thought that he would smell the odor when he came in.

"He'll back out in disgust." She saw him in her mind's
eye holding his nose and staggering out of the room, pretending to be asphyxiated. She heard him say: "They're
dropping like flies." She thought, also very fast, of sprink-
ling perfumes about, but the time it would take to get
them . . . and they might not destroy the smell. The key
was inside. Jean's mother leaped to the door and threw
herself against it just as Erik, after knocking, was turning
the knob.

"Don't come in! No, don't come in!" she screamed.

She pressed against the door with her foot, shod in a
pink satin mule.

"But, darling . . . open up . . . open up . . . it's me."

Her pushing lover kept forcing, but the mother held
out and turned the key.

"I don't understand. . . . I don't understand why . . . what's happening, my God, what's happening?"

Behind the door Erik was uttering the same words I uttered in the presence of the sacred corpse. Death had shut the door. Though I questioned myself and questioned death with all kinds of precautions in my voice, that giant and yet ideal door was keeping a secret and allowing to escape only a very light but sickening smell over which the corpse drifted, a smell of astonishing delicacy which again made me wonder what games are played in the chambers of the dead. If death turned the key, what would one find? The seconds went by. Erik could have cried. He felt death in his love. He heard a window being opened and almost immediately after that the key turning in the lock. He pushed the door violently, surged into the room, which had been sprinkled with eau de Cologne and dashed to the open window in order to see the back if not the face of his fleeing rival. The street was empty except for a little girl who was carrying a loaf of bread in her arm. Erik leaned farther out. He suspected a bend as deep as a bowl of concealing the guilty one, and then, more disappointed than reassured, with the feeling of having been fooled, he straightened up and went back to his mistress. She was standing by the bed, inhaling the pure air through her nostrils, mortally anxious lest he still be able to smell the odor and understand the whole mechanism of the scene, and the thought really made her look like a guilty woman. He moved forward:

"Why didn't you open the door?"

The woman huddled against her lover's chest in such a way as to put her fragrant head of hair by his nose. The scene ended the way all scenes created by suspicion end: with the confusion of the jealous party. There were suddenly the classic embrace, the desperate body, the mouths caught in each other, the knotted arms, the crushed bosoms, the genitals hampered by their violence and surging. The mother opened her eyes. She looked at her lover. She was victorious. Then she took him by the arm, stepped a little away from him, and gravely said, "Well, darling. . . ."

He did not answer.

Juliette was a witness, though she felt no envy, to what went on between Erik and her mistress. She grieved for neither Jean nor her daughter. She simply slept. When lunch was ready, she did not come and sit down at our table. She served us.

"Perhaps it's a good thing for the girl that her child died. She wouldn't have been able to bring it up."

The voice of Jean's mother was meant to be sweetly compassionate. As she was the only woman at lunch, it was up to her to display deep feeling. And she used the word *child* for what she thought of in private as "the *lousy brat*." Her lover listened to her. Was it a canticle of the fairest love that the gestures of his mistress sang to him? Her way of rolling the macaroni around her fork, of swallowing, the slight sniffling of a constantly moist nostril, the quickness with which she caught the napkin that slid off her lap, in short, everything, did it all compose a hymn in his honor, a song?

"In short, do I love her enough? God," he secretly invoked, "tell me whether I love her enough."

They spoke of the maid again. Paulo did not defend her. I noted the impassiveness of his features and his mean look. The mother opened her mouth, and noodles fell out onto her plate.

"Anyway, today she didn't spit in the food."

"Gisèle!"

It makes no difference which of the two men uttered

that cry of revolt, for the other would have made it with the same vigor.

"In the fried eggs. Don't defend servants. They spit in the food."

There is no telling whether Juliette heard her or not. She seemed indifferent to our talk and indifferent to the strange impression she created. It was enough that she be there for the most magnificent landscape to become as dismal as a heath in winter. And her mere presence in that little dining room stripped all the trees of their leaves. All that remained was sloes and withered red berries on black branches. The sky was overcast. One could wet one's feet in the muddy water of the swamps which that cunning fairy traversed in her veils of sadness. When she came in with a dish of steaming cabbage, the deep mono-tone that welled up from each of Erik's gestures and even from his immobility seemed to rise over the Breton moors from the puddles in the clay that reflected a frozen azure, gorse, and a bush with thorns. In Erik's vicinity, that whole landscape, wingèd as dead hair, loosed a slow but lordly music. The maid was singing. She put the dish on the table. There were still swamps around us, but elves were dashing through them. Paulo was a silent and impassive witness of that fête, and had I wished to participate, I had only to shed a tear.

"And I can tell," added the mother as she raised her fork to the level of her voice. "I can tell when she spits. I recognize the bitter taste, the taste of a maid's mouth, the bitter taste of all the bitterness accumulated in the bottom of the stomachs of all high-class servants. . . ."

Paulo shrugged. He was eating his noodles and bread. His mother swallowed a mouthful and continued, as she watched her lover:

". . . a high-class servant is a servant who's really low,

that is, more and more of a servant. That's why when you tell them to keep quiet they shut up, so that you can't smell the foulness of their guts. I hate. . . ." She opened her mouth wide, and, a mouthful being ready on the end of her fork, she stuck it in. With her mouth full:

"Servants. Their bodies have no consistency. They pass. They passed. They never laugh, they cry. Their whole life cries, and they soil ours by daring to mingle in it by way of what ought to be most secret, hence most unavowable."

. . . . . . . . . . . . . . . . . . . . . . . . . . . . . . . . . . . . . . . . . . . . . . . . .

In the dangerous darkness, a song seemed to merge Erik and Riton. Each of them would have wished to writhe to happiness, to kiss, to squirm with pleasure, but other sounds, along with the waiting, caused weariness and sleep to leave them unsatisfied, bound to each other in the darkness by Riton's hand.

Was it true that every child, little girl, and old woman in Paris was a soldier in disguise? Erik was seized with fear at being alone with his weapons amidst a people of monsters mysteriously armed with knives and charms and knowing an art of camouflage that reduced to child's play the one used by German soldiers to disguise themselves as lizards, as zebras, as tigers, as moving, vertical graves that preserved a fresh, light-footed, blue-eyed blond corpse. He could not shake off the memory of a soldier wearing flesh-colored silk stockings and a pink dress, of a fifteen-year-old soldier dressed up as a journeyman baker, or that of a tank beset by strange warriors whom he had often brushed against in the street, bare-legged warriors in sweaters and often sneakers, warriors with delicate faces pale and drawn by the will to kill Boches,

with terrible hands whose delicacy drew tears. All the
glory of nations was for a long time revealed by the
splendor of military apparel, by the red, gold, and azure
of glittering ranks, by white gloves, handsome eyes behind lacquered visors, noble shoulders, twisted torsos,
horses, croups, and sabers whose very arrogance bespoke
loyalty. Falling into rank, the virtue of chameleons became the greatest virtue of the soldier. Deceit and
hypocrisy (in technical language, camouflage) were so
perfected as to give France the quiet, friendly look of a
vicarage garden. The Germans, knowing they were the
masters of costumed war, did not think that one could
transform one's face, wear a wig, paint one's eyes, dress
up as a girl, undress, be reamed by the male, and, without even wiping one's pussy or bronze eye, slit his throat
when he dozed off. I'm amused by this game of recording
here the shame of a country to which I belong by virtue
of language and of the mysterious threads that bind me
to its heart and that bring tears to my eyes when it suffers. It pleases me that France has chosen the charming
disguise of a hideous religious whore so as, no doubt like
Lorenzaccio, the better to kill her pimp.

Standing sadly at the summit of the Bavarian Alps in
the glass cage of a fortified chalet, Hitler towered over
history. Nobody approached him. At times he would go
to the edge of the great esplanade that separated him
from a void bristling with the highest peaks in the world.

. . . . . . . . . . . . . . . . . . . . . . . . . . . . . . . . . . . . . . . . . . . . . . . . . . . . .

Jean! Young tree with thighs of water! Blazoned bark!
Endless and amazing revels took place in the hollow of
your elbow. The shoulder of the Parthenon. A black
clover. I am a wad of tow pierced with gold pins. The

taste of your mouth: deep within a silent vale a mule made its way in a yellow cassock. Your body was a fanfare into which water wept. Our love! Remember. We lit up the barn with a chandelier. We woke the shepherds dressed for their Mass. Listen to their songs merged in a light blue breath! I fished in your eye! The sky opened its gates. Thin out my sleep on the brow of stillborn children, thin out our love over the world, thin out the world on our beds. Leave in your veiled wagons. I sleep beneath your door. The wind sleeps standing up. All these are themes with which my voice could go in quest of you! Jean, I'm abandoning you. The firs are moving by themselves. You live elsewhere, stronger than I who am here among the dead still unborn. All day yesterday I adorned a dog with my tenderness for you; a kind of St. Bernard, very white and very strong. I feared for a moment that I did not have enough tulle and roses. The box of matches was easier. Today you will be a branch of holly that I found, no doubt broken by a young monk on a flat, mossy stone. I haven't put you into a vase or behind a frame, but with the help of one of the lace curtains I made a kind of altar on the night table and put you there. I realize that this book is merely literature, but let it enable me so to glorify my grief that it emerges by itself and ceases to be—as fireworks cease to be when they have exploded. The main thing is for Jean or me to gain thereby. My book will serve perhaps to simplify me. I want to make myself simple, that is, to be like a diagram, and my being will have to gain the qualities of crystal, which exists only by virtue of the objects that can be seen through it. Rags, poverty, even a careless or untidy way of dressing, enable pathos to enter easily, more easily, into daily life. To be buttoned. Faultlessly. Apparently inaccessible. If I desire saintliness, let it come wholly from within! A torrent flowing into me from head to heart and circulating. A very simple ribbon. I would hate a crease, a silk pocket handkerchief, a badly pressed crease, a down-at-heel shoe to allow me the slightest self-pity, the simplest casualness with respect to strictness, to make disobedience easier. Where I was heavy with so many furs! Where the snow isolated each of us—we who lived, nevertheless, in the same thick darkness of a tank—in the middle of a vast plain of silence.

"They tortured women and children."

The French papers say that about us. In Russia I planted patches of forest between women's teeth. We had to make the Russian girls and their brother (seventeen years old) talk. There were four of us: the lieutenant, the corporal, a fellow private, and I. The girls were silent. The boy too.

The lieutenant said to me, "Slap him."

I was already smiling a bit because the officer was held in check by those Russians, and it was with a broader smile that I gave the kid a big, thick smack on the cheek. He made a faint, very faint move to hit back. He didn't dare.

"Talk."

He remained silent. Still smiling, I gave him another slap. He was still silent. I turned to the officer. The corporal and the other private also smiled, probably because I was smiling.

"Do the same to the girls."

I slapped them. They staggered, and one of them fell. The brother didn't bat an eyelash.

"The young man isn't very chivalrous," said the lieutenant.

We laughed, and all three of us laughingly indulged in a merry slapping game. We were in a transport of joy. We knocked the girls down and kicked them with our

heels. We were amused at their ridiculous postures, at
their rumpled hair, at their losing their combs, at their
groans. We tore their clothes. The girls and the boy were
naked. Within my joyous drunkenness I felt the very
grave presence of a touch of sadness. I felt it so precisely
that I knew it could become *the sorrow of not being able
to indulge in pity.* I kept punching away, but with a smile
that was no longer the same: it was now the motionless
sign of a joy stained with a misfortune that had to be
hidden. Because of that smile our game continued to be
a game, and was to seem harmless to us. We tore out tufts
of hair, the women's pubic hair, we pinched, twisted the
brother's balls. Our three partners had joined the game;
they were not laughing, but their dances and grimaces
were worse than laughter: they were the counterpart of
our drunkenness, an apparent despair at the heart of
which was contempt. And I knew that they had to indulge
in those grimaces because their contempt was in danger
of becoming *indifference to evil, to the point of their feeling pity for those who commit it,* and no doubt the officer,
who was standing behind the table and watching us with
a smile, knew it too. I hardly had time to feel all that,
as it swept me along, as it governed me, but the officer
had time to take it all in. He was there to know that we
would perhaps be dead the next day. He was also the
representative of so many heroic deaths, of so many
smoking homes, ruins, griefs, miseries, he knew that that
day we could indulge in joyous despair. And we invented
very funny pranks that made us laugh. . . .

. . . . . . . . . . . . . . . . . . . . . . . . . . . . . . . . . . . . . . . . . . . . . . . . . .

A posture of Erik's: his thumb was in the space between
two of his fly buttons. Like Napoleon, who used to hook

his thumb on his vest. A sick man fearing the rush of
blood to his bandaged hand.

. . . . . . . . . . . . . . . . . . . . . . . . . . . . . . . . . . . . . . . . . . . . . . . . . . .

   If Paulo's meanness kept him from betraying, it was
gentleness and tenderness that made Pierrot a traitor. For
two days the inmates, after forcing the doors of the cells
and getting hold of some weapons, became the masters
of the prison, which will be the place where uncontrolled
force is law. The inmates frightened themselves. The
guards had fled, closing the outside gates, and we went
into the rat trap, unable to get over the walls behind
which the armed soldiers and police lay in wait. If one
of us showed himself at a skylight, a policeman aimed
and fired. We had hardly any ammunition. We were in a
panic and didn't know whom to fight. The walls had us
well in hand. We had already eaten all the provisions in
the stockroom. The water supply had been cut off from
the outside. The guards fired from the gates at every
shadow they could see in the corridors. We always moved
slowly, cautiously, with a thick pallet in front of us to
protect ourselves a little. We were trapped; they could
let us die of hunger. Or thirst. Or toss grenades. They
could smoke us out. Among the minors, fear and the sublimity of the adventure, its exceptional strangeness, the
approach of punishment, which they assumed was bound
to be cruel, drove the children to love each other, also
to seek out oldtimers in whose arms they huddled in the
pretense of helping in a fight that already was dragging
to a close. I longed to betray. I felt myself delightfully
capsizing, as when certain tangos turn a cabaret into a
steamer that sinks amidst a smell of decaying flowers.
My soul visited Pierrot. When the white flag was waved

at the end of a broom, the militiamen entered, cooped the prisoners up in a few cells, and demanded the guilty ones. The captain questioned a few prisoners, one after the other. Some of the kids knew nothing about the beginning of the revolt.

"It's the political prisoners, eh?"

The captain asked his questions with a toss of his head and a faint grin of complicity at the corner of his lips.

"I don't know, boss. I didn't see."

"Take him away. We'll see later. Next!"

Another kid replied:

"I was sleeping, sir."

Grabbing him by the shoulders, the captain shook him and roared, "What do you take me for?"

He drove him with a slap to the opposite wall.

"Next!"

A youngster entered.

"Were you sleeping too?"

"No."

"Oh, that's a surprise. Well, what do you know?"

Paulo remained silent. He looked straight ahead. The gleam of his gaze was as rigid as a metallic beam. Without his realizing it, his hands went to his pockets, but only the thumbs entered, and hooked on the edge of the opening. And he stood there without moving.

"Well?"

The skin of his little face seemed to have tightened over an indestructible framework of bone.

The captain flicked his keys impatiently and said, "I've got to have them. I want the ringleaders. Otherwise, I'll give the prisoners more than they bargained for!"

Immediately, Paulo's taut metallic gaze seemed to be adorned with frail spring blossoms. His face lit up a little in a strange way: that is, it became darker. Paulo realized that his silence would cause a lot of trouble for the captain and might even bring on a catastrophe. He thought of nothing definite but yielded voluptuously to a wave of refusal. He said, through clenched teeth, "What do you want me to say? Someone opened my cell. . . ."

"Number what?"

"426."

"And. . . ."

This "and" was stressed by a movement of the foot with which the captain kicked against the opposite wall a little piece of wood that had been on the floor. It was a soccer player's movement. Paulo immediately felt a brief twinge of shame that reminded him that *he* was not an athlete.

"I don't know what it's all about."

The captain looked at Paulo. He stared mechanically at the bridge of the boy's nose where he saw the eyebrows meet and give the face that stubborn look which meant he would get nothing out of him.

"Get the hell out!"

Paulo left. Other kids had their turn, were questioned gently or violently. No one talked, since no one knew anything. Pierrot entered. He denounced the twenty-eight inmates who were executed. Accompanied by the warden, the captain of the Militia, the chief guard, and four turnkeys, he made the round of all the cells. He pointed out the fellows in each of them who had prepared the job, the kids who first had knocked at the doors, those who had been most zealous—the spark plugs, the bold, daring, fierce ones. The captain and the warden stood by without batting an eyelash. The kid entered the crowded cell—for all the inmates had been rapidly locked up in batches of twenty in cells meant for a single man—and he stood on tiptoe in order to see the faces at the back, and

because he did not know any of the names, he pushed
aside the men who were standing crammed in the sweat
and heat of July, the smell, the shadow, bumping against
their knees, their chests, their elbows. From the darkest
corner of the cell he brought back, at the end of a body
that he pulled by the jacket or shirt, the face of a child
whom the four turnkeys took in tow.

The night before writing what follows I had a dream,
which I record too late: "I was imprisoning a boy's cock
in a special chastity belt to which there were five keys.
Out of *hatred* (I remember that the feeling which made
me commit the act that follows was hatred) and of a love
of the irreparable, I tossed the keys into a torrent of mud."

Pierrot did not take revenge. He was among the first
to be captured by the militiamen, and as the captain
asked him, just as he did all the captives, whether he
knew the ringleaders, he, and he alone, said that he did.
He did not know any names.

"If I saw them," he said, "I'd point them out."

I had been arrested along with the others, but when I
was released I felt such joy, such gratitude, that I was
unable to keep my self-control. It was at the very
moment when my joy opened wide that the captain—was
it chance or the result of a very delicate observation or
shrewd guess?—asked me whether I knew the ringleaders.
I was not afraid. It did not seem to me that I was yielding
to a threat but, on the contrary, that I was in a state of
happiness in which to refuse would be a crime, one of
those states in which you give to a beggar. . . . As the
inmates were still confined in the upper section, nobody
bothered about me. I was hoping they would forget about
me. I was really hoping, but the warden had made a note
of my name. Three hours later, when the revolt was over,
a guard came to get me. The captain put his gun to my

temple and said, "Either you point out the ringleaders to me or you'll be rubbed out."

To a lover of justice this method would have seemed abominable. He would have feared that in order to save my hide I might accuse innocent men. The captain wanted only to execute men in order to make an example of them, as a measure of reprisal, and particularly to prove to himself that he was brave since he dared punish with death. This method proved to be an excellent one. The first twelve who were pointed out were real ringleaders. The explanation is as follows: the captain's terrifying face and tone of voice and the coldness of the muzzle of the revolver, which was ready to fire at my temple, caused me such fright that I had no doubt about my death. I felt I was turning white from head to foot or that my whole being was draining out. Instantly a lyric farewell to all that I loved was formulated within me. Everything around me changed meaning. Woods, rocks, sky, women, flames, sea, were suddenly present. The sun lit up the prison. The flowers, the hedges, the accordions, the waltzes, a beach of the Marne, loomed before me and were immediately regretted to a point of despair beyond tears. The accordion! It was through the accordion that my body screamed as it unfolded in pain.

"They are making one end of it writhe, to right and left."

Then and there everything seemed remote to Pierrot, to belong to another world, to be subject to other laws. Then, his life ended that very moment. Through a thick glass he saw and heard things and people, all except the captain, his voice, his face, his gesture, and his "icy fire." Pierrot opened his mouth and said nothing. His eyelids burned. He was obsessed by the following thought: "The captain's sore. Anything can make him shoot." He saw the danger instantly. He articulated with difficulty:

"I'm going to try to see if I recognize them."

His mouth immediately shut, its corners drooped, it seemed drawn with dryness. His face, which already had the paleness that is called, I think, the greenness of fear, grew uglier with the sagging of the flesh. I could read in it an anguish as grave as that expressed by a landscape in which, beneath the trees of an estate, German officers bury the uniforms, helmets, and guns of a conquered company that has dispersed. The kid felt his life was linked with cruel certainty to the finger which was on the trigger but which he could not see, for he dared not move his head. He feared lest his slightest movement be taken for an act of rebellion. He was subjugated by a kind of hypnosis. The captain's severity was too tense with a will to death and so wavered a little. This wavering was dangerous. It might have made him think that he was acting in a dream and that he would not kill anyone by shooting. Then awareness returned. He looked at Pierrot with more flexibility. He saw his delicate face, his long eyelashes, his freckles, the roundness of his lips, and he saw that despair was like a dead rose upon them. He thought of shifting gently and thus introducing the muzzle of his weapon into the mouth.

"That's how the Militia loosens a tongue," he thought. "That'll make him come around."

The warden's presence made him feel uncomfortable. He lowered the revolver. The moment which had lasted God knows how long, with Pierrot's life in mid-air, was thereby broken. Gone too was the extraordinary impression of despair which, by desensitizing him, had placed him above his body, leaving it without a mind. He saw the warden look for a cigarette; he felt as if he himself were standing on his stiffened legs, in the military position of attention. He flexed his right calf a little so as to rest on that leg. His body grew a little suppler, and he put a hand into his pocket. But though death could not take hold of him in a twinkling (the captain now needed time to aim at the temple), it was present, on the alert, ready to seize upon the first mistake, and in order to succeed he had to remain in a state of hypnosis into which only the highest pitch of danger could put him.

"Come with us."

They left for the cells where the prisoners were parked in lots of twenty. No doubt the movements of his legs and the necessity of climbing stairs made him realize again that he was still in a world where one suffers and bleeds. The beginning of that walk was for him a march both to death and to the light. But, unlike the victim who is awakened at dawn and whose last walk is a march to the light and to death, Pierrot felt, from the hope that reanimated his body, that light would be. However, the gravity of the act he was about to perform, the dignity with which it was invested, which was all the greater in that the gestures were familiar, and the solemnity of the moment, without destroying his fear, which idealized it by destroying everything around it and allowed to subsist only the extreme limit of his being and his memory of his despair, without destroying his panic desire by leaving him insensitive to consequences, that is, to life outside of self since it became a cause, met within him at the same instant and made of it a pure act of faith. Even the all-too-present death to which he still belonged invited him to be honest, to be straightforward. Death is sacred. Any being it has touched, if only with the tip of its wing, is taboo. He knows that it is stronger than he, he blesses it for having spared him, and, in order to tame or perhaps discourage it when it is too close, he makes himself a carapace of the brightest virtues, particularly of the justice that makes man unassailable. Anyway, Pierrot thought that his denunciations would be verified. Without making any mistakes at first, he pointed out those who were responsible. The gravity of his act and his almost automatic movements did not permit him to be seriously concerned with his cronies' indignation. He perceived their contempt only through the mist of his lucidity. The captain and the warden accepted his decisions without examination. They recognized the choice of heaven. The finger of a child. Perhaps they were under the sway of his pure and fresh authority. For those brutes the child was playing the role of the pendulum. His very silence added to the exceptional nature of his case, dehumanized him. In the first three cells—there were twenty in all— Pierrot chose ten victims. Having reached that number, he hoped that the captain would say that he was satisfied. He was expecting others; he did not say a word. The very slight scruple that Pierrot had had at first when he was threatened with the revolver and thought it was a matter of offering up several lives in exchange for his own, completely disappeared.

"It's not possible that they're going to butcher all those guys," he thought, "but it would be some job punishing them all!"

From then on, he felt a certain shame. He thought less of himself for not sending a few men to the scaffold and he thereby felt less afraid of himself and his act. He felt that his feet were burning, not as if he had walked on live coals, but with a slow, imperious heat that rose up all through his legs. With the passing of fear the blood circulated faster. I thought of my youth in winter, when before I left for school my mother filled my sabots with embers and shook them until the wood was warm. I would then trudge through the snow along roads edged with slush. In the seventh cell, he designated the victim simply with a gesture of his chin, but it was so haughty that he felt he was defying ten thousand years of morality and disposing of them. When he inspected the other cells, every gesture, look, and sigh of the huddled men seemed to him charged with contempt. When he plunged into the midst of their warm, damp mass, it was disgust that seemed to separate them so that he could pass. The cells were as jammed as a subway during rush hour, and Pierrot dug his way in, wormed through the crowd, pursued by disgust. The atmosphere of the cells was too like that of the subway the night Riton met Erik there for me not to speak of them. Riton was seventeen. It was the same night that he had executed the rebels who had been betrayed by Pierrot. Just before eleven he bought a ticket at the La Chapelle station to go back to the barracks. As the tracks are above ground at that station, he had to wait in the darkness because of the general blackout. Yet Riton was able to make out the face of the German tank driver who stood behind him. A face of about twenty-two, fierce eyes, a blond curl that stuck out impertinently from under the black police cap set on the eyebrow and supported by the ear. The neck was massive, as I have already said, and it shot straight up from the collarless uniform that was black down to the boots. Erik was holding a pair of brown gloves. He stood right behind Riton, who was leaning out into space against the central bar, opposite the door. The crowd was dense. People were crushing one another in silence, and, despite the silence, before the train entered the darkness, Riton could see on all the faces the contempt of an entire people. He was alone, young, and already conscious of his solitude and strength, and proud too. No sooner did the train get under way than the shaking of the car flattened the belly of the Frisou (as the Germans were called) against Riton's behind. The kid thought nothing of it at first. Then he was surprised at continuing to feel a weight and heat against him. In order to verify his impression he ventured a wiggle to disengage himself, though he wanted it to be very slight so as not to discourage the soldier if his impression was correct. The soldier pressed all the more; he had a hard-on. Riton remained still. At each station the car lit up, but no one noticed anything, for all that could be seen was heads and hands clinging to the bar. At most, the sight of the kid provoked disgust, which took the place of thought and prevented observation. Erik was staring straight ahead. As his head was slightly turned so as not to seem to be kissing the kid's hair or beret, his gaze passed beneath the arm of a waiter who was leaning against a post.

He thought to himself, "He must feel my hard-on."

Then he couldn't get rid of the idea. He hoped and feared that the child would feel it. He dared not press too much and at the same time he pushed very hard, for he retained the image—more exciting in the dark—of the slender, slightly curved neck which he managed to catch a glimpse of at each station.

"Even if he doesn't like it because I'm a German, he won't dare make a scene."

The stations rolled by. Erik tried to dig his left arm (which he held above the passengers) into the human mass. The arm slowly descended. The hand sought a hollow between two shoulders with the cautious intelligence of the head of a snake that seeks a cavity. Riton wiggled his hips again. He was almost not thinking. He was letting himself be carried along by a happiness that at bottom was a kindly torpor. The male, the soldier, and the German dominated him. There was a luminous

pause. It was Jaurès Station. Passengers got off. By virtue
of an understanding that had already been reached,
neither Riton nor the Fritz stirred, except that Riton took
his right hand out of his pocket.

The train rolled into the darkness. He did not move.
For the first time since that morning he felt somewhat
peaceful. What the German soldier was granting him was
perhaps not yet affection. Nevertheless, Riton rested in
that warmth and physical force, forgot his heinous crime.

"He'd understand me."

Holding his cock horizontally—but behind his buttoned
fly—Erik withdrew his belly from Riton's behind and let
his tool be guided by the movements of the car. Thus,
each jolt made him ram it into the kid's buttocks. And
each time the contact was broken Riton grew aware of
his solitude. Renewed, it calmed and reassured him, made
him feel at peace with the world.

"The thing is, how far's he gonna go?"

And Erik: "I'll follow him when he gets off."

The subway went on with the speed and sureness of a
frieze around a Greek temple. The train gave a violent
jolt and in order to regain his balance Erik put his left
hand—the one that was holding his gloves—on Riton's
shoulder. The boy felt he was bending under the weight
of Germany. He leaned his head forward a little so that
his cheek would graze a finger of the gloves.

Erik wondered: "Is he smiling or does he look
annoyed?"

He would have liked Riton to make a little pout. Yet,
from almost imperceptible signs, from a kind of increasing force that was mounting within him, from a certainty,
from the greater effort, from beads of sweat on his
temples, and also from less sureness in his rod, Erik felt
that he was winning. The kid was caught. He was granting

his dearest treasures. If he hoped for a peevish pout on
Riton's face, it was in order to tear away a last veil of
modesty, and because a pout would have gone well with
the grace of such hair, with the beret that hung way down
on one side like a big ear of a hunting dog. There was
another jolt, of which Erik took advantage to flatten his
chest squarely against Riton's back.

"The boy's letting himself go. What'll they take me for
if the light goes on?"

This thought did not trouble him. In fact, it gave him a
kind of joy, for he hoped he would be compromised and
have to brave additional disgust. Another jolt and the
German's thighs stuck to his neatly.

"The guy must be having a great time in his mourning
outfit. And I don't know where he's getting off!"

The light went on. The car was almost empty, and all
the faces were looking at the two soldiers, whom fear
prevented anyone from chiding and who were stuck
together back to belly, caught in their amorous adventure
and as impure and serene as dogs on a public square. Both
Eric and Riton immediately saw their immodesty. Without a word between them, they got off. It was Parmentier
Station. Certainty of your beauty gives great assurance,
as do muscular strength and, behind you, like a protecting
wall against which you lean, the dark, gloomy mass of the
Reichswehr. Yet as soon as he stepped out of the train
and onto the platform, Erik felt a slight shyness. It was
Riton who took the initiative and spoke first. He had
jumped off the train while it was still moving. The jump
and a brief run on the platform made him feel at ease
and then made him joyful. He took off his beret with a
laugh, tossed his head as he ran his hand through his
hair, and said, looking at Erik, "It's warm, eh?"

"It is." And Erik smiled. He spoke perfect French, with

a somewhat heavy accent. Walking at Riton's side, he readjusted his short black jacket, his belt, and his revolver. He passed a candy-vending machine and saw his black sleeve in the narrow mirror: to the already sublime fact of being a tank driver in the German army was added the brilliance of his name. Deep inside the dark block of his funereally garbed body he guarded that name: Erik Seiler, followed by a magical expression, and around them, though less precise, for it was only the pretext for the scintillating of the name, a whole amazing adventure that was set in Berlin. The expression: the executioner's lover. Erik had no vanity. His reputation for scandalous love affairs had satisfied him in the past, but this was because they prevented his diverging from his singular destiny.

"I alone am Erik Seiler." This certainty exalted him. He was sure that no one recognized him in the street, but he knew that the crowd knew of the existence of Erik Seiler, whom he alone could be. Renown suffices, even if it be of an ignominious kind and thus the opposite of glory, if *fama* is glory. To have been the executioner's lover sufficed for his glory. He was famous, young, handsome, rich, intelligent, loving, and loved. In short, he had everything that is implied, everything that is specified, when people say: "He had everything to make him happy." The unhappiness or sufferings of that exceptional being could therefore have had only a noble source. His sufferings were of metaphysical origin. As others are isolated by an infirmity, so he was isolated by that bouquet of multiple gifts. From his solitude sprang his qualms about the problem of evil, and he had opted for evil out of despair. His having seen himself—though just a glimpse —in the mirror of the candy-vending machine fortified him against his image of himself. He was under the protection

of the headsman of Germany, of the executioner with the
ax, and when he emerged from the subway into the
darkness of the street, he stroked the militiaman's delicate
neck, and the boy nimbly turned halfway around and
placed one of his legs between Erik's.

. . . . . . . . . . . . . . . . . . . . . . . . . . . . . . . . . . . . . . . . . . . . . . . . . .

Pierrot was not the administrator of justice but a mer-
chant. He was afraid of what Paulo would think if he
heard about the adventure. And he *would* hear about it.
Little by little he lost altitude. He was being abandoned
by his sublime rectitude. Death was withdrawing. He was
walking on earth. At the same time, his mind got busy,
and his intelligence told him that it was impossible for
anyone to check upon his choice. He pointed to faces that
he hated then and there, and, as he himself was a minor,
in the minor section he pointed out only the younger ones.
The contempt of all the men—and chiefly that of the
adults who saw squealing pass by in the garb of youth
and beauty—was more and more evident. In order to appear casual, indifferent to his role and to the contempt
he aroused when he went to point out the victim, he
forced his way through the herd of brutes with his hands
in his pockets. To escape their gaze, that is, in order that
his own not be caught in that of someone sterner,
tougher than he, he drew his hands together in his pockets
till they almost met over his belly, so that the cloth of his
trousers tightened around his behind and made him pivot
on one heel with so nimble a movement that his locks got
mussed and the flap of his muffler slapped an old man in
the face. As he progressively lost his haughty rigor, the
captain's blind confidence in him declined. A bit of hesitation, a more bullying manner, gestures that were more

insolent because of the contempt that had to be pushed aside, were perhaps signs warning the officer that the kid was lying. For a moment he thought of checking, but his laziness, first of all, and his indifference to the lives of others made him more or less drop the idea.

"What a little bitch the kid is!" he thought to himself. And he could not refrain from loving him, from secretly forming an alliance with him. He was even grateful to the boy for reminding him that the Militia played the same role in the life of France that the kid was playing in the present life of the prison. He more than anyone else knew that the Militia existed in order to betray. It bore a burden of shame. Every militiaman had to have the guts to despise courage, honor, and justice. It's hard at times, but laziness helps us just as it does the saints. The kid is worthy of a militiaman. While he was pursuing these thoughts, with one hand immobilized in his pocket on his keyring and the other resting on his yellow leather holster, a kind of grin twisted his mouth, but actually the laugh continued inside the closed mouth with a slight ironic sound in mockery of that thought, and his eyes suddenly grew fixed so that his mind could see it more clearly in a crueler light.

"And what the hell does it matter if we do shoot innocent ones?" He had this thought the moment preceding the choice of the twenty-eighth victim, whom the kid had just designated by standing in front of him and repeating for the twenty-seventh time the following words: "He's one too." The kid was leaving the cell. The turnkey was about to lock the door, but the captain turned to Pierrot and asked, "Did you look carefully? Are you sure he's the only one in that bunch?"

An unexpected gentleness in the captain's voice disturbed the kid, who thought it had been feigned. He had spoken in a theatrical tone in which the kid thought he detected a fierce irony. He was seized with fear lest his imposture be discovered. He turned pale. If after such a betrayal the power that had demanded it on pain of death turned against him or even abandoned him to the hatred of the prisoners, he would have to swallow his tears and, bent endlessly over the rag with which one washes the steps of a staircase, endure eternal humiliation. And it was a poor, humble little housemaid, subjected to all kinds of whims, who, trembling like a dog, answered:

"No, sir, no. . . ." His voice remained suspended, not daring to say "He's the only one," for that sentence contained the statement "He's one," which he had not the courage to proclaim, for fear of suddenly hearing a frightful burst of laughter in the sky, that is, in all things, in doors and walls, in eyes, in voices, when they heard so monstrous a statement. And he quickly calmed down, for he told himself that such monstrousness had been possible because fate had made an error and had used him to commit that error. "And if heaven recognizes the error," he thought to himself, "there will be such joy in our Father's dwelling that my reconciliation with the order of the world will take place by itself." In short, that's how I express what he felt.

Then he came down to earth. He was afraid and did not want to find a single condemned face in any of the four remaining cells. He went up to a kid of about sixteen whose jacket, which was simply thrown over his shoulders, fell to the floor. Pierrot picked it up very politely and helped him slip it on. Souls have been saved for less than that. For a caterpillar that has fallen from a tree and that is put back on a leaf, for a little blue flower that the foot refuses to crush, for a kindly thought about a toad, nature sings a hymn of joy, all the censers swing in your honor. A child was sure that no harm would befall him because one afternoon, in the empty church where he was about to break open the poor box, he was so kind as to close the open door of a stall, thereby re-establishing the destroyed order, repairing an error, perhaps a tiny one, but there is nothing to which one does not cling, and Pierrot knew that he would be forgiven everything for that one charitable gesture. It is not surprising that he has such difficulty in climbing the rungs of evil and that he seeks help. He did not cheat. When the Yogi makes his way to knowledge, he is always accompanied by a master who guides and helps him. It is right for the murderer to help himself along however he can.

Pierrot, the captain, the warden, the chief guard, and three other guards (for one of the three turnkeys led each chosen victim to a cell elsewhere) formed a group which at that moment was at the end of the fifth section. With his soul utterly distraught, Pierrot stood stock-still and awaited the announcement of a frightful judgment. The captain went up to him and put out his hand, which the kid shook. He said: "My boy, you've done your duty. You've just performed an act of courage, and I congratulate you."

Then, addressing the warden, he demanded that the guards treat the squealer decently. And then he asked what would be done to protect him from the prisoners' revenge and persecution. It was quickly arranged that he would be a librarian until he was freed by an early pardon. A guard escorted him to the library. Two hours later, another guard, whose voice he could feel was charged with hatred and disgust, informed him that an emergency court composed of the warden, the captain, and an official delegated by the secretary to keep order had just issued a blanket verdict sentencing the twenty-eight child victims, minors all, to death by a firing squad.

. . . . . . . . . . . . . . . . . . . . . . . . . . . . . . . . . . . . . . . . . . . . . . . . . .

The prison chaplain suffered from aerophagia, and, in order to release his gases in silence, he would squeeze his buttocks together with one hand. The farts, instead of exploding, would fizz without making a loud noise. Being close to fifty, he was almost bald and his pudgy face was grayish, not because of the color of the skin but because it was completely expressionless. On the morning of the execution, as soon as he got up, he ran to the crapper at the far end of the garden without buttoning his cassock. All went well, and when he wanted to wipe his ass, he reached out mechanically for the tissue paper. But his housekeeper had once again hung the pages of *The Religious Weekly* on the nail. Usually he didn't give much of a damn. That morning he dared not drag the name of Jesus or Mary through the shit. He ran his fore-finger over the shitty hole and tried to wipe it, as he often did, on the door (the swimmer does it on the rocks, as the athlete on the boards of fences). Whereupon he noticed that the comma which his finger had just shaped there formed, at the top of the heart bored in the door, a bouquet of flames that made a Sacred Heart of Jesus out of the empty heart through which could be seen in the dawn a priest's garden and, to be more exact, a clump of white phlox. The heart, suddenly consummated by the sublime distinction of its flame, burst into a blaze, and the abbé thus received the baptism of fire. He did not reflect upon what he should do in the presence of that simple prodigy. He did better than think, he acted.

Frightened by the sight of God—and not because God manifested himself in the crapper by transfiguring an image of emptiness and shit—but because of the suddenness of the grace that had been granted and because his soul was not, he thought, quite ready to receive God, on account of a terrible sin—whereas that sin alone had put him in a state of grace—the priest tried to kneel, but his knees banged against the door, which opened and presented in the trivial daybreak the shit-adorned heart that had gleamed in the darkness of the outhouse but that was dismally dirty in the morning light. Confronted with this new miracle—the disappearance of the first—his agitation increased. He rushed out and did violence to his feelings in order not to slam the holy door. He ran through the garden, which had been dampened by the night mist. He stepped over a lane of strawberry plants and entered the presbytery, which was on the street. Three minutes later he was at the Militia barracks. In a few amazingly supple strides he dashed upstairs to the captain's office and opened the door without knocking. Then he stopped, out of breath. "God," he said to himself, "is first making me perform a little act that has a social meaning."

If I am relating the inner adventures of a Catholic priest, do not think that I am satisfied with probing the secrets of the mechanism of religious inspiration. My goal is God. I am aiming at Him, and since He hides Himself in the jumble of the various faiths more than elsewhere, it seems clever of me to pretend that I am trying to track Him down there. Priests think that they are with God. Let us assume that they are with Him, and let us see ourselves in them. Despite his devoutness, the captain was infuriated at the interruption. Nevertheless, he stood up. The priest made a gesture of peace with his right hand. He said:

"Remain seated, captain."

His breathlessness made him actually say "main seated."

The captain was standing behind his desk, at the right of the glass cabinet containing the French flag, the silk cloth of which was double, heavy, and motionless.

"In case of trouble," he thought, "I'll wrap myself in its folds."

His pale clenched hands were pressing against the black wooden desk over which his body was bent. A sunbeam, coming from the window like grace from heaven, separated him from the priest, whose face was enough for him to understand the significance of the priest's behavior, thus justifying his casualness. He said:

"Monsieur l'abbé. . . ."

The abbé had already taken a paper from his cuff, but he did not use it. "Is the captain baptized?" he wondered. "Where are the baptismal certificates?" He saw the roster on the wall. . . . "Join up. . . ."

"Captain, what I have to do would be painful if it were not ordered by God. . . ." He stopped, embarrassed by the beginning of the sentence. The solemnity of the order and the majesty of Him who had given it were too great for him, were not in keeping with the place, with the posters, the pencils, the ordnance survey maps. He looked at the officer.

"It was in the crapper, in the form of shit. . . ."

The captain's cold eyes stared at the bridge of the abbé's nose. Beneath that gaze, which was visibly ready for anything, even for the most dangerous weapon, irony, the priest had a burst of courage and wild hope. Still winded by his tirade, he cried out with a sputter, in a high-pitched voice:

". . . God. . . ."

Uttered in such a tone, that burning and desperate

name, which was now outside of him, could have been a
threat, an appeal, an invocation. It emerged from the
priest's mouth amidst a spray of spit that crossed the
field of blond light from the panes and became the golden
rays of an extremely delicate sun in which the name appeared suddenly glorious, alone, and so intimately mingled
with those tenuous rays that it scattered itself in droplets which sprinkled the captain's clothes with an invisible and perhaps dangerous constellation. The captain
did not move under the onslaught. Thanks to the fixity of
his eyes, he was master of the situation. There was a
moment of silence. It was a July morning. Each guarded
within himself a treasure that was his strength and behind
which he took shelter. The priest had God since he spat
Him out piecemeal as a tubercular spits out his lungs.
France and, better than France, a tricolored banner of
thick silk embroidered and fringed with gold were a
magnificent cope for the captain.

"Tell me about it," said the captain, who immediately
thought to himself with gravity, "You could have wiped
your ass."

"It's . . . very grave. . . . It's. . . . I know . . . today,
this very morning. . . ."

The captain had regained his self-possession. Fully
absorbed in higher contemplation of the disaster, he was
master of the moment. He pulled himself together, and
this betrayed him, for he replied haughtily and arro-
gantly:

"What do you mean?"

The admission was in the tone.

"Captain, what I know . . . if. . . ."

"If what? . . . If what?"

"Save those children. I have. . . ."

"What? . . ."

"Proof."

"You have proof? What proof?"

"I'll strike. I'm a priest and God is my strength. . . ."

All the same, the captain began to be afraid, but it was a fear of the moment and not of social and official consequences. Anything was possible with a man dressed as a woman, in a black robe beneath which were no doubt hidden at night, clinging to the hairs on the balls, to the balls themselves as to the rocks of the Sierra, armies of policemen with muscular thighs who might at any moment open the cassock and handcuff him and extradite him from *public barracks*. He overcame this idiotic fear and said:

"That paper of yours. . . ."

The priest, who had just held the paper out, tossed it on the desk, and the captain saw a cartoon of a soldier teasing a servant girl.

"Revelation. . . . Revelation. . . . Revelation. . . ."

Once the word appeared, it proliferated in the ecclesiastic's head with an abundance that left no room for any idea. Threatened by a military man who seemed very self-possessed, the priest had no time to think, but he was suddenly struck, with lightning speed, by the following: "God *reveals* himself to me who *reveals the sin of others*." The word revelation meant both glory and its exact opposite. God was backing away from France but was thereby triumphing over it.

"My son. . . ."

The abbé put out his hands, and his arms, which for a few seconds were parallel, motionless, and stiff as marionettes, then crossed on his chest. The captain walked around his desk and kneeled before the priest, who blessed him and left the room, murmuring:

"Compose yourself. God needed that admirable sin."

A Militia company had put down the prison rebellion. Riton was not a member of it. He was among those who were chosen—or picked at random—to execute the twenty-eight victims. When he learned that hoodlums were to be shot, nothing within him rebelled. On the contrary, he was filled with a kind of gladness. His eyes gleamed. We can be sure that none of the following ideas occurred to him, but I am trying to explain why he was joyful. Fed by the gutter, the entire soul of the gutter would be in him until he died. He liked hoodlums and respected the strong and despised the weak. It was hunger that had made him a militiaman, but hunger would not have been enough. He had learned from pals of his who had joined up earlier that the Militia recruited from among riffraff. They were birds of a feather that would never include squares who wore glasses, noncoms of the destroyed army, hollow-chested bureaucrats, but only former thugs from Marseilles and Lyons. The Militia was hated by the bourgeois before it was formed. Its purpose was to spread fear, to spread disorder. It seemed the materialization of what every thief desires: that organization, that free, powerful society, which was ideal only in prison, in which each thief—and even each murderer—would be openly appreciated for no reason other than his worth as a thief or murderer. The police make associations of felons impossible, and the great gangs that are not fantasies of journalists and policemen are quickly broken up. The thief and the murderer know camaraderie only in jail, where their worth is finally recognized, accepted, rewarded, and honored. The "underworld" no longer exists, except that of pimps, who are stool pigeons. The burglar and the killer are alone, but they sometimes have friends. Though pals may hang out together, you must always be on guard, must always give vague answers: "Oh, I manage," must never give any publicity to jobs, which are veritable jewels, except when you're nabbed. But the great happiness of knowing your name is under a photo, of thinking that the pals are jealous of that glory, is paid for with freedom and often with life, with the result that every job, every burglary or murder, will be a wonder of art, for from the last one of all will come your death and your glory. The felon is a Chinese, a Burmese, who prepares his funeral all his life. He works on the coffin, splendid lacquers, skillful paintings, gold and blood-red lanterns, cymbals. He invents processions of Laotian priests wrapped in their white linen bands. He pays embalmers. He organizes his glory. Each act is a phrase of our overlong funeral. Though the police serve order and the Militia disorder, they cannot be compared socially. The fact remains that the latter also did the work of the former. It was at the ideal point where the thief and the policeman meet and merge. They achieve the following exploit: fighting the cop and the thief. In like manner, the Gestapo. On June 23, Riton and one of his cronies were summoned to the captain's office. The chief was sitting on the edge of his typist's table and smoking a cigarette. When the two kids entered, he turned his chest a little. The new leather of a complicated outfit (belts, holsters, cross-belts, etc.) creaked.

"I've had my eye on both of you. You feel up to an expedition?"

"Yes, I do, chief."

"Okay, load your guns."

The two boys felt the presence of the seated woman. She was blonde, commonplace, but her make-up was fresh and quite became her. Had she not been there, the captain would have handled the two rookies better. Flowing from her deep, limpid eyes, from her smile, from each

of her gestures, or given off, rather, like the smell from
a flower, that corolla of black silk in which her pink
crossed legs were knotted stigmata, the femininity of that
pink, clever doll spread through the office and discon-
certed the males. None of the three was quite in possession of himself. Their quivering created around each of
them an aura of desire, pride, and vanity that became
tangled in that of the other two. They had stage fright
as the motionless typist stared at them. The two kids
gravely took their revolvers from the leather holsters, and
Riton said:

"Mine's ready, chief."

"So's mine, chief."

"All right. Okay then?"

"Right, chief."

They answered at the same time, whereupon the captain swept up with one hand two pairs of handcuffs lying
on the table and with the same quick gesture tossed one
to Riton and the other to his pal.

"Put them in your pocket. They're for later. All right.
Stick around, I'll send for you."

As they left, the handcuffs in Riton's hand made the
metallic sound that for years had been for him the sound
of misfortune, and immediately a tremendous sadness
clouded his heart. Handcuffs are the indispensable acces-
sory of an arrest. They are so powerful a symbol of it that
the sight of them in even the friendly hands of certain
cops is enough to make me feel, not fear, but, as it were,
the reflection of a great grief. Riton felt like running
away. Since the handcuffs were open in his free hands, it
was, so it seemed for two seconds, because he was released from them. For the first time, the victim held and
was frightened by the knife of the sacrificer. This ambi-
guity did not last. A great force hardened him. The feel of

that contrivance in his hand, in the presence of a woman, made a little man of him. He put the handcuffs in his pocket, saluted, and left without any betrayal of his emotion. The kids had the courage not to stop when they got outside, but Riton's walk grew heavier, his strides were slower and longer. Though he had just received an investiture, the sign had, above all, metamorphosed him into his own enemy.

Riton had become the man who can arrest and also the man who cannot be arrested, since he is himself the one who arrests. That steel object was booty taken from the enemy, a trophy. His hand was clutching the handcuffs, which were in the pocket of his breeches, and he walked with a heavy step to keep his joy from being visible. And the force conferred by the handcuffs gave him the authority of men who are armed or rich, an authority that is almost always manifested by a heavier gait. Hoodlums themselves say, "He's a guy with authority" or "a guy that has weight." At a bend in the corridor his pal took out his gadget.

"Nice toy! Let's see if the moonlight bounces off it!"

Riton took out his pair.

"Look at that, I can't believe it."

He was pensive for a moment, not listening to the other say:

"Who'll we stick 'em on? Got any ideas? Say, your mind's wandering. . . ."

Riton looked at the handcuffs. He had locked up one of his wrists.

He said: "I can't count how many times they slapped the bracelets on me! It's my turn now. I'd like to stick 'em on a cop."

"It'll probably be a Jew. Don't you think?"

Actually, it was a matter of arresting two patriots who

had made their way out of the underground for a moment in order to go to Paris for instructions, but Riton did not learn this until the following morning, after the arrest of the two men, one a chap of twenty-three and the other of twenty-four. They refused him the fierce and exalting joy he expected of the adventure, and all he had was a furious satisfaction. They were arrested quite simply, in a hotel room. And when, though proud to see that their victims were older than they, the kids, with a bluffness stolen from genuine cops, imprisoned the four sturdy, dark, hairy wrists in a pale steel retreat, the captives, strong with the live force of forests, with the sap of an eternal April, with verdant violence at liberty, glanced at the handcuffs with such a look of contempt that the three hunters felt a shame which expressed itself at once by bullying. The captain put his gun back into its holster so as to confront them more squarely with his hostile humanity, to fight them with his enraged flesh, which was thereby more relieved. He looked at them angrily. He said coldly:

"You bastards, you don't expect to get away with it, do you? I was waiting for you. We knew you were coming. Someone ratted on you. There are stool pigeons among you."

While the elder of the two smiled, the other dared say:

"Sir, it's wrong of you to insult us and to insult the patriots. Furthermore, it's not for you to pass judgment. Your function is simply that of a policeman."

The captain hesitated. For a moment the prisoners and the militiamen saw anguish not painted but sculpted on his face: he was mentally seeking, very fast, and was in a panic at not finding, deep down in his throat, a tone of voice of unheard-of force and violence, one that had hitherto never been used, a voice calling upon all his vigor and every part of his body, which he would have exhausted, so that it would have remained alone, vomited out until it dragged along the bones and muscles, and the whole body would have been charged with hatred in the vomit so as to give him the strength to blot out the two impertinent ones. The captain, bewildered, wild with rage, plunged into himself. He explored his depths, but the voice did not go down far enough. He put his hand to his throat. His anguish was visible. His eyes were rolling wildly. Rendering secret tribute to poetry, to the Word, he felt obscurely that men must be dominated only by the voice but, unaware of the wondrous ways of language, he sought the tone that confounds. After ten seconds, weary and exhausted by the quest in the depths of his cavern, he said quietly, his mouth dry:

"I'll give you the works."

The patriot smiled sadly. Then, his face became impassive. Unable to throw his enemies out and shut the door on them, he shut his face on them. The two militiamen felt the same shame and fury, which bound them then and there in deep friendship. Only a common hatred can give friendship such strength. The two kids escaped the patriots' gaze. Riton raised his revolver, and the other boy, who was more nervous, shivered on his legs. Had the patriot made a move against one of the militiamen, the other, that pendant of love, would have risked his life for his friend. When the captain motioned to them, Riton pressed the muzzle of his revolver into the elder patriot's back and said, as he pushed him:

"Get going."

Despite himself he had used the formal form of address. The two handcuffed men went down the stairs of the hotel and stepped into a car. Riton was struck by their beauty. The men in the underground had a finer bear-

ing than the militiamen of the same age. Certainly they
were of nobler metal. Coming from me, this is no com-
pliment. I mean by nobility a certain conventional combi-
nation of very beautiful lines, a certain physical and moral
carriage. The noblest metal is that which goes through the
fire most often: steel. One cannot regret that they were
not on the German side, for the Germans were all the
more handsome for having handsome enemies. Out of a
sort of sadistic refinement I would have liked the men
of the underground to fight for evil. Those whom I saw
were good-looking and too brave. In their presence neither
Riton nor his pal lost anything of his vicious grace, but
they thought of other militiamen who wore glasses, who
were weak, round-shouldered, dirty, fat, or sickly. They
felt the same sadness that I myself did at Santé Prison
when I saw hoodlums who had neither good looks nor
shrewdness, although I had the strength and boldness to
imagine pious church clubs full of splendid fellows in
which, however, the outlaw element was represented by
the handsomest boys. The militiamen copied the youth
of the Reich, and the patriots had the advantage of
originality and its freshness. Although people feared that
everything was ersatz and a mere pretense of serving a
fine cause, splendid youths, drunk with freedom, lived
in the woods. That amazing godsend had been the result of despair. The Resistance sprang up in the under-
brush like a nervous prick in the hair around it. All of
France rose up like that prick. If he were sitting in his
armchair or lying on his couch, the French bourgeois
would have stood up when he heard the *Marseillaise*, but
Riton was standing near a window; if he were wearing a
hat, he would have removed it; but he was bareheaded.
To honor France, with a magnificent gesture of his right
arm he removed from his nose, as one unsheathes one's

sword, his tortoise-shell glasses with thick temples, and held them at his chest until the end of the anthem, which was being played on the hills in the twilight. The *Marseillaise* was emerging from the woods:

"You won't take it with you!"

The young patriot responded thus to a kick from Riton, who was humiliated by all that glamor.

"I'll let you have it in the shins. That'll put your pal in his place!"

As the arrest had taken place in the morning, Riton's entire day was as if bruised by that shame, not that he thought about it or, above all, that he could carefully analyze the reasons why he was sad, but he felt uneasy in his mind. It was not until that evening, when he met Erik on the boulevard, that he felt a bit calmer. Although the Militia was an astounding association of hoodlums, who were almost always cowardly and indulged in looting (for their monthly pay of eight thousand francs could only be called part of the booty), it was also a police force, since it made arrests, and always in accordance with a certain social order, never freely. It could perform its police functions only with excess, with the very excesses that magnified it. Drunk with the thrill of finally being the police, it acted drunkenly. Beneath an appearance of legality and probity, it tried at first to mask its looting and murdering, but the joy of being able to steal without danger made it cynical. However, the militiamen kept their distance from the hoodlums who had remained pure and anarchic to the marrow of their bones. The entire Militia thought it was ready to betray what it served. We shall see that, to a certain degree, it was unable to.

A firing squad was appointed to execute the twenty-eight victims. Thirty-five men. I have referred to the joy that Riton felt when he learned he had been chosen. He

was in the barracks room when the sergeant informed
him and the other fellows in these words:

"You'll be on the firing squad."

Riton turned slightly pale. But he immediately sensed
that all eyes were watching him. Pride lifted him up, it
made him stand erect. His body vibrated at once, even
the curly lock that fell over his eyes. He replied, a bit
more curtly than firmly, "Okay, chief," and stood stock-
still, with a fixed stare.

"Clean your gun. The corporal'll wake you up at three
A.M."

This detail terrified him, but he betrayed no emotion.
He repeated:

"Okay, chief."

The sergeant went off to inform others. Riton's two
bunkmates who had also been chosen went over to him.
They were not pals, but at that moment a kind of complicity was born among them. The three kids displayed
the same casualness of gesture, but their eyes were gleaming. One of them made the first comment:

"Three A.M. What a lousy break! Tomorrow's Sunday."

Riton gave a shrug of his shoulders that meant: "Tough
luck, it's fate."

Just one fellow in the room muttered:

"What a business. . . ."

But his voice was quickly drowned out:

"So what, it's our job."

"It's what we're here for."

"That's what we're paid for."

A voice said:

"That's not the point. After all, they're thugs."

"So what? Who the hell cares!"

He dared not say "All the better," but they were all
willing to see that job as the extreme activity for which

they had come together. It was the climax of their life as militiamen, the act that wholly fulfilled them, since it made them then and there, without danger, murderers, traitors, and cops. To have killed bourgeois would doubtless have charmed them, since it meant killing in order to be a tough. They would have known the pleasure of revenge, but perhaps with a certain horror of that mass murder which was of no use to them. Yet they felt a need of help. And when they cleaned their rifles, they quickly realized that grim cruelty could do away with the slightest remorse, with the greatest shortcomings.

A thought:

"Are they going to get it in the belly or the ass?"

And the snickering that followed made cruelty dawn in the room. A fang, an eye, a snicker, and they immediately realized the advantage it meant.

Someone answered with a laugh:

"You'd rather squirt it up their ass, huh, you bastard?"

"I'm going to aim at the heart."

"Me, between the eyes. The bullet'll bounce off the bone."

They laughed. They were vying in ferocity, wallowing in murder, their legs, thighs, and hands were full of blood.

Looking at his shiny steel weapon, Riton declared:

"It's a fact, when it comes to being fierce we know a thing or two."

And turning to his pals, smiling, but with solemn eyes:

"Am I right, you big bruisers?"

He was filled with intense joy at being the delegate of the willful cruelty of a whole barracks room. A young militiaman, who was on his way out with a pal, said:

"That's not revolutionary."

At the break of day, on Sunday, July 17, the whole prison was awakened by a salvo and seven finishing shots. Three others were heard. Dawn was being greeted. Twenty-eight youngsters collapsed in their blood at the foot of the outer wall. In the cell where he was alone, Pierrot thus received confirmation of his glory. He instinctively assumed the supplest moral attitude, which enables one to absorb hard blows.

"Don't tighten up."

"Mustn't tighten up."

Despite him, his mask assumed a tragic character: his eyes stared in the dawn, his mouth opened, his lips contracted around an O, but he quickly loosened his face a little by shaking his head, running his tongue over his lips, yawning, stretching.

"Got to be natural. The situation is so natural. And besides, that means they weren't meant to live after twenty. That kind of zeal requires a will whose source can be found only in love, in passion. But if I display such passion in discarding good, it's because I'm passionately attached to it. And if evil arouses such passion, it's because it itself is a good, since one can love only what is good, that is, alive.

"And, after all, that means you were meant to live only until twenty. Jean, I'm talking to you because you can understand me. We mustn't get worked up, either of us, that wouldn't get us anywhere. Let's remain calm. You've got to make the best of it. . . ."

Thinking them was not enough. These words, if they remained ideal, would have still been too noble. I had to utter them. With my elbows on the coffin and my feet and legs against the flowers, I was bent over his face. In the presence of the flowers I got a hard-on, and it made me feel ashamed, but I felt that I could oppose the stiffness of the corpse only with the stiffness of my prick. I had a hard-on and desired nobody. I replied to myself: "It's fatigue."

The death of Jean D. reveals to me the meaning of the great funerals that nations grant their heroes. The grief of a people that has lost the man who had captured its attention makes it indulge in the strangest fancies: flags at half-staff, speeches, radio programs, streets named after him. By that funeral Jean's family knew display, princely pomp, and the mother was ennobled by the escutcheon on which a capital D was embroidered in silver. With my eyes closed, I heard in the silence the echo—the prolongation rather—of a wail or a very faraway call, which was being uttered within me but which had the overtones of the long-drawn-out calls of farmers' wives on the heath, calls that are heard on a late afternoon in autumn behind a thornbush, near a swamp, by the little girl who has lingered with her geese and who goes to get her afternoon snack. It was a similar cry that I heard, and in its physical unreality and human reality it seemed to me to be related to the images which escape from the pupil of the eye when one is greatly fatigued and which engender a spectacle that is truly fantastic. Jean was rotting among the roses, but he seemed to understand the situation very well. The very silence of his pale, narrow face was intelligent. He visibly knew that the cries and tears would plunge me into great tragic eddies, into workings of the mind from which I would be unable to extricate myself. I would founder. And his attitude was advising me to be careful, not to give too much credit to the drama. Fortunately, certain thoughts are not uttered aloud, and when they are not formulated in your depths by very precise words, the cruelty of those thoughts is frightful. How many deaths I have desired! I keep within me a charnel house for which poetry may be responsible. How many devoured hearts, stabbed and slit throats, opened chests, how many lies, poisoned weapons, kisses! I am surprised by the daylight, surprised by my cruel and ridiculous game. I am told that the German officer who was in charge of the Oradour butchery had a mild, rather likeable face. He did what he could—a great deal—for poetry. He deserved well of it. My deaths rarely dare express my cruelty. I love and respect that officer. Jean was listening to me:

". . . You're twenty, and that's not bad. You couldn't, believe me (I softened my voice even more to avoid the somewhat declamatory tone of repetition), you couldn't live past twenty. As for me, I'm going to go on. They'll arrange things for you, they'll enclose you, you'll have a nice grave. . . ."

Despite my efforts, my face remained drawn. I would have liked to smile a little, but I couldn't. None the less, that conversation in a familiar, slightly silly tone, did a great deal toward calming my suffering. If it had been caused by the disappearance of Jean's friendship, when I think I am experiencing this suffering, should the cause of my friendship, which I almost said was impaired, rather be said to have been revealed and exalted by this death? I have gradually been able to grow accustomed to the strength and comforting inner warmth of that friendship, and do I perhaps feel that pain because I no longer receive its rays? Was my extreme sensitivity able to perceive that an astral body had died? What means have I of knowing whether it was the birth into the light of my friendship for him or the death into the light of his for me? I would like to indulge in words as little as possible, but I let myself think that that friendship perhaps fed on the mad, violent, consuming love (fed friendship . . . consuming love) I felt for Jean years ago. My present feeling can be measured only by the violence of my pain as I record my friendship (and its strength) at the very moment when the one for whom I feel it escapes (exactly the right word) me, and I truly think that in the past my love caused me the same pains when I felt that Jean was out of sight or far away because his heart was indifferent. The adventure of Jean's death became natural. The porter of the amphitheater came up to me, put his hand on my shoulder, and said, "You mustn't stay, sir. You've been here a quarter of an hour. Be reasonable."

I said all right, without looking at him. He released my shoulder and added: "It's warm. They'll take him down to the refrigerator."

I bent over the forehead that was already beginning to turn green, I kissed it, and, still bent over it, I murmured:

"Yes, you'll be more comfortable in the refrigerator. Come now, be patient a bit longer. Good-by, my dear."

No doubt, I said to myself, the refrigerator is a very clean, hygienic invention, and since Jean's body is now only a corpse, it's good that it'll be preserved there. However, he'll fulfill his dead man's destiny when his grave is filled. He therefore should be buried as soon as possible.

After leaving the amphitheater, I tried hard to maintain within me the tone of my conversation with Jean, but though I managed a few reasonable reflections I felt the fragile crust being threatened by the surge of a terrible muffled grief that was rumbling in the profoundest depths of my misery and that awaited only a lapse of my attention to burst into sobs and despair. Nobody, nothing would prevent the fête's taking place that evening, the delicate and private feast at which I would sit down alone *around* the corpse. The back room of a store would do. Mirrors, gilding, stucco, became unnecessary. The sacrifices most acceptable to God are offered up on a makeshift altar. I will, without respect, undo the blood-stained white cloth on the body lying on the pinewood table. First a sheet, then a long white linen shirt. Body and cloth were frozen. They had just come out of the refrigerator. There were three holes in the chest. I did not recognize the body. I took the stiff arms out of the sleeves. I removed the pins at the bottom of the shirt which made a bag of it. Jean's bare feet, legs, thighs, and belly appeared, frozen. What bread the feast brings me! In my memory, his prick, which used to discharge so calmly, assumes the proportions and at times the serene appearance of a flowering apple tree in April. Even when eating one's friends, one has to cook them, prepare the fire, the pots. It was a long time before I sat down to table with a fork, like Riton with the cat. And now you are only that thorny branch which tears my gaze. What could I do to the holly that you have become for a day? In the past, I would have stroked your delicate cheeks with it until they bled. Its points would have caught in your skin and hair, they would have ripped your breath and perhaps the holly would have clung to it. Today I dare not touch you. Your very immobility claws the void. Those stiff, glazed leaves are the color of spitefulness. I must put on my gloves to place you in the garbage can. For you were also, for a few minutes, a garbage can on the edge of a sidewalk, full of a heap of rubbish, broken bottles, eggshells, wet bread crusts, wine, combings of hair, bones in evidence of the feasting on the upper floors, leek tops. On the edge of it, down to the foot of the garbage can that stood in the spilled ashes, flowed a violent disorder of withered chrysanthemums, one of which, spotting, ripping, wounding the side of that privileged garbage can, adorned it with a sumptuous order. With my pious hands, I spread my tenderness and veneration, letting them come to rest rather than setting them

down, like the veil of a blonde or a brunette, and, lest
the wind blow them away, with the delicate and fluttering
gestures of the wardrobe mistress of a star I kept them in
place with wreaths of flowers and laurel. I placed my foot
and some huge blocks of stone, that had come running
when I called, on the torn ends of these veils. The ash can,
thus decked out, had the charm of living-room chandeliers
that are protected against flies by a sheet of muslin knotted
at the bottom, or of a face behind a veil, of a sick prick
wrapped in lint bandages, of a bread crust under cobwebs
and dust. Yet it was not without danger that I introduced
such an emotional charge into that metal can which my
fervor transformed into an infernal machine. It exploded.
The most beautiful pyrotechnical sun, developed by the
soul of Jean, scattered a spray of glass, hair, stumps, peels,
feathers, gnawed cutlets, faded flowers, and delicate eggshells. And yet in the twinkling of an eye everything was
in earthly order, except that I was left in that kind of
depression that follows the act of love, a great sadness,
and I felt as if I were an alien in my own country. I am
coming out of a dream that I cannot relate. A dream
cannot be set down. It flows, and each of its images is
constantly transformed since it exists in time and not in
space. Then, oblivion, confusion. . . . But what I can tell
is the impression it made on me. When I awoke, I knew
I was emerging from a dream in which I had done evil
(I don't know by what act: murder, theft?) but I had
done evil and I had the feeling that I knew the depths of
life. Somewhat as if the world had a surface on which we
slide (the good) and a thickness into which one sinks
only rarely, more rarely than one thinks (I note at once
that the dream was about a stay in jail). I think that this
rejection of the world by the world can produce humility
or pride, can oblige one to seek new rules of conduct, that

this new universe enables one to see *the other world*. It would be hard to explain why the funeral procession of all the kings of the earth went through the yard of that prison. Yet this is no time for being imprecise. Actually, each king, each queen, each royal prince, all of whom were wearing trailing court cloaks of black velvet and closed gold crowns and most of whom were veiled with crape, were in mourning for all the other kings. Almost all the kings in the world—which means those of Europe —had already passed by her when the maid saw a gilded carriage drawn by white horses draped in black coming toward her. A queen was in it, with a scepter in her hand and her hand on her lap. She was dead. Another queen, whose face was veiled, was following on foot. They could not be recognized. One could tell they were kings, queens, and princes by their crowns and the somewhat shy stiffness of their gait. Despite the dignity and forced remoteness that life requires of them, these monarchs seemed very close to the maid, who watched them file by. She was astonished but was no more afraid or wonderstruck than if she had been watching a flock of geese led by a gander. The procession really gave an impression of wealth. There was a profusion of mourning jewels, though there was not a flower or any foliage, except what was embroidered in silver on black. The Queen of Spain, who could be recognized by her fan, wept abundantly. The King of Rumania was skinny, almost fleshless, and white. All the German princes were following him. And each member of the procession was alone, captured in a block of solitude from which he could see nothing but himself and the exceptional splendor, not of a destiny, but of the trail of the destiny that he continued. Their solitude and indifference made it possible for the maid to be *mistress of herself* in the presence of those lofty personages.

She watched them the way her employer stood on her balcony and watched marriage processions go by on Saturdays.

I am suddenly alone because the sky is blue, the trees green, the street quiet, and because a dog, who is as alone as I am, is walking in front of me. I am moving slowly but with a firm step. I think it is nighttime. The landscapes I discover, the houses with advertisements on them, the posters, the shopwindows I pass as a sovereign, are of the same stuff as the characters of this book, of the visions I discover when my mouth and tongue are occupied in the hairs of a bronze eye, visions in which I think I recognize a recurrence of my childhood love of tunnels. I bugger the world.

. . . . . . . . . . . . . . . . . . . . . . . . . . . . . . . . . . . . . . . . . . . . . . . . . . . . .

When it came to the second murder, Riton was calmer. He thought he was getting used to it, whereas they had just done the greatest harm. He was already dead to pain and quite simply dead, since he had just killed his own image.

. . . . . . . . . . . . . . . . . . . . . . . . . . . . . . . . . . . . . . . . . . . . . . . . . . . . .

Before being assigned to Paris, Erik spent several weeks in a château in Loiret which he occupied with five men from his battery. They were five young Germans. The grounds were always closed. Nobody looked after them. The soldiers took their midday and evening meals at the mess hall in town, which was a half-mile away. They ate and then returned to the château where an observation post had been established. All the disorder in that life, which could have been quiet, in the heart of an estate

in France, was brought about by Erik, the handsomest
and boldest of the five, a kind of delegate of Evil among
us. The château slept during the day and came alive at
night. The relations of the five young men became strange.
They went in and out of the drawing rooms, library,
attic, and up and down the stairs in accordance with a
mechanism of love, formalities, and hatreds that were
even more complicated than that which governs, binds,
and unbinds palaces. Their youth, beauty, solitude, night
life, and the strictness of their laws, being active, charged
the château with a violence that succeeded in making
people think it was damned. At one of the windows, the
noblest, floated the red banner with the swastika. The
photo of Hitler was pasted on a mirror in the main drawing room. The one of Goering, on the opposite wall,
stared at it. That double presence interfered with the
love affairs and exasperated them. When the soldiers
went out in the evening with their friends in the town,
they got drunk, and when they returned to the château,
the mirrors in the entrance hall reflected sparkling images
of warriors lit up by wine. The first evening, Erik, drunk
with wine, drunk with being in his own presence, looked
at himself in the hall with curiosity. The seven bulbs of
the chandelier and the four wall lights were lit. Erik, black
beneath his hair and his tank driver's uniform, was standing, alone and stiff, in a fire of live coals that was the
center of the night. He stepped back a little. His image
in the mirror moved away from him. He put out his
arm to draw it to him, but his hand encountered nothing.
He felt, despite his drunkenness, that he had only to
move forward to make his reverse image come to him, but
he also felt that, being only an image, it had to obey his
wishes. He became impatient. His red face in the mirror
became tragic and so handsome that Erik doubted that it

was his own. At the same time, he demanded that he
master such a male, one which was that strong, that
solid. He was dead set on doing so and took a step back.
The image stepped back. A hoarse, inarticulate cry of
rage took shape in his throat and reverberated in the corridors and empty drawing rooms. The beast in the mirror tossed its head, the forage cap fell off, and the
blond curls scattered over the face, the lower jaw of
which became slack. Erik trembled. With drunkenness
helping him founder, he was within an ace of losing his
reason in his own beauty. Mechanically, that is, in a way
that was surer and more skillful than if it had been apparently deliberate, he took a firm stand, with one leg
tensed and itself tensing the black cloth of the trousers,
his left hand pushing back the locks of hair over the
left temple, and his right hand, leaning, resting, on the
yellow leather holster. The gesture begun by Erik was
continued by the image with set eyes. Its left hand
opened the holster and took out the revolver, aimed it
at Erik, and fired. A burst of laughter burst with the shot.
It came from the five others who were returning. A salvo
resounded. All five shot at their images. The same orgy
was repeated every evening, but whereas they aimed at
the heart, Erik fired at his sex and sometimes at that of
the others. Before long, all the mirrors in the foyer,
drawing rooms, and bedrooms were pitted with rimy
stars. Killing a man is the symbol of Evil. Killing without
anything's compensating for that loss of life is Evil,
absolute Evil. I rarely use the word absolute because it
frightens me, but it seems imperative here. Now, as meta-
physicians will tell you, absolutes cannot be added to
each other. Once the absolute has been attained as a
result of murder—which is its symbol—Evil makes all
other bad acts morally useless. A thousand corpses or

only one, there's no difference. It is the state of mortal
sin from which one cannot be saved. One can line up the
bodies if one's nerves are strong enough, but the repetition will calm them. One can then say that the sensibility
is blunted, as it is whenever an act is repeated, except
in the act of creating. For the last time the thirty-five
militiamen lowered their rifles and stood with arms at
rest. They were in groups of five, each group ten feet
away from the next, facing the twenty-three-foot wall.
Seven groups commanded by only a lieutenant. A sergeant fired the coup de grâce. The prison assistants carried off a first batch of seven corpses. On the same spot,
on the blood of the first, the next seven were set up and
awaited their turn, astounded by the game at the wall
so early in the morning. Astounded by the white label at
heart level. Their faces remained surprised. They were
taken away. Seven others came up, standing, shivering
with cold, anxious about the result. Fire! . . . They died.
Finally, the last seven. The thirty-five men of the firing
squad were pale. They tried to march away, and their
wobbly legs could hardly support them. Several were
haggard, and none of them would ever in his life forget
the eyes or periwinkle faces of the twenty-eight murdered
men. If they were still on their feet, it was because of the
block they formed. When they reached the circular drive
each was given half a glass of rum. They swallowed it
in silence. The rum wasn't theirs but that of the condemned men, and they felt that all the importance of the
adventure was being taken away from them for the benefit of the twenty-eight innocents. The main door of the
prison was open. The chief ordered:

"Attention!"

The militiamen brought their heels together and drew
themselves up. The immobility unsettled their eyes and

minds even more. On a boat rushing to the abyss they were being made to perform so stupid a gesture as polishing their shoes or saluting a corporal.

"Forward, march!"

A sunbeam gilded the top of the wall. And the militiamen entering that Sunday whose threshold led out to death went through the doorway. They were given the day off. They went into town, stern in body and gaze, just as I am now.

Pimps offer me a very fine example of sternness. I want to retain that apparent vigor of bearing, not that I am afraid, as they are, of being drawn into nonchalance, of succumbing to it, but because that attitude appeals to me aesthetically, it seems to me beautiful, even if it contains a wily, suppler, more sinuous moment or some very soft magma to which it gives form. Impelled by a single—aesthetic—motive I vainly provoke the erection of a tough, handsome being, although writing often embarrasses me. Writing and, before writing, taking possession of that state of grace which is a kind of levity, of detachment from the ground, from what is firm, from what is generally called reality—writing involves me in a kind of bizarreness of attitude, of gesture, and even of language. Thieving—and even living among thieves—requires a flesh-and-blood presence, a positive mental presence which manifests itself by gestures that are brief, deliberate, sober, necessary, practical. If I displayed that flightiness among thieves, that waiting for the angel and the gestures that summon him and try to win him over, I would no longer be taken seriously. If I submit to their gestures, to their precise speech, I shall stop writing, I shall lose the grace that has enabled me to seek news from heaven. I must choose or alternate. Or be silent.

. . . . . . . . . . . . . . . . . . . . . . . . . . . . . . . . . . . . . . .

Riton went out alone. He wandered from one café to another, drinking a few glasses of dark beer, as one does in Germany. An uneasiness as delicate and fragile as a myosotis blossom—though quite perceptible—had flowered within him. He was carrying the sprouted sorrow of that morning's act. He finally felt calm toward evening, in the subway, leaning against Erik's warm belly. When they got to the street, the tank driver drew the kid to him with one arm, kissed him on an eye (thereby scraping his mouth on the edge of the tilted beret) and disappeared into the night. A terrible emptiness filled Riton, who returned to the barracks, alone with his solitude in the midst of himself.

"Maybe it's the cat that made me like that," he thought to himself.

He heard a murmuring at his ear, in the darkness:

"You're a dead man."

And it was the very same anguish that was about to come down on me, to make me give up, when, at night, I chanced upon riderless horses browsing on the frozen grass of the ditch. What soldiers could have abandoned them there, what lovers? No doubt to wander about near an old monastery at the edge of a torrent, I had assumed the form of Erik, his grim face, and I camouflaged myself in the mist that always emanates from a gloomy hero. I felt protected by the fabulous power of the Reich. Nevertheless, I was aware of the sharp, luminous presence within me of Jean Genet, mad with fear. But perhaps I had never been so aware of myself as at such moments. When I kept Jean clinging by the teeth to the muzzle of my revolver, fear also shrank my center of consciousness by making it more acute. The fear of firing was combating the fear of not firing. Jean was living his last seconds more than I. Anyway, Riton's peace was definitely restored one morning, ten days later, when he was called to the guardroom. Someone wanted to see him right away. It was a civilian.

"Oh! Paulo!"

They embraced each other like two brothers, two children. They immediately moved away from the men on duty and spoke in low voices.

"You're out?"

"Yes, how're things going? Anything cooking?"

"Me? Nothing."

Riton thought that Paulo didn't know about Erik. And suddenly he asked:

"You talk German?"

"No, why?"

"Nothing."

Paulo shrugged.

"Things got you down, huh?"

I know the answer. I miss neither Mettray, which was at the time as frightful to me as the camp to Paulo, nor the state prison. Those years of unhappiness carpet the depths of our memory with a kind of moss and shadow into which I sometimes let myself sink, where I feel I can find a refuge when life gets rough, but innumerable confused desires also arise out of those disrupted depths, desires which, if one knows how to go about it, can be formulated so as to compose a group of movements which will make one's life beautiful and violent. I venture an image. Those years deposit within us a mud in which bubbles form. Each bubble, which is inhabited by an individual will to *be*, develops and changes, alone and in accordance with the other bubbles, and becomes part of an iridescent, violent whole that manifests a will issuing from that mud. In my fatigue between waking and sleeping, between pain and what combats it (a kind of will to peace, I think), I am visited by all the characters

of whom I have spoken and others too who are not clear
to me. They seem to emerge from limbo, that is, from a
region where bodies are imperfect, misshapen, somewhat
plastic, like clay figures in the hands of children . . . "to
emerge from limbo." It's worse, they have just emerged
from one of those chapels that surmount burial vaults in
cemeteries. I am not asleep. I know that they are informed of Jean's doings out there, in his death. They live
in the tomb to which they return.

*
* *

Let us continue the account of the events on the rooftops. Anxiety prevented the sergeant from sleeping. He
got up during the night and made the rounds of the
apartment. In the bedroom, the three soldiers were
sleeping on the bed in a tangle that the most indulgent of
men would have regarded as scandalous, but it was
fatigue alone that thus entangled the soldiers at the edge
of the grave. He entered the dining room, carefully direct-
ing the beam of his flashlight. At his feet he saw the sight
I have depicted. Riton was sleeping with his arm out and
his hand almost entirely buried in the trousers of the
sleeping Erik.

At daybreak, when they were awakened, caution
obliged the soldiers to remain sitting where they were
lest their walking make a sound that would worry the
tenants on the floor below. Nevertheless, they would have
liked to explore the conquered rooms that were still warm
with the life of the occupants who had fled. Apartments
offer themselves to the burglar with painful immodesty.
Without looking for them, we find the very personal
habits of the bourgeois, and I can say for a fact that I have
opened drawers in which there were underpants with

shit stains, and hard, dried, crumpled socks that emitted their sad fragrance when spread out. I have even found abandoned fragments of shit in the drawers of elegant commodes. For a long time I thought that women are the dirtier, but actually men are. As for the imagination of both, it's on a par with that of the police. If they have hidden the hundred francs in a fold of the window curtain, under a pile of sheets, or behind a frame, their mind is at rest. At rest, except for the mortal anxiety that is the very stuff of their life when they are more than fifty feet away from the hoard. But who am I to talk, since I piss in the sink, I forget turds that I leave in old newspapers in the wardrobes of hotel rooms, and I don't have the guts to leave my money in my room for an hour. I walk with it, I steal with it, I sleep with it.

The soldiers did not wash themselves. Nothing came out of the taps. The lack of water made them panicky. There was hardly any left in their canteens. The sergeant allowed them to talk in an undertone, for the noises of day drowned out their murmuring. Their blond hair was in their eyes, and at the corner of their eyelids were bits of white mucus. It was a miserable awakening. The apartment seemed the domain of death to the soldiers. It was as disturbing to be there as in certain regions where the land is mined, where snakes bulge their delicate throats, where rose-laurels grow. We were afraid. Not of the danger but of the accumulation of fateful signs. At each window the sergeant posted a man who could fire on the insurgents. Then he divided the day's food into eight equal parts. Although he did not want to talk about it, he twice made smiling remarks about Riton to Erik, which showed that he knew what had happened. Erik smiled and, in the presence of his joking comrades, admitted the night's adventure. There was no scandal.

They laughed a little and were silently amused as they looked at the kid whose beauty was suddenly revealed to them. He was squatting on the bed and eating bread with chocolate. Riton bit into the chocolate and took a canteen in order to drink, but Erik snatched it from his hands. The child's astonished eyes looked into his. Erik murmured with a gentle laugh as he handed the canteen back to him without having drunk:

"I'm German."

Riton smiled back. Erik pointed a finger at him:

"You're French," and he laughed a little more loudly.

And I can understand polygamy when I realize how quickly the charms of a boy-girl are exhausted and how much more slowly those of a boy-male disappear. Erik tried to act as if he were joking about that pretension, but the fact that it was already stated, even though in an ironic tone, indicated sufficiently that it was at the basis of his relations with Riton. The pride which he sensed, instead of saddening Riton, afforded him a kind of repose. Five Germans were in the room. Erik was standing behind the bed. His comment distracted the attention of the soldiers, who spoke about something else, but a soldier smilingly stroked Riton's tousled hair as he walked by him. The kid was filled with surprise and then anxiety. He tossed his head to shake off the hand, but he didn't dare make a gesture or scowl, not even frown. And immediately he realized, from the soldiers' looks and laughter, that they knew. He thought they were mocking contemptuously. He blushed. Not having been able to wash, his face shined and the blush seemed sparkling, then warm. One of the soldiers saw him in the mirror, and, without showing the kid that he had noticed the blush, revealed it smilingly to Erik, who gently went up behind Riton, took him by the neck, pulled him back a little, and kissed him very sweetly on the hair, in the presence of his comrades and the sergeant. Nobody commented on the gesture, which was natural and charming. Riton smiled, for, though he pretended not to care, he was so in love with Erik, whose sovereign person had just compelled everyone's recognition by that quiet kiss, that he was willing to announce his marriage.

Then Riton suddenly felt he was falling over a precipice. Did Erik really love him? He would have liked to tell him that at the hour of their death in each other's arms, the most human thing was to grant each other the greatest happiness. But that was hard to say. He did not know German. He felt like crying. For a moment they all looked at one another gravely, in silence. The soldiers who had been posted at the half-open windows with instructions to shoot were lying flat on their stomachs on the rug so as not to be seen from the houses opposite. When they assumed that position, the sun was hardly up. The light was gray, though the weather promised to be fine. They saw nothing on the boulevard, which was slightly blurred by a light mist. They were watching listlessly. Erik cleaned his revolver and Riton his machine gun. The others dozed off. An hour later, the sun had driven off the mist, and when Riton went to the window, behind a tulle curtain with lace designs, after a moment of amazement the strangest emotion took hold of his mind and body, twisted him, and left him in tatters. He did not cry. The whole boulevard was decked with two rows of French flags. He solemnly bade France farewell. The flags were out for his treason. He was being thrown out of his country, and upon awakening, every Frenchman waved at his window the flag of freedom regained, of purity recaptured. He was going to the realm of the dead that day, and it was a fête on earth, in the sun, in the blue air. He was in the realm of the dead. He did not cry. But he realized that he loved his country. Just as it was on the day Jean died that I knew I loved him, so it was on losing France that he knew he loved her. The English and American flags were at the windows along with the French. A tri-colored shit and spew was dripping from everywhere. Riton realized the meaning of the house's silent activity. All night long the whole city had been spinning yards of red, white, and blue cotton fabric. And that morning, the *Marseillaise*, weary of flying over Paris, had dropped to the streets, torn and exhausted. That miracle had taken place on the day of his death. For a second Riton thought he could still go down the stairs without the Boches' knowing it (the Boches—the word clearly shows that grief invents a whole symbolism whereby one hopes to act mystically: I hesitated to write the word Boche with a capital B, out of contempt, in order to make it a *common* noun—the Boches and the Militiamen killed Jean, whom I revere, and as I see it this is the finest story of Boche and Militiaman, which I offer up to his memory. Erik has my favor). Or spring from the balcony to the street. He would not hurt himself, for this was the day when to wish for a miracle sufficed for it to take place. The Fritzes would no doubt shoot, and he then thought very seriously of running the risk of death from a German bullet. A feeling of purification, of redemption, was involved in the idea, bringing to his eyelids a tear that did not flow. He had betrayed France, but he would be dying for her. He very nearly performed a heroic act, a tailspin among the three colors.

"What the hell do I care about France? They're all jerks. Fuck 'em all on foot and on horseback."

He was bound to think that. But he was still too young for his face to remain serene, and the corners of his puffy little mouth drooped painfully at the thought of what France was doing to him, at the thought of the joy he was losing, and also because, despite its force, the bitterness of losing the things of the world always accompanies the gravest joy of marvelous expeditions in forbidden lands. He made a face. It did not occur to him that he had gambled and lost and that he was paying. What he felt was not comparable to the pain caused by turning up the wrong card. It was due mainly to the decision taken by France, his friends, his family: to expel him from joy, from play, from pleasures, and to display the flags in honor of that exile. His mouth was still pasty after the bread and chocolate. It was dark in the room where the Germans were sleeping. He was not combed. Hairs from combs and brushes were strewn all over the bedroom. An untidy soldier whose belt was unbuckled and whose shirt was half out of his trousers, playing the role of a bare-headed girl getting out of bed, went from the bedroom to the living room. Riton sniffled. A drop of snot had just started dripping from his nose. He would never again wash his face. He tried to clean the corner of his somewhat rheumy eyes with his fingernail. A slight breeze stirred all the flags.

> *It's bright and gay!*
> *Good morning, swallows, it's bright and gay!*

He whistled a measure of the tune between his teeth. The first car that passed in the street was white and had a red cross on the roof. There were more wounded Frenchmen. He had fired. A slight pride at the thought of it cheered him. He had killed young men on the bar-

ricades. He had wounded others with the machine gun.
With Mademoiselle. Girls were looking after the wounded,
were kissing them. France would make speeches. France.
France, France, forever. He had Erik. Then and there
that love did not fill him enough. There was a place for
regret in him. The Germans suddenly—for a great sorrow
gives you extraordinary lucidity, things which do not go
together dovetail, and others that appeared to be decked
in splendid cloths look scraggy in their bony nakedness
—the Germans seemed to him to be what they were:
monsters. It was not because they shot Frenchmen. Riton
did not regret those they had killed. He regretted not
being able to be near those who sniveled for them. The
Germans did their job. Everything about them was monstrous, that is, was opposed to the joy of the French. The
Germans were dismal, black, but the others were green.
In that room they had the gravity of people whose destiny
is only pain. Riton was not good at thinking, nevertheless
he ventured the following reflection to himself:

"Who are my pals now, my com-rades? It's them, it
ain't my Paris pals. I'm washed up, and that's no shit,
I'm washed up, Riton my boy."

The soldiers were snoring. A subterranean soul animated that exceptional tomb which had been raised to
the top of a giant building from which Riton, his heart
overflowing with peace, could watch the naive joy of the
inhabitants of the earth. He stood stock-still, his face
still ravaged. His grief lasted five to six minutes, long
enough to prepare him for what follows. He squatted
with his back to the window and looked at the loose-leaf
calendar on the wall, the block calendar that showed
August 15, Assumption Day, and he loosened his belt a
bit. The sergeant was rereading his letters. Erik was
gazing sadly at his harmonica, he was waiting for a

screaming of sirens to be able to play a little, if only in a muted tone. Three shots shook the apartment. The soldier in the bedroom had fired at some fellows crossing the boulevard. The question of shooting had been discussed. They had decided to fire only when it was essential so as to husband ammunition, and particularly so as not to give away their hideout. The house was certainly not abandoned. They were to shoot mainly to help German comrades who were grappling in the street with insurgents. The sergeant seemed frightened by the sniper's firing. They no doubt had a plan of escape over the rooftops, but they could not have gone very far since the block of houses was only a steep rock cut out among four streets. If they were found, it was sure death. After the shots the silence became crueler. Anxiety made its way into the apartment in the form of signs revealed by the objects. It seemed impossible that a radio would be there or that the frame of a photo would be turned or that a spot on the wall would be visible if they were not to die that day, if they were not to be blasted. The seven males and the kid, who were all tired from the struggle, which had lasted perhaps a quarter of an hour, were caught in the pose in which the burst of gunfire had stopped them. An anguish had been floating in the apartment since morning, an anguish so painful that it made the air in the rooms and the look of the faces almost black. Every angle, every sharp point of a motionless gesture, a badly wrinkled fold of cloth, a hole, a finger, instantly emitted distress signals. They were extremely nervous. The anguish with which the rooms were mined increased a hundredfold in two seconds. The sergeant muttered reproaches to the sniper, who answered in a scarcely higher tone with another mutter whose meaning was conveyed chiefly by the lips. The sergeant mastered his desire to scream an order, but the impossibility of expressing his rage exasperated him. He made the unfortunate gesture of pushing the soldier away from his weapon and giving it to a comrade whom he posted in his place. The sniper's little mug, buffeted by locks of hair, contracted, the look on his face hardened. Under constraint, the anger grew. This rapid and necessarily silent scene was prolonged as the men waited anxiously. The soldier had half sprung up, with one knee barely touching the floor and his hands empty, one of them hanging at his side, the other clutching his hair, but quivering with an uncompleted movement, somewhat like that of the runner set to go waiting impatiently to continue—and already continuing by the quivering of his body—with a run or a leap. Anger contorted his mouth, turned his face pale, the accompanying hatred brought his knitted eyebrows together into a mass of darkness from which lightning flashed at regular intervals to strike the sergeant and destroy Germany. Cowed by the necessity of being submissive even at such a moment, the soldier remained in that position, stupefied and motionless. But anxiety had made its way into the apartment. Sitting at the foot of the bed, on the edge, Erik, without realizing it, kept his dry lips on the bee's nest of his harmonica. He didn't give a damn. They waited. The sergeant, who, after his short-tempered gesture, had remained still for a moment, hesitated a second and went into the living room. As he walked out, his body discovered Riton, who was crouching, gaping, as the sniper stared at him. It was nighttime. Unless it was continually day. I even think there was neither night nor day at the top of the tall building. In broad daylight they were sometimes in utter darkness, that is, every moment revealed a nighttime activity. They went through space so gently, the movement of the Earth was so slow, that the soldiers' gestures were all gentleness. A body was asleep with its head on a heap of rope. Or a boy was whispering. A boy was dreaming. The maneuver was muted. Riton got up. Suddenly he was concerned with what day it was. He went to the wall to tear off the pages of the calendar. This gesture drew him out of the tragic a little and then put him back into it more deeply.

"It's ass-headed, but I've got to see what day it is."

As he stood up, his trousers, which had no belt loops, slid completely out from under the belt, and the shirt bunched up against his chest and back. He was hardly aware of it, yet he made the gesture of pulling up his pants with his hand. In order to go to the wall, he had to push aside or disturb the sniper, who had not moved and whose eyes, which had been hostile since the sergeant had left the room, weighed on Riton. When the kid neared him, the soldier, on seeing the sloppiness of his attire, finally found an excuse for releasing his anger. He roughly grabbed the belt and pulled the kid, whose torso was delicate despite its hardness. It was also flexible, and it bent back, as if to regain its balance, or to escape, but the soldier prevented it by putting his left hand even more angrily around his waist. Riton thought he was being playful and, though he had seldom fooled around with that soldier, supported himself with both hands on the curly head which the swiftness of the whole rather brusque movement had knocked against him. Now, the soldier, despite his anger, was unable, on feeling the irony, to keep from being (in, to be sure, a very imprecise way) under the charm of the noblest posture of respect and faith. A kind of confusion ruffled his soul and made him slightly dizzy. The child, who saw in the mirror over the fireplace that Erik was watching him from behind, tried to get away. The soldier felt it and tightened his embrace, and Riton, clutching the Fritz's hair, pressed the head harder against himself. The forehead rested on his belly, in the space between the belt and the trousers, while the mouth was crushed on the stiff blue cloth of the fly. The significance of the posture was changing. The German seemed to be clinging to the kid by the belt, as to a life-buoy. The wounded male, who was in a rage, was on his knees before a sixteen-year-old Frenchman who seemed to be his protector and to be indulgently crowning his head with two strong clasped hands. Everyone in the room waited in silence. The soldier refused to let go of the kid, holding him firmly with his muscular arms, furious and humiliated at the fact that his face was lost in the shadow of the trousers, whose smell he breathed in with his open mouth. He tried to raise his head, but the buckle of the belt scraped his forehead. Pain made him finally make the gesture toward the performing of which everything was converging, the gesture after which the day was later named: with wild fury, the German, whose arms were tensed and whose torso had suddenly come to life on his thighs, which were buttressed by his rising motion, bent the kid under him. Riton's eyes became those of a hunted animal. He wanted to flee, but he was trapped, and his head banged against the wooden bed. The three other soldiers were silently watching this almost motionless *corps à corps*. Their attention and silence were part of the action itself. They made it perfect by making it public and publicly accepted. Their attention—their presence, at three points in the room—enveloped the action. Two men and a soldier were on guard at the sixth-floor windows of a mined building, which was menaced by a hundred rifles, so that a black pirate could bugger a young traitor at bay. Fear is a kind of element in which gestures are made without their being recognized. It could play the role of the ether. It even lightens acts that are not conditioned by what caused it. It quickens one's knowledge of them. It weighs down and blurs others. This fear that the nest would be spotted, that the house would explode, that they would be drilled, did not seem to preoccupy them. Rather, it made a kind of emptiness inside them, in which there was room only for that extraordinary fact, which was really unexpected at the hour of death. Since they were at the edge of the world, at the top of that rock posted at the outermost point of Finis Terrae, they could watch with their minds at ease, could give themselves utterly to the perfect execution of the act. Since they could view it only in its closed form, which was cut off from the future, it was the ultimate one. After it, nothing else. They had to make it as intense as possible, that is, each of them had to be as acutely conscious of it as he could be so as to concentrate as much life as possible in it. Let their moments be brief, but charged with consciousness. A faint smile played over their lips. Erik's hand, which was lying on the bed, was still holding his harmonica. He was smiling with the same smile as the others. When Riton's head banged against the wooden bed, there was a dull but weak thud, and he uttered a very faint moan of pain. The three witnesses of the struggle, who felt no pity but were very angry with the one who threatened to botch everything, made the same gestures of the arms and silently articulated, opening their mouths wide, the same threats whose meaning the kid understood from the hardness of their features and expressions. Instead of cursing the torturer, their hatred was directed toward the child who was capable of depriving them of the joy of his tortures. Finally sure that the thud would be without danger, the hatred subsided when silence was restored. The subtle smile flowered on their mouths again, but the kid, who had been knocked out by the blow on the chin, from which blood was flowing, was already lying on the bed, with his pants down, his face against the sheets, his body pounded by the husky body of the soldier, who had the self-possession to lay down his burden delicately so as not to make the spring of the mattress groan. There was only the barest creaking. For Riton it had happened. . . . Unable to imagine how far that fury would go, he nevertheless made the movements that might help calm the soldier. The militiaman on the mattress placed his legs, which had been dangling down to the floor, next to Erik, who had remained seated, with his harmonica in his fist. The other soldiers looked on.

"Good thing I cleaned my hole a little."

The sergeant, who was at the door, was also watching. Annoyed at having been too rough with a soldier who was fighting and who would probably die that day, he dared not interfere. Besides, he was under the sway of a feeling that I shall speak about presently. In the silence of the city, which was at times disturbed by the sound of a Red Cross car carrying arms, there entered through the half-open window, from a thin, cracked voice, purer for being cracked—a broken toy—the following song, composed of the tenacity of the weak, which rose up from the pavement and, passing through the foliage of the trees, reached the ear of Riton, to whom the melody seemed radiant:

*They have broken my violin . . .*

Riton, who had been knocked senseless by the Fritz, bit the bolster so as not to scream. The brute stopped and panted a little, letting his cheek rest against the

back of Riton's neck. He snorted. A short rest, a lull in
the fellow's fury, enabled the kid to make out the end
of the stanza, which the fragile voice was repeating:

> *For its soul was French.*
> *It fearlessly made the echoes*
> *Sing the Marseillaise.*

Riton dared not stir. He first wondered anxiously
whether he should clean himself or simply suck the jissom
in. And what could he clean himself with if there was
no water? He could only wipe himself. With his handkerchief. The soldier, whose bearded chin Riton felt on the
back of his neck, gave a shove, which made the kid groan.

> *. . . Sing the Marseillaise . . .*

Erik had not stirred. He had to watch the kid who had
been downed by force get sawed in half.

Riton wanted the rape to be over with, and he feared
the end of it.

Surely they would all take a crack at him. Erik's
presence, which he still felt at the edge of the bed, kept
him from moving his rump to make the soldier come
more quickly.

> *. . . made the echoes . . .*

Finally the warmth of the liquid escaped in slower
and slower throbs, like the blood of a cut artery. The
fellow from the North was discharging into his bronze
eye. . . . When he raised himself up, gently so as not to
make any noise, the soldier was calm. He was smiling.
He remained standing beside the bed for a moment. He

looked defiantly at his smiling cronies, then, slowly, smiling more broadly and tossing back his blond hair with a flick of his head, he adjusted his trousers and little black tank driver's jacket and rebuckled his belt. He said to the soldiers:

"What are you waiting for?"

He looked Erik in the eye. Riton, relieved of the bruiser but still outstretched, had pulled up his pants and tucked in his shirttails. Turning his head, he waited with a feeble smile on his lips. One of the soldiers who was sitting in the armchair was about to follow up, but he changed his mind and, turning to the door, laughingly invited the sergeant to enjoy himself first. The sergeant looked at Erik and signaled to him. Erik whispered a word, and they all went out. Nothing happened. They had to flee by the rooftops.

. . . . . . . . . . . . . . . . . . . . . . . . . . . . . . . . . . . . . . . . . . . . . . . . . . . . . .

The little housemaid left the tomb toward evening and returned on foot by narrow, shadowy roads. She was alone, with a daisy in her hand, and was amazed at being free. She was losing her flesh-colored stockings. She hardly noticed it and did not notice that she still had on her head the wreath of glass pearls with the little pink porcelain angel, who trembled at every step at the end of a brass prong wrapped in green silk thread. She kept the crown on, tilted over her ear like an apache's cap, all the way from the cemetery to her room. A fart that had been rolling in her stomach for some time broke free with such a burst that she thought she had been transformed into a seashell.

"A seashell doesn't have feet," she said to herself. "How am I going to get home?"

She had had no news of Jean for a long time. He
shifted from one underground group to another and no
longer came home. It was she who occasioned my love for
Erik. I had been at the home of Jean's mother for some
minutes, chatting with the Fritz, when I tried to cover up
a yawn.

"Are you hungry?" he asked.

"A little."

He stood up, opened the door, and through the opening I caught sight of Juliette, who was walking through
the other room. She was wearing a gray apron over a
short black dress, so that my whole image of that vision is
gray and sad. Her hair was uncombed, and there were a
few tufts of wool or bits of fluff in it. Had she perhaps just
been cleaning the bedroom? So the most palpable remains
of Jean, his fiancée, were in the likeness of a dirty, unkempt housemaid. What was there about Jean that had
made him love so unlovely a creature? Had he chosen her
out of excessive humility, because he himself was equal
to assuming the beauty of the couple? Erik had pushed
open the door with his foot and then kept it open with
his big arm, so that it was beneath that arch that I saw the
maid go by and disappear. The sadness I felt did not
lessen my love for Jean, but I felt furious with him for
leaving me that girl with the hideous function as memento
of him. I felt abandoned, weary, wretched. Erik called
out:

"What time is it?"

His voice was heavy and hollow. I looked at his face,
which I saw in profile, for his head was turned, and my
anguish latched on to the hard, long muscle that bulged
in his neck. The sight of the maid had just opened my
heart to weariness. My muscles themselves were numbed,
and my mouth and throat were clogged with a wad of

dirty hair. Had I been smoking too much, or was Erik's presence acting thus, by that indirect means, so that I would love the deserter?

Never would I have the strength to bear my love for Jean if I leaned on that wretched girl. On the other hand I could indulge myself completely if I were supported by Erik. My heart had been opened by disgust, and love swept into it. A transport swept me toward the Boche. I clung to him in thought, grafted my body to his, so that his beauty and hardness would give me strength to bear and repress my nausea. I loved Erik. I love him. And as I lay in the Louis XV bed, Jean's soul enveloped the bedroom in which the naked Erik was operating with hard precision. I turned away from Paulo. With my head in the hollow of his legs, my eyes sought the sacred crabs, and then my tongue, which tried to touch that precise and tiny point: a single one of them. My tongue grew sharper, pushed aside the hairs very delicately, and finally, in the bushes, I had the joy of feeling beneath my papillae the slight relief of a crablet. At first, I dared not remove my tongue. I stayed there, careful to keep the joy of my discovery at the top of my tongue and of myself. Finally, having been granted sufficient happiness, I let my head and closed eyes roll into the hollow of the valley. My mouth was filled with tremendous tenderness. The insect had left it there, and the tenderness descended into me by the throat and flowed through my body. My two arms were still encircling Erik, and my hands were gently grazing his back and the root of his buttocks, and I thought I was stroking the hairy slopes of a wondrously large crab, which I would have worshiped. "A louse," I said to myself, "would have transported and fixed my love better. It's bigger, has a more beautiful shape, and, when enlarged a hundred thousand times, its features are

more harmonious." Unfortunately, Jean had not left me
any lice. Then, with my teeth pressing hard on the
muscle of the inner thigh, I tried to mark off a sacred
area, a garden even more precise and precious than the
rest of the forest. My hands, which were in back of Erik,
dug into his buttocks and helped my head, which was
slightly cramped by Erik's belly and cock. I felt in my
mouth the presence of the insect that was the bearer of
Jean's secrets. I felt it getting bigger. I heard a noise. I
turned around. Paulo was entering. His rifle was slung
across his back. We were already friendly enough for him
to shake my hand. He did so casually.

"How goes it?"

"All right, and you?"

"All right."

He said nothing to Erik. He went to the window and
looked into the street without removing his gun, which
intrigued me. Paulo could no doubt have joined the
liberators of Paris, but I could not keep from thinking
that he was tied up with the Germans, and I included him
among the militiamen who, at the beginning of the insurrection, had joined the French Resistance. They fought
at the side of sincere Frenchmen, but within the ranks
they continued their struggle. Though almost all of them
realized that the German card had lost, they kept playing
it on the sly. They sped through Paris and France in cars
that sent out volleys of bullets and were described in
posters on all the walls. I am still amazed at the thought
of that riffraff carrying on an underground struggle on
behalf of a fallen master for whom they never felt any
love. But Paulo seemed, under his dirt, to be fighting for
freedom. Erik had shut the door again. The sight of Paulo
beneath that burden and in that posture, which defined
his avenging activity, made me feel a little ashamed of
loving a Boche. I said:

"The Germans had better behave with Paulo around."

I was smiling, but I felt like being spiteful, and Erik sensed it. He looked at me. He was pale. No doubt my spitefulness was meant mainly to cover up my love. My comment wounded Erik. He said nothing. I added:

"Aren't you scared?"

Paulo had heard the first sentence; he had come in. With his gun over his shoulder, he was leaning on the table with both hands and watching us. I mechanically took a pack of cigarettes out of my pocket. I took one and handed the pack to Erik. He shook his head and said, "No, thanks."

"You want one?" I asked, turning to Paulo.

He moved his hand. His gesture, which was contained in the whole bearing of his body, was about to unfold, to unroll, to emerge from those eyes, from that body, from that arm, and to extend all the way to me. . . .

"Me? Oh, no!"

He shook his head just as Erik had done.

"No, no," he said, "I don't want one."

I put the pack back into my pocket and lit the cigarette that was in my mouth. I was less annoyed at their refusing my offer than at discovering to what degree Paulo secretly loved Erik, since, unwilling to leave him there alone, he was bent on sharing his solitude. I did not think I could declare my love to Erik yet, nor to Paulo either. For he had never made any allusion to my affair with Jean. The maid opened the door and said:

"It's a quarter past twelve."

. . . . . . . . . . . . . . . . . . . . . . . . . . . . . . . . . . . . . . . . . . .

The German soldiers and Riton had gone back to the roof. They felt they were being pursued less by the tenants of the building than by fear. They were fleeing from it. Slowly, in broad daylight, following the least exposed slopes of the roof, they got to a corner formed by three chimneys. The hiding place was narrow. It could hardly contain them, though they squatted together in a kind of cluster from which the notion of the individual disappeared. No thought was born of that armed mass, but rather a somnolence, a dream whose chief and mingled themes were a feeling of dizziness, the act of falling, and nostalgia for the Vaterland. No longer worried about being heard, they spoke aloud. Riton was caught in Erik's legs. They crouched against each other, and they spent the day that way, crushed by the five soldiers who at times overflowed onto the sky. There were potshots all around them, but they could see nothing, not a single patch of street, or a single window of an apartment. The heat was overpowering. Toward evening, the mass of males was loosened by a little elasticity. Numbed limbs came to life again. Erik and Riton awoke. Beneath the shelter of the chimneys, the sergeant divided the remaining food and they ate their last meal. The general idea was to get down under cover of darkness and make their way to the Bois de Vincennes. There was much less shooting. Evening was imposing its calm. There was nothing visible on the rooftops; yet they felt that every windowsill, every balcony, concealed a danger, the side of every chimney was capable of being a soldier's shield and the other side that of his enemy. The sergeant and the men crawled off to explore. Two Germans remained in the hideout with the weapons and water. They were to shoot only in case of emergency. Erik and Riton went around the chimney and sat down at the foot of that cliff, with the machine gun between Riton's legs. Erik was weary. His springy blond beard softened his face, which was hollowed by fatigue. Neither of them spoke.

They were coming out of their tangled sleep. Their eyes were dim, their mouths slack. The visibility was a little better from their observatory and they could see a few housefronts and windows. Opposite them, about two hundred yards away, one of the windows lit up with a faint, shifting light. A man's silhouette stood out in the rectangle. Riton aimed and then fired a burst. The silhouette moved back into the shadow. Erik's firm, imperious hand came down on Riton's.

"Don't."

Riton pulled away impatiently and his nervous finger let loose a second burst.

"Don't," Erik repeated hoarsely in a scolding but low tone.

He was again traversed by rivers of green anger. They were sailing at night, beneath a sky streaked with heat lightning, down a river full of alligators. On the shore where ferns grew, the savage moon-worshipers were dancing around a fire in the forest. The tribe that had been invited to the feast was reveling in the dance and in anticipation of the young body that was cooking in a caldron. It is nice and comforting to me, among the men of a black, disrupted continent whose tribes eat their dead kings, to find myself again with the natives of that country of Erik's so that I can eat the flesh of the tenderest body without danger of remorse, so that I can assimilate it to mine, can take the best morsels from the fat with my fingers, keep them in my mouth, on my tongue, without disgust, feel them in my stomach, and know that their vitals will become the best of myself. The boredom of the preparations was spared me, although the dancing helped the cooking, the digestion, and the efficacy of the virtues of the boiling child. I was dancing, blacker than the blacks, to the sound of the tom-tom, I was making my body supple, I was preparing it to receive the totemic food. I was sure that I was the god. I was God. Sitting alone at the wooden table, I waited for Jean, who was dead and naked, to bring me, on his outstretched arms, his own corpse. I was presiding, with a knife and fork in my hands, over a singular feast at which I was going to consume the privileged flesh. There were no doubt a halo around my head and a nimbus around my whole body: I felt I was shining. The blacks were still playing the bamboo flute and the tom-tom. Finally, Jean appeared from somewhere or other, dead and naked. Walking on his heels, he brought me his corpse, which was cooked to a turn. He laid it out on the table and disappeared. Alone at the table, a divinity whom the negroes dared not gaze at, I sat and ate. I belonged to the tribe. And not in a superficial way by virtue merely of my being born into it, but by the grace of an adoption in which it was granted me to take part in the religious feast. Jean D.'s death thus gave me roots. I finally belong to the France that I cursed and so intensely desired. The beauty of sacrifice for the homeland moves me. Before my eyes smart and my tears flow, it's by my beard that I become aware of the first manifestation of my emotion: a kind of gooseflesh that is made more sensitive by the presence in the epidermis of the rough hairs of my beard, which suddenly gives me the sensation of being a field of reaped rye—of stubble— over which two bare little feet are running. Perhaps my chin trembled like those of sorrowful children. I have my dead who died for her, and the abandoned child is now entitled to the freedom of the city. The lovely moon was motionless in the clear sky.

"Don't."

Erik uttered the word more calmly, more gently, he seemed to be roaring from a deeper, more mysterious part of the forest. His hand remained, preventing Riton from continuing to shoot.

"Not . . . (Erik hesitated, trying to find the word) not . . . now."

Riton's hand lost its will power and Erik's became more friendly. Gently, with the other hand, the German took the machine gun and put it down at his side. He had not let go of Riton, in fact he made his hug more affectionate. He drew the kid's head to him. He kissed him.

"Up. . . ."

This single word had the curtness of an order, but Riton was already used to Erik's ways. He stood up. Leaning back against the brick monument, facing a Paris that was watching and waiting, Erik buggered Riton. Their trousers were lowered over their heels where the belt buckles clinked at each movement. The group was strengthened by leaning against the wall, by being backed up, protected by it. If the two standing males had looked at each other, the quality of the pleasure would not have been the same. Mouth to mouth, chest to chest, with their knees tangled, they would have been entwined in a rapture that would have confined them in a kind of oval that excluded all light, but the bodies in the figurehead which they formed looked into the darkness, as one looks into the future, the weak sheltered by the stronger, the four eyes staring in front of them. They were projecting the frightful ray of their love to infinity. That sharp relief of darkness against the brick surface was the griffin of a coat of arms, the sacred image on a shield behind which two other German soldiers were on the lookout. Erik and Riton were not loving one in the other, they were escaping from themselves over the world, in full view of the world, in a gesture of victory. It was thus that, from his room in Berlin or Berchtesgaden, Hitler, taking a firm stand, with his stomach striking their backs and his knees in the hollows of theirs, emitted his transfigured adolescents over the humiliated world. But Erik's fatigue was already, and more obstinately, drawing him back. He was re-entering himself, was recapturing his youth, his first marriage with the executioner in the shrubbery when each of his hands, which were equally skillful in wielding the ax, unbuttoned a fly, pushed aside a shirt, took out a prick, and Erik raised his frightened eyes to those of the brute and said to him sweetly:

"Don't be angry with me if I don't do it well, but it's the first time."

Standing against a tree, the executioner made Erik face him, and he put his member between the kid's thighs. Riton's arms grabbed Erik's disheveled head and pressed the strong, famous neck, which bent forward, Erik's head finally touched the pale face, which was an utter appeal, a dying concert. Riton's arms quivered around the captured neck and enclosed it in a basket of tenderness and roses, of children's frills, of lace, and the kid's voice murmured against the ear of the half-naked warrior:

"All right now. Come in, it's time."

In passing through all his flesh, the memory of the executioner obliged Erik to greater humility toward the child. All his excitement receded. The executioner's hideous but hard face and sovereign build and stature, which he could see in his mind's eye, must be feeling freer, either the thought of them gave him greater pride in buggering Riton and caused him to beat and torture him so as to be surer of his freedom and his own strength and then take revenge for having been weak, or else he had remained humiliated by past shame and finished his job with gentler movements and reached the goal in a state of brotherly anguish. Riton, surprised at the respite

of love, wanted to murmur a few very mild words of reproach, but the vigor of the movements gave him the full
awareness that great voluptuaries always retain in love.
He said, almost sobbingly:

"You won't have me! No, you won't have me!" and at
the same time impaled himself with a leap.

"*Einmal. . . .*"

With my head bent back, I observed the solitude of the
chimney, alone against the starry sky, like a cape outlined in the sea. They—the chimney and the cape—seemed
to me to be conscious of their beauty and driven to
despair by that consciousness. The whole member entered
in, and Riton's behind touched Erik's warm belly. The
joy of both of them was great, as was their confusion,
since that joy had been attained. In the kind of swing
which is in the form of a closed cage, the kind you see at
country fairs, two kids pool their efforts. The cage goes
up. Each oscillation acquires greater amplitude, and
when the cage reaches the zenith after describing a semi-
circle, it hesitates before falling in order to complete its
perfect curve. For two seconds it is motionless. During
that moment the kids are upside down. It is then that
their faces come together and their mouths kiss and their
knees get entangled. Beneath them, the crowd, whose
heads are inverted, looks on. Riton became even more
tender. He murmured as one prays:

"Say, listen, see if you can't get it all in!"

For Erik this sentence was only a graceful song. He
answered with an equally lovely sentence and in an
equally hoarse tongue. And Riton:

"You're right, try."

Then suddenly Erik's body arches a little.

. . . . . . . . . . . . . . . . . . . . . . . . . . . . . . . . . . . . . . . . . . . . . . . . . . . . .

When the grave of the housemaid's child was filled, the hearse left the cemetery. The choirboys ran off among the graves. They laughingly scaled the wrought-iron railings and made a few rips in the lace of their surplices. Suddenly stopping face to face, they looked each other in the eye. For a moment they did not move, and suddenly they burst out laughing and, with their cheeks flushed, fell on each other in the grass, under the cypresses, where the roses known as "chiffon roses" twined. The younger escaped from the other's embrace with his hair mussed, and dashed to the cemetery wall and climbed over it. In the distance, the empty hearse was on its way back to the garage. The kid turned around and shaded his eyes with his hand, and what he saw hurled him down from the wall. His friend was naked in the black cassock, which was open on a muscular body. He got a hard-on. I approached and lay down near Erik. A tornado of petals came down on our heads from the roses twined about the cypresses. Only two sturdy arms struggling in the position that sailors call "an iron arm" survived that avalanche. He made Erik stay there without moving so as to be completely aware of being possessed in the silence of immobility. Only white roses could emerge from Erik's member to enter the bronze eye. They flowed out slowly with each quick but regular pulsation of the prick, as round and heavy as cigar smoke rings from pursed lips. Riton felt them rising within him by a path swifter than that of the intestines all the way up to his chest, where their fragrance spread in layers, though surprisingly it did not perfume his mouth. Now that Riton is dead, killed by a Frenchman, if one perhaps opened his chest would one find, caught in the trellis of the thorax, a few of those slightly dried roses?

Erik covered the sweating face with kisses. The perfo-

rating tool so hurt the child that he longed for an increase
of pain so to be lost in it.

"*Ich.  . . .*"

Erik's mouth was speaking, breathing on the kid's
shoulder. And his back kept thrusting. His eyes, which
he had kept closed, opened on those of Riton. It's banal
to say: "Those eyes have beheld death." Yet such eyes do
exist, and after the ghastly encounter, the gaze of the
men who possess them retains an unwonted hardness
and brilliance. Without wanting to speak too long in this
tone about the eye of Gabès and create a confusion close
to punning, I wish to say that Jean's eye became funereal
to me. When I stretched out on his back, when I went
farther down, I sharpened my tongue to a very fine
point so as to burrow neatly into that crack which was as
narrow as the eye of a needle. I felt myself being (I've
got him by the ass!) . . . I felt myself being there. Then
I tried hard to do as good a job as a drill. As the workman
in the quarry leans on his machine that jolts him amidst
splinters of mica and sparks from his drill, a merciless sun
beats down on the back of his neck, and a sudden dizziness blurs everything and sets out the usual palm trees
and springs of a mirage, in like manner a dizziness shook
my prick harder, my tongue grew soft, forgetting to dig
harder, my head sank deeper into the damp hairs, and I
saw the eye of Gabès become adorned with flowers, with
foliage, become a cool bower which I crawled to and
entered with my entire body, to sleep on the moss there,
in the shade, to die there.

In my memory, that purest of eyes was decked out
with jewels, with diamonds and pearls arranged in the
form of a crown. It was limpid. Erik's eyes: Erik had
known the snows of Russia, the cruelty of hand-to-hand
fighting, the bewilderment of being the only survivor of

a company; death was familiar to his eyes. When he opened them, Riton saw their brilliance despite the darkness. Remembering all of Erik's campaigns, he also thought very quickly: "He's been face to face with death." Erik had stopped work. His eyes kept staring; his mouth was still pressed against Riton's. "I now have the impression I love you more than before." This phrase was offered to me three months ago by Jean, and I put it in the mouth of a militiaman whom a German soldier has just buggered. Riton murmured:

"I now have the impression that I love you more than before." Erik did not understand.

No tenderness could have been expressed, for as their love was not recognized by the world, they could not feel its natural effects. Only language could have informed them that they actually loved each other. We know how they spoke to each other at the beginning. Seeing that neither understood the other and that all their phrases were useless, they finally contented themselves with grunts. This evening, for the first time in ten days, they are going to speak and to envelop their language in the most shameless passion. A happiness that was too intense made the soldier groan. With both hands clinging, one to the ear, the other to the hair, he wrenched the kid's head from the steel axis that was getting even harder.

"Stop."

Then he drew to him the mouth that pressed eagerly to his in the darkness. Riton's lips were still parted, retaining the shape and caliber of Erik's prick. The mouths crushed against each other, linked as by a hyphen, by the rod of emptiness. a rootless member that lived alone and went from one palate to the other. The evening was marvelous. The stars were calm. One imagined that the trees were alive, that France was awakening, and more intensely in the distance, above, that the Reich was watching. Riton woke up. Erik was sad. He was already thinking of faraway Germany, of the fact that his life was in danger, of how to save his skin. Riton buttoned his fly in a corner, then quietly picked up the machine gun. He fired a shot. Erik collapsed, rolled down the slope of the roof, and fell flat. The soldiers in the hideout neither heard the fall nor noticed the oddness of the shot. For ten seconds, a joyous madness was mistress of Riton. For ten seconds, he stamped on his friend's corpse. Motionless, with his back against the chimney and his eyes staring, he saw himself dancing, screaming, jumping about the body and on it and crushing it beneath his hobnailed heels. Then he quietly came to his senses and slowly made his way to other rooftops. All night long, all the morning of August 20, abandoned by his friends, by his parents, by his love, by France, by Germany, by the whole world, he fired away until he fell exhausted, not because of his wounds but with fatigue, as sweat glued desperate locks of hair to his temples. For a moment, he was so afraid of being killed that he thought of suicide. The Japanese, according to the papers, advised their soldiers to fight on even after death so that their souls could sustain and direct the living. . . . The beauty of that objurgation (which shows me a heaven bursting with a *potential* activity and full of dead men eager to shoot) impels me to make Riton utter the following words:

"Help me die."

. . . . . . . . . . . . . . . . . . . . . . . . . . . . . . . . . . . . . . . . . . . . . . . . . . . .

The little maid returned to her room. It was nighttime. She did not let anyone know.

She sat down on her cot, still wearing her wreath at a

rakish angle. Sleep crept up on her as she sat there holding her faded daisy and rocking her leg. When she woke up, late in the night, a moonbeam was shining through the window and brightening a patch of the threadbare rug. She stood up and quietly, piously, laid the daisy on that grave. Then she undressed and slept until morning.